Dark On The Inside

"Cantorna paints with her words. She conveys the atrocities of war with vivid imagery. She shows you what it's like to be confused about love, life, hate, and suffering. Hers is a book that will make you feel. A gifted writer."

— Jasmyne Boswell,
Author of *What If the Problem's Not the Problem???*

"Virginia Cantorna's novel is a touching, gripping, sad, insightful, and artfully constructed portrait of a family who must endure a culture gap, a generation gap, and a socio-economic gap. This novel reminded me of my parents and the sacrifices they made to create the good life for their children. It made me weep. It made me rejoice. It takes guts to write about prejudice, the haves versus the have-nots, the givers and the takers, what is fair and unfair. We each have judged others yet believed ourselves to be above being unjust. This book may shake that belief. Virginia Cantorna is a courageous author, very courageous indeed."

— Cornelia Soberano,
Co-Founder of the Maui Filipino Working Group

"A staggering, lyrical, and powerful story about a poverty-stricken family in a Filipino barrio during the invasion of the Japanese during World War II. Virginia Cantorna's riveting, deeply human characters come off the pages to touch your hearts in a tale that addresses the universality of pain and suffering. There are surprises throughout the book that make this a page-turner you will not want to put down."

— Patrick Snow,
Publishing Coach and International Best-Selling Author of
Creating Your Own Destiny

"A highly entertaining, heart-wrenching story that affords an intimate view of life in a simple Filipino village during the time of the Japanese invasions of the 1940s. Drama, intrigue, and tenderness carry the reader into another era as cultural beliefs and prejudices are played out and lives are forever changed."

— Pamela Saharah Dyson,
Author of *Premka: White Bird in a Golden Cage*

"An epic tale set against the backdrop of the Philippines, while being occupied by the Japanese during World War II. The author paints a canvas rich in the colors and textures of Filipino life, and wartime suffering, with well fleshed out characters who come alive off the page. A journey that begins in the rice paddies of a Filipino barrio and ends in the fields of a Hawaiian sugar plantation, follows the main characters from the horrific darkness of war into the promising light of a new life in a peaceful land."

— Robert DeVinck,
Author of *The Pono Principle and The Ascension Within*

"Virginia Cantorna transports the reader to a small Philippine village where the women are robbed of something precious, and the men fight to avenge the devastating loss. Haunting, riveting and unforgettable."

— Elizabeth Ayson,
Author of *Anak* and Co-Publisher of *Fil-Am Voice*

"On December 7, 1941, the Empire of Japan launched a surprise attack on the U.S. Naval Base at Pearl Harbor on the island of Oahu, Hawaii. Virginia Cantorna's debut novel, *Dark on the Inside*, begins the following day with the Japanese invasion of the Philippines, an event that was to cause devastation and suffering for Ligaya and her sister, Gloriana. The riveting climax describes immutable loss and sorrow. The sisters must find courage and a sense of self through their struggles for empowerment, liberation, and survival."

— Kenn Grimes,
Author of the *Booker Falls Mystery* series

DARK *on the* INSIDE

A Novel

VIRGINIA CANTORNA

Published by:
Aviva Publishing
Lake Placid, NY 12946
518-523-1320
www.avivapubs.com

Hard Cover ISBN: 978-1-63618-014-4
Soft Cover ISBN: 978-1-63618-015-1
E-Book ISBN: 978-1-63618-017-5
Audio Book ISBN: 978-1-6318-017-5

Library of Congress Control Number: 2020951954

Editor: Tyler Tichelaar, Superior Book Productions
Author Photograph: Jack Grace
Cover Design and Interior Layout: Meredith Lindsay, Media Mercantile

DARK *on the* INSIDE

A Novel

VIRGINIA CANTORNA

DEDICATION

This book is lovingly dedicated to the memory of my parents, Ramon Dagdag and Valeriana Donia Dagdag. By taking the courageous step of immigrating to Hawaii, they became the catalysts for creating significant change for generations. I honor my dear husband, Alfred, who helped me launch the dream of penning the stories embedded in my soul. To my precious daughter, Emily, and all of her cousins: Be proud to be Filipino. Learn about and treasure your heritages. A big hug to my little grandson, Mateo Cantorna-Aina, who never fails to make me smile through the challenges of my writing process. To my sisters, Evie Chargualaf and Sandy Hew, I relish sharing the "second-generation" Filipino-American experience with you. I also remember my ancestors and living relatives on both the Dagdag and Donia sides of my family, whose support continues to be expansive and much appreciated. I love you and appreciate you, all of my family, so very deeply.

CONTENTS

AUTHOR'S NOTE

When I was a young girl, my mother, a Filipino immigrant, shared a secret with me that would turn out to be the seed for this novel. She said, "The women in our village were raped by the Japanese." It was as if she dropped a single-sentence bomb. She did not repeat it nor elaborate, and I was afraid to ask the question, "Were you raped, Mommy?"

Over the years I heard stories and read articles and memoirs about World War II and the heinous acts that the Japanese inflicted upon the Filipinos. My own father sustained a bullet wound. The fictionalized atrocities described in my book are based on my memories of true accounts and research.

Growing up Filipina, I faced some prejudice and discrimination because of my gender and brown skin. Growing up in Hawaii, the so-called "salad" of many races, I watched as others from marginalized communities either learned to work with others or fueled their dislike of people who were different from them. I lived on the East Coast for eleven years and witnessed divisiveness and derision enacted upon myself and other minorities.

This novel, one of a planned series, is relevant especially now when the United States is experiencing stark political, religious, homophobic, and racial divides. My book is dark--meant to teach about the ravages of war, hate, crime, poverty, isolation. I want my readers to also learn the importance of culture, differences in world views, gender roles, and ways of coping. Pain, loss, and suffering are universal themes. But so are courage, love, hope, and faith. The characters in this novel are resilient, empowered. They exude these qualities and arise, survive, and thrive.

The beginning of every war

is like opening the door into

a dark room.

One never knows

what is hidden

in the darkness.

– Adolph Hitler

HISTORICAL CONTEXT

PRE-WORLD WAR II — THE SPANISH AMERICAN AND PHILIPPINE-AMERICAN WARS

Many countries regarded the Philippines as a vital Pacific hub for commerce and military protection. In the 1500s the Philippines was colonized by the Spaniards who stole lands and charged exorbitant taxes. A caste system was created with the top of the hierarchy consisting of wealthy landlords, the church elite, and ruling nobility. At the bottom were Filipinos forced to be chattels and cheap laborers who were poorly treated by the Spanish colonists.

In the late 1800s, Filipinos were able to study in Europe and brought back the concept of self-rule. After three hundred years of oppression, a revolutionary movement was initiated, influenced by Dr. Jose Rizal, who was executed for treason in 1896. He is regarded as a national hero. The Americans entered the Spanish-American War, promising to help Filipinos gain independence from Spain. Spain lost and ceded the Philippines to the USA which, despite promises of freedom for the Filipinos, claimed the country for itself as an American territory. Filipinos were provoked by the idea of not being in charge of their own country. This led to open warfare in the Philippine-American War. The Philippines lost and continued to be an American commonwealth until Japan invaded and took over the country on December 8, 1941. The Philippines finally became independent in 1946 following Japan's surrender and liberation from the United States.

WORLD WAR II IN THE PACIFIC

World War II began in Europe in 1939 and is best remembered for the holocaust under Adolf Hitler. Less known is that the United States only entered World War II after the bombing of Pearl Harbor in Hawaii on December 7, 1941. The surprise attack on American soil galvanized the U.S. Congress to declare war against Japan and its allies—Nazi Germany and Benito Mussolini's Italy.

Imperial Japan then invaded the Commonwealth of the Philippines, at the time, a United States territory like Guam and Puerto Rico are today. The combined army of Filipino and American soldiers under the command of General Douglas MacArthur failed to contain the Japanese. President Franklin D. Roosevelt, afraid that MacArthur might be taken prisoner, ordered the brilliant military tactician out of the Philippines to defend the Southwest Asian Pacific. He famously promised the Filipinos, "I shall return." General MacArthur did come back to the Philippines in 1944 to overtake the Japanese. Many major battles ensued. The Japanese surrendered in 1945 but by then over one million Filipinos had lost their lives.

GEOGRAPHY

The Philippines is an archipelago of seven thousand large and tiny islands. Only one-fourth of the Southeast Asian country is inhabited. The majority of people live on three clusters of islands—Luzon, Visayas, and Mindanao. The Japanese once occupied all three areas. The remote barrios in this story and the capital of Manila are located in northern Luzon. Many areas were decimated during World War II.

COLONIZATION AND CULTURE

Filipino is not a pure race; it is the result of thousands of years of intermixing African, Mongolian, Polynesian, Malaysian, Muslim, Asian Indian, Arab, Chinese, Spanish, Japanese, and Caucasian blood. Filipinos have a wide range of skin color, with fairer complexions the most desired and esteemed.

Significant influences on Philippine culture (architecture, religion, language, literature, cuisine, clothing styles, music, higher education) have been from the Spanish colonists (1565-1898) and American occupiers (1898-1946). The Spaniards pressured the Filipinos to convert to Catholicism; it is the dominant religion today. Filipinos seem able to face extreme adversity with their strong religious belief that "God will take care of things." Their fatalism can sometimes deteriorate into passivity, submissiveness, and resignation. Public education was introduced during the American occupation and English was taught. In fact, Filipino (Tagalog) and English are considered the official national languages of the Philippines. Many Filipinos have tried to protect and preserve their heritage despite outside influences as evidenced by an ongoing, widespread belief in superstition, traditional mores, and the practice of indigenous healing and rituals. Life revolves around the care of extended family which is built on a foundation of respect, hard work, altruism, loyalty, and generosity.

TIMELINE

March 16, 1521
Explorer Ferdinand Magellan reaches a Pacific island chain and claims it for Spain.

1543
The region is named after the Spanish heir to the throne, Prince Phillip.

1565
The first Spanish colony is established in the Philippines. The Spaniards rule the natives for over 300 years.

December 30, 1896
Dr. Jose Rizal, whose novels stoked nationalism, is executed for treason.

April 25, 1898
The US supports the revolution against Spanish rule and launches the Spanish-American War.

December 8, 1898
The US defeats Spain. The Philippines is ceded to the US.

1899
The US claim ownership of the Philippines but the Filipinos want independence.

February 4, 1899
The Philippine-American War begins.

July 2, 1902
The Philippine-American War ends.
The US controls the Philippines.

November 15, 1935
The Commonwealth of the Philippines is established.
The US promises independence in ten years.

December 7, 1941
The Japanese bomb Pearl Harbor.

December 8, 1941
Japanese forces invade the Philippines.

1942 – 1944
The Japanese control all of the Philippines.

March 11, 1942
General Douglas MacArthur is reassigned and leaves the Philippines, promising to return.

October 20, 1944
General Douglas MacArthur returns to the Philippines, leading the way to recapturing the Philippine islands.

May 8, 1945
World War II in Europe ends.

September 2, 1945
The Japanese formally surrender.
Over one million Filipinos die during World War II.

January – April 1946
Six thousand laborers arrive in Hawaii to work for sugar and pineapple plantations.

July 4, 1946
The US grants full independence to the new Republic of the Philippines.

ACCENTS AND DIALECTS

Filipino accents are generally unfamiliar to most Americans. I have limited the dialects and accents in my novel with readability in mind. In the majority of this book, the longer sentences written in English reflect the ease with which the characters speak their native language. Shorter, broken sentences appear when the characters, struggling with English as their second language, are trying to speak pidgin, an English-based creole language. In these parts of the book, I have used atypical syntax and alternative spellings to help develop my characters. In the Philippines, the placement of the accent can change a similarly spelled word drastically—I have indicated the accented syllable in a word with all-capital letters.

PRONUNCIATION GUIDE

Phonetics for sounds that are different in Filipino, Spanish, and English.

A	Sounds like the *a* in the English word *father*.	Papang, Mamang, Nana, Tata
ANG	Sounds like *ahng*. Closest pronunciation in English is *among*.	Papang, Mamang
AY, AI	Sounds like the *ie* in the English word *pie*.	Ay, Jaime, Pinay
E	Sounds like the *e* in the English word *set*.	Bartolome, Jaime
I	Sounds like the *ee* in the English word *sheep*.	Pinoy
O	Is a shorter sounding *o* as in *frog*.	Apo Dios, Japon
U	Sounds like the *oo*, as in the English word *food*.	Luna
J	Sounds like *h*, as in the English word *hi* or the *j* in the Spanish word *jalapeño*.	Jaime, Japon
R,RR	Trilled or rolled *r*.	Gloriana, Barrio

GLOSSARY

Aloha – (Hawaiian) Hello, farewell, and fare well

Americano – (Spanish and Filipino) American

Anata – (Japanese) Intimate term of address; darling

Apo Dios – (Filipino) Father God

Ay – (Filipino) Oh

Banzai – (Japanese) A Japanese battle cry

Barong Tagalog – (Filipino) Embroidered shirt or top sewn from thin material. The national attire of the Philippines

Barrio – (Spanish and Filipino) A district, town, or village

Bati-cobra – (Filipino) Batting game using bamboo sticks

Bayag – (Filipino) Scrotum and testicles

Bushido – (Japanese) Code of honor developed by the samurai

Carabao – (Filipino) Water buffalo

Centavo – (Filipino) The smallest unit of currency in the Philippines. One hundred centavos are equivalent to one peso.

Chichis – (Japanese slang) Breasts

Cigarillos – (Spanish) Small cigars

Doctora – (Spanish and Filipino) Female doctor

Fiesta – (Spanish and Filipino) Festivities or celebration

Filipina – (Filipino) Female Filipino

Halo-Halo – (Filipino) Ice cone dessert covered with coconut, condensed milk, and tropical fruits

Japon – (Filipino) Japan; Japanese

Jeepney – (Filipino) Public transportation vehicle modified from army Jeeps

Kuso – (Japanese) Swear word. "Fuck" or "Shit"

Loco – (Spanish) Crazy

Lola – (Filipino) Term of endearment for grandmother

Lolong – (Filipino) Term of endearment for grandfather

Loris – Slow-moving primate

Luna – (Latin) Moon

Mabuhay – (Filipino) Used as a toast – "Long life"

Nana – (Filipino) Term of respect used when addressing an older woman

Nipa – (Filipino) A long-leaf grass used to make thatched roofs and walls

Parol – (Filipino) Ornamental, star-shaped Christmas lantern representing the Star of Bethlehem

Pesos – (Spanish and Filipino) The official currency of the Philippines

Pinakbet – (Filipino) Stew made with Filipino vegetables

Pinay – (Filipino) A woman of Filipino descent

Pinoy – (Filipino) Man, person, or group of Filipino descent

Policia – (Spanish) Police

Sakadas – (Filipino) Laborers recruited from the Philippines to work in the USA

Saké – (Japanese) Alcoholic beverage made with fermented rice

San – (Japanese) Honorific title used after one's surname

Stupido – (Spanish and Filipino) Stupid

Tata – (Filipino) Term of respect used when addressing an older man

Tinikling – (Filipino) Traditional folk dance where the performers step over and between long bamboo poles that are rhythmically slapped together

PRINCIPAL CHARACTERS

FILIPINOS

The Ugale Family

Ligaya "Liling" Ugale – Young Filipino woman working for the Americano doctor

Gloriana "Glory" Ugale – Liling's flirtatious older sister and best friend

Jaime ("HI-meh") Luna Ugale – Glory's sweet-natured, young son

Felipe "Boy" Ugale – Liling's older brother, a sugar cane irrigator living in Hawaii

Bartolome Ugale – Liling's nearly blind eldest brother, a tobacco farmer

Corazon "Cora" Meili Gotiangco Ugale – Bartolome's loving wife

Pacencia Ugale – Bartolome and Cora's school-aged daughter

Rosa Ugale – Bartolome and Cora's baby

Luisa Rose Ugale – Bartolome and Cora's newborn

Maria Ugale – Devout mother to the Ugale siblings

Respicio Ugale – Maria's husband, the physically disabled patriarch of the Ugale family

The Cruz Family

Soledad Cruz – Maria Ugale's opinionated elder sister

Vicente – Soledad's young, mischievous grandson

Villagers

Father Benito – Catholic priest and Bible-thumping pastor of the village church

Raul Hidalgo – Next-door neighbor and Liling's betrothed

Gilberto "Berto" Abueg – Raul's best friend and fellow military man

Agapito "Pitong" Macadangdang – Filipino soldier betrothed to Salome in an arranged marriage

Salome – Agapito's missing wife-to-be

Santiago – Glory's lover, a fisherman who pursues a different vocation

AMERICANS

Dr. Billet aka *Dr. B* aka *The Americano Doctor* – The Caucasian physician for the region

The Americano doctor's wife – The woman who recognizes Liling's intellect and gives her gently used items

The Americano doctor's son – The university student who has a crush on Liling

JAPANESE

"Gorilla" – A hairy Japanese soldier

Captain Fuku – The "Oriental Bull," a Japanese soldier of high rank

Bald Japanese soldier

PART I

FOREBODING

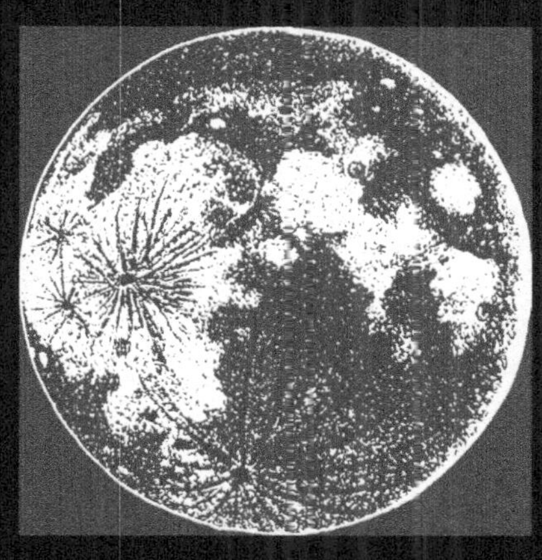

Chapter 1

LIGAYA "LILING" UGALE

December 8, 1941

She had a tendency to blow things out of proportion. What was all the commotion about? I dropped my crocheting, pushed out the plywood awning, and leaned out of the opening in our bamboo hut. Auntie Soledad, my mother's know-it-all elder sister, looked like a cackling hen, wings akimbo as if darting from a savage dog. "Pearl Harbor! Attacked! Japan! The Philippines!" My auntie could hardly catch her breath.

"What is that foolish sister of yours up to?" My *papang* turned abruptly toward *Mamang*. He seemed annoyed.

"Oh no! The Japanese invaded the Philippines a few hours after Pearl Harbor? The shocking news was difficult for me to believe. My head hurt; my bewildered brain turned into a whirling mist.

Auntie Soledad, the self-proclaimed nexus of warnings, shouted in front of almost every house in our tiny Filipino *barrio* or village. Her piercing voice seemed to send electrically charged waves over the rice paddies. The volume and agitation in her staccato drew the neighbors out of their homes.

I hurried my mother, Maria Cruz Ugale, and father, Respicio Ugale, to the Chinese restaurant where there was one of only three existing radios in our poverty-stricken village; the mayor and *Americano* doctor owned the other two. My pulse quickened, but I could not tell whether it was because of my fear of war or the sight of my betrothed, Raul.

The crowd was divided into two camps, each displaying one of two prevailing emotions—fury or fear. The listeners converged near the radio, conversations at high pitch.

"Quiet. Quiet down."

The Chinese restaurant owner motioned for silence. He turned up the radio's volume. The newscaster reported in a somber voice, "At approximately 8 a.m. Hawaii Standard Time, the Empire of Japan attacked Pearl Harbor." He quoted President Franklin D. Roosevelt, "December 7, 1941, a date which will live in infamy…."

"*Ay, Apo Dios.* Oh, Father God. Liling, is the sugar plantation near Pearl Harbor? I'm scared. Liling, Hawaii was bombed. My son is dead?"

I was worried about my thirty-year-old brother, Felipe "Boy" Ugale. He had immigrated to Hawaii seven years ago. I prayed aloud, hoping to ease Mamang's concern. "God of Far Away Places, I petition Thee to protect Felipe. Amen." *Is Boy safe?*

With a mother's panic caught in her throat, Mamang made the sign of the cross.

Where were the Japanese now? Fortunately, our remote barrio is well-hidden, nestled in the mountains, a long distance from the Philippine capital, about four-hundred kilometers.

My God! *The Philippines is at war.*

...

The villagers gathered at the Chinese restaurant almost every evening for the latest bulletins. The newscaster described military action in Manila and the rest of the country as if recounting spooky tales to an audience huddled around a campfire. I felt a sense of doom and could hardly concentrate, hearing only fragments of the war reports. "Terror-filled civilians fled to churches for sanctuary...fortified walls did not offer protection. Babies bashed like bowling balls against the base of a Virgin Mary statue. Dozens of involuntary martyrs littered the tessellated tile floors of the Basilica. Worshipers' corpses..."

I pictured bodies like slender sacks of loosely packed rice draped over the pews and spattered blood drops staining the altar linens. My trepidation increased exponentially with every telling detail of the atrocities.

Papang joined his cronies, who were sitting in a corner of the restaurant as they drank their first round of beer. They slammed, pounded, and clinked their beer bottles much harder on this day. Glass shattered and liquor sloshed everywhere. I quickly picked up the broken shards so the Chinese owner wouldn't fuss, but mostly because I wanted to catch the local information that the men shared among themselves.

"Did you hear about the Mountain Mansion Massacre?" asked Papang's closest friend.

"They jammed hundreds of Filipinos into the house. You know how big the property is, right?" This man's potbelly shook with each word he shouted.

"Yes, *Tata*," I said, using the honorific term that Filipinos use to address elder males. "I know the place. I passed the enormous, fancy two-story house on a school excursion long ago," I said as I reached across the table to collect the empty bottles. "I'm sure Mamang and Papang remember that trip because they had to scrape for my fare."

"The Japon blasted a hole into the flooring of an upstairs room. One by one, blindfolded men, women, and children—"

"And children?" I picked up the last piece of broken glass and wrapped it in a banana leaf for safe discarding.

"—were shoved into a kneeling position. Forced to lean over the opening."

My vivid imagination afflicted me. I felt sure that, deprived of sight, the prisoners' sense of hearing was sharpened. I closed my eyes and "heard" the whistle of swords slicing the air. The cleaving sounds of metal blade against human flesh, the macabre sounds of decapitation fueling their wildest terrors. Knock, after knock, after knock, in a litany of percussive sounds, skulls crashing onto the growing mountain of heads in the abyss. The cracking of cheekbones upon the marble floor below resonating like goblet drums.

I envisioned faces frozen with grotesque expressions carelessly discarded like old Saints Day masks. My eyes flew open. That was enough of the movie in my head. I rubbed my temples; a headache was coming on. I sensed Raul's pitying eyes on me.

The man with the potbelly petted the dog the proprietor kept indoors, easy cleanup of scraps from the restaurant floor. "My cousin said he came across one of the heads. Must have rolled out the doorway into the street." Mr. Potbelly pulled his hand away from the fur. "He said the dogs were licking the blood off its neck and nipped on its ears. My cousin shit his pants and ran all the way down the mountain to his hut."

The remark would have normally elicited a laugh, but no one even gave a smile.

"You don't say!"

"I can't imagine being that frightened," Mamang said as she helped the restaurant owner pass around more bottles of beer. Round five. I signaled my mother to stop. Papang could be aggressive when drunk.

Auntie Soledad joined the men. "Did you know that in Manila the Japon are throwing Filipino babies in the air and skewering them upon their bayonets?" Mothers who had gathered in the restaurant pulled their children closer. "The Japon push our people into the social halls. They lock the buildings, then light them on fire. The enemy is marching this way, toward our village." How did Auntie already know of these horrors?

One of Papang's friends chopped a banana with too much force, then passed the plate of mangled slices to share. "At the meat processing plant, they butchered our Pinoy people. If me, I would squeal like a pig."

"Filipinos, slaughtered like animals." Papang shook his head.

Mr. Potbelly threw a scrap to the mongrel. "Who are the animals? This dog? The Filipinos? Or the Japon?"

...

The intricate patterns on the white curtains that I, Ligaya Valeria Cruz Ugale, was crocheting, danced like angels with wings of lace. Was it a phenomenon caused by the strobe effects of sunlight through walls of bamboo slats or an aura warning me of an impending migraine? Or could it be that the horrific news about Pearl Harbor and the Japanese invasion of the Philippines caused anxiety-induced hallucinations? "God of Peace, I humbly ask Thee for mercy upon my country. Amen." I shut my eyes and opened them. Still, the images before me were blurred. The optical illusion caused me to blink, and blink again. I paused, but only momentarily, to wiggle my weary fingers. I willed the pain to disappear from the orbits of my eyes. "God of Perfect Health, I trust Thee to remove my affliction and reduce my suffering. Amen."

"Where is your sister Glory? Why was she not at the restaurant?" Papang slumped onto his seat with a huff.

I saw Mamang shudder.

"Auntie Liling, like this?" I welcomed the child's interruption. Pacencia showed me the valance she was crocheting. The stitches were surprisingly straight for an eight-year-old.

"You learn quickly, niece."

"It's not good enough, Auntie."

"Yes, like that. Don't pout. Be patient, dear one. Your work is improving every day. I'm proud of you."

"Thank you, Auntie."

"Remember what your name means?"

"Pacencia?"

"Yes, patience."

Bartolome's daughter was very helpful and very attentive. A sensitive and serious child. My kindred spirit. Cute, with straight bangs, and braids of brown-black hair. She smiled easily and sometimes jabbered too much.

I moaned and rubbed both temples.

"Auntie, another headache?"

"Yes, niece. Sorry. It is best that you go. Pain makes it difficult for me to teach and crochet this curtain. Your parents have been working extra-long hours, but they should be home by now."

Pacencia kissed me on the cheek. The girl gave a cheerful shout to her grandmother, "Bye-bye, *Lola*."

"Tomorrow, you help your grandfather glue the paper and bamboo for the *parol*, yes? He's cutting the bamboo strips for the star lantern right now." My mamang loved the Christmas season.

"Oh, Lola, I can't wait."

"Remind your mommy to bring paper for the star. We'll hang up the parol in one week."

"Yes, I will, Lola."

"Oh, and by the way, I heard your mommy is not smoking anymore."

"Not anymore, Lola."

"Is Cora pregnant again?" I paused my crocheting to ask.

"I don't think so. She just quit cigarettes recently."

Pacencia hopped down the steps of the bamboo hut. "Bye-bye, chickens!" Her playfulness caused the flock of birds to stare and cluck. She shooed the big-combed rooster. It escaped into the banana grove.

"Be careful, Pacencia. Watch out for the Japon!" I called after her.

I watched as my niece skipped past the banana trees. There was movement. A flash of something red. I decided it was just the breeze showing me it was time to prune the overcrowded stems and suckers.

The girl paused a half-dozen times to adjust her frayed dress. The garment was so oversized that it slipped to expose one shoulder or the other. She fussed with one of the thin straps, which fell to reveal a breast bud the size of a five-centavo coin.

I heard a trickle and a shuffle. I shot a glance at the banana grove. Was that a man licking his lips, slowly buttoning his trousers? I shook my head to shake off the illusion. Psychosis? God of Suffering, let it not be so.

Mamang waved to her granddaughter. "Pacencia needs little girl clothes, not hand-me-downs from her teen-aged cousins. That girl will be entering puberty soon."

"I know, Mamang."

"Her mother will have to teach her the cycles of her moons. Pacencia will have to learn to wash and fold her rags. And that she shouldn't bathe during her menstruation; it will make her blind."

I rolled my eyes. "I'm sure Cora will teach her daughter that her hygiene is important, Mamang." I do not believe in unhealthy Filipino superstitions.

"Blindness runs in our family."

"Not so, Mamang. Bartolome is the only one with vision problems. Brother needed a new eyeglass prescription."

"Ay, my poor son." As is her habit, Mamang made the sign of the cross.

I pulled some fabric out of a basket. "As soon as I feel better, I shall sew a new dress for Pacencia. The doctor's wife has given me three meters of this material. The Americanos are generous."

Mamang did not appear grateful. "Upholstery cloth."

"Stiff, yes, but pretty."

The gift of cloth was placed next to the Americanos' latest donations—candy and several books. The missus had called me "a voracious reader." She included a history text, a biography about our national hero José Rizal, and a couple of romance novellas in the basket. I devoured books by the dozens, especially those that gave me a vicarious journey to other lands, other times. Although I had not gone past the sixth grade, I had learned English well and had a pretty good vocabulary; the family counted on me for many tasks such as negotiating contracts, making bus reservations, and translating for the Americano doctor. My sister, Gloriana Consuelo Cruz Ugale, was not bad herself at speaking English. I think that is why the physician employed us both at his clinic.

I was eager to read the love stories. The heroine and hero's deeds piqued my curiosity about intimacy. The "happily ever after" endings satisfied me emotionally. I ran my fingers over a book jacket and studied the illustration of a handsome man with long, dark wavy hair embracing his beloved fair-faced maiden. This would be Raul and me on our wedding day. Soon. I must be patient.

Once heart-shaped, the now melted dark chocolate seeped out of a tinfoil wrapper labeled with my name. Every December, the Americano doctor's son returned from college and persisted in expressing an interest in courting. I feigned naïveté and ignored his advances. I could never consider such a proposition. Dating him was impossible.

I was already locked into an arranged marriage with Raul Hidalgo, since childhood. Besides, a racially mixed marriage would have been scandalous. I knew the Americano physician would never approve; he called his Filipino patients "the poor, sickly Brownies." Furthermore, Papang said many times that he regarded white Americanos as entitled, arrogant, and stingy, even though they offered their gently used effects to the Ugale family.

"You know, your sister is not interested in books," said Mamang, interrupting my reflection on prejudices.

"I agree. Glory has literature far from her mind. Mamang, you know that in her spare time, she prefers to cut through the rice fields, past the ditches and to the river where tilapia is plentiful and many young men fish."

I glanced at my reflection in the small, inverted hand mirror that hung on a rusted nail. The strands of hair loose around my ears bothered me, and I tried to tuck them back into the bun at my nape. My eyebrows were scant, unlike Gloriana's. I wished I had Glory's thick lips and her lashes, so lush.

We sisters were often compared. I had been told that I had a "delicate beauty."

On the other hand, Gloriana was deemed "handsome." The features of her face, taken individually, were remarkable, but the sum of the parts was slightly askew. She was born with a small congenital mole on her right jaw, adding to the asymmetry. It was incongruent to refer to it as a "beauty spot." Glory was by no means ugly. However, I noticed that my sister counterbalanced her perceived plainness with behaviors that were flirtatious, forward, and feisty. Of considerable consternation to Mamang and Papang, Glory attracted the attention of males of all ages and reputations.

Our parish priest, Father Benito, seemed to treat my sister with disdain. He once compared me to a shepherdess who tends flocks of children; elderly, polite businessmen and persons of a spiritual ilk. Surprisingly, he seemed to approve of me.

Chapter 2

LIGAYA "LILING" UGALE

December 9, 1941

"Mamang, stop! Please. All that Bible talk is torment right now. My headache is getting worse." I wished my mother hadn't enrolled in Father Benito's Bible study class. She now uses Scripture as if it gives her divine authority over her adult children.

"In Genesis it says, 'God finished his work and on day number seven he rested.' You see? You have been working one week on those curtains; it is time to take a break."

Her earnest Bible recitations—I am never sure whether Mamang knows the exact wording of verses in the Catholic Bible; she's illiterate and doesn't own the holy book. However, Mamang has a keen memory and can reel off any passage she has heard at Mass.

"You must rest, Liling."

Mamang stood behind me and rubbed my shoulders, digging her thumbs deeply into my muscles the way I liked. Already, the intensity of my headache was decreasing. The blue veins on her wrinkled hands were prominent, coursing with the blood of fierce Spaniards, indigenous mountain people, maybe Chinese, maybe Middle Eastern

Muslims. Who knows? Filipino is not a pure race but an amalgam of long-ago ancestors who visited the archipelago over thousands of years.

She pressed harder into my flesh.

"I cannot rest, Mamang. I must continue."

"There is tightness in your back. I can feel it in your muscles. Do not let your suffering distort your designs or your curtains will not be salable."

Fallen tears moistened a spot on my newly crocheted work. "Massage helps, Mamang. Thank you."

"You're too young to be troubled by such intense headaches, Liling. You must see the Americano doctor."

"I'll see him tomorrow when I go to work." I am employed as maid to the doctor's family. Gloriana is the clinic janitor.

I resumed my crocheting. "If I hurry, perhaps I can meet the deadline set by the Chinese merchant."

"For your papang's chair?"

I nodded. I have been hoping to save enough for a simple mahogany-framed chair. The living area of our one-room hut is sparsely furnished, with only a table pushed against the bamboo wall and three unpainted wooden benches that offer no back support. My father's seventy-year-old spine has gradually shown considerable signs of deterioration from decades of rice farming. When I saw that Papang could no longer safely stand from a sitting position without occasional assistance, Dr. Billet prescribed analgesics, a cane, and a chair with arms.

"Your papang is especially violent when *debilitated*." Mamang didn't say *when drunk*.

"I know, Mamang. He drinks more when his back is in pain."

"The Japon attacks will, of course, add to his worries."

"Papang keeps showing us his scar from the Spanish-American War."

"He practically brags about that bullet wound. But I know it is a reminder of how devastating war can be."

"He seems to be drinking more since Glory began—"

"—carousing," Mamang finished and shook her head.

"Your papang has been mean ever since we lost…we lost…" Mamang was unable to finish recounting the deaths of her other children. "Do you think we lost Boy, too, in Pearl Harbor?" She was silent for a long time.

"What were you saying about Papang?"

"He used to be a decent and thoughtful man."

I cannot imagine being married to an abusive drunkard like my father. I think of my fiancé, Raul. He is a gentle man. A gentleman.

"I remember. When we were little, Papang cuddled with us and said, 'Good night.'"

Mamang stomped her foot for emphasis. "His beer is like fuel for a bonfire where he burns me at the stake." She complained of weariness. "Sometimes I wish we could escape; follow Boy to the United States of America."

"I know, Mamang. You keep saying that."

"And you, dear? What are your plans with Raul? Will you relocate to Hawaii?"

"No, Mamang. Who will take care of you and Papang?"

She nodded and looked relieved.

"Besides, we don't have a large enough savings. No, I don't want to go to Hawaii. Goodness, no! Pearl Harbor is in Hawaii, Mamang."

My mother is diminutive in stature. In her mid-sixties, her hair is still jet black. Sometimes a single filament of gray will sprout, but she tugs on the stray strand to uproot it. Except for a tiny bit of slack on her jowls, her skin is taut and porcelain smooth. Her eyes are exceedingly expressive; she can convey the emotions of a Greek tragedy with one look.

My father is hunchbacked but destined to farm until death because there is no such thing as a paid retirement. Papang's spinal deformities have prevented him from working for prolonged periods. At home, he putters about idly, treating his wife and children like slaves, ordering us to maintain the house and farm.

"I would be content with my lot in life after a fourteen-hour day of farming," said Mamang, "as long as your papang did not beat me."

"What kind of life is that, Mamang?"

"Sometimes, it is easier to surrender."

"Why do you stay with that madman? Forty years of marriage?" Auntie Soledad had asked on one of her visits. That day, I had served Mamang's famous sweet rice cakes and listened in on their sisterly conversation. "Why do you settle for him like a dog satisfied with bones?"

"In all my life, no one has offered me steak. I must accept what Apo Dios has given me. It is part of God's plan." Mamang made the sign of the cross. She repeated the fatalistic message. "He is my damned husband, and I shall not leave him. It is God's will."

"If you expect bones, Maria, you will get bones."

Over the time of poverty and plagues, my father's "friendly" whacks had escalated into assaultive behavior. His unrelenting abuse caused each of his two living sons to break free, one by one, regretfully choosing to leave their mother and two younger sisters behind.

During last week's argument between Mamang and Papang, I was forced to intervene by physically inserting myself between them. When will the next beating be?

Mamang pressed a fading bruise on my shoulder, which made me wince and pull away.

...

My mother has much to bear. An abusive husband. All six of my brothers, either emancipated or dead. Two unmarried daughters, both now in our mid-twenties, still living at home—Gloriana, the eldest girl, seventh in a string of eight births—and me; I am the youngest.

Only two of my six brothers are alive. Bartolome and Felipe "Boy" say they were intimidated by our father, at best. At worst, they were terrorized and tormented by Papang's unpredictable and unyielding temper.

Both my brothers moved out of our family home when they arrived at the age of majority. Most male offspring would have willingly remained to assist aging parents on their family farms, but the promise of inheriting that tiny piece of low-producing land was not a good-enough incentive for my brothers to stay.

The first-born, Bartolome, crossed paths with one Corazon Meili Gotiangco—Cora for short—as he delivered boxes of Bartolome's Sweet and Dark Cheroots to the Chinese merchants. She is petite, with dainty hands and feet, skin like sun-bleached capiz shells but with a bronze undertone, and naturally coral pink cheeks and lips. They fell deeply in love, and soon he married the nice Catholic girl. After their wedding, the newlyweds relocated to the part of the village farthest from our parents' place, where Bartolome established an even bigger tobacco farm and cigar manufacturing plant. Papang became bitter because he had expected his eldest son to run the family's rice farm.

...

The sugar plantations in Hawaii lured my youngest brother, Felipe "Boy." The company sought strapping young bachelors as *sakadas*, farm workers, to emigrate from the Philippines.

I was still a teenager when a rusted *jeepney* waited outside to take my brother to the dock. Boy said, "I'm sorry, Mamang. I *must* go. The sugar company pays far more than the net profits of our farm. I will send you money and then come back for you, and Glory, and Liling. I promise to rescue you from Papang." Felipe had once told me that guilt punched him in the gut for leaving us behind.

Boy bit his lower lip as if doing so would dam the tears welling in his eyes. He squeezed Mamang and latched his overfull suitcase.

Mamang made the sign of the cross. Holding a red bandanna to her cheeks, she wept silently. "Will I ever see you again, Boy?"

Felipe tried to sound optimistic. "Don't worry, Mamang. Of course. I will come back home often." He didn't sound convincing. It's been seven years and he hasn't returned.

My dear brother works for the sugar cane plantation on the island of Oahu. Pearl Harbor is on Oahu. Is he hurt? Dead? A jolt of electricity seemed to pierce my head. I jerked. A line of crochet stitches unraveled.

Chapter 3

LIGAYA "LILING" UGALE

December 9, 1941

"Oh, Lee-ling. I have a see-cret." A sexy sing-song voice.

A familiar shuffle along the path that fronted our hut signaled the arrival of my sister and best friend. Gloriana moved through life spry and energetic like a dancer, ever-ready to use her charisma and coquettishness to seduce a man. She was dressed in a blouse, a little too sheer; a skirt and crinoline that lifted to mid-thigh when she twirled; and a cluster of jasmine blossoms in her hair. She looked like a groomed poodle, a little on the wild side.

"Oh, Lee-ling. Come with me to the ree-ver." Glory always displayed a cheerful disposition, even after cleaning the Americano doctor's clinic. She didn't just scrub the latrines and sanitize the bedpans. She sterilized Dr. Billet's surgical instruments and sharpened the hypodermic needles.

"I can't come with you."

"And why not, Miss Cannot, Queen of Crochet?"

I shrugged.

"It's time for you to escape. I overheard Mamang say so just now."

"My head is throbbing."

"Well, I prescribe an excursion to the river." Gloriana's voice dropped to an excited whisper. She looked about to see if Mamang was eavesdropping. "Come with me and you can meet my man, the best-looking in the province."

"Glory, what are you talking about?" I allowed her to drag me in the river's direction.

"Santiago. *Santiago*. Remember? I told you about my secret. Perhaps you'll see your Raul there."

I stared ahead intently, beyond the trees where a confluence of smaller creeks joined the river. Indeed, perhaps my lifelong friend and fiancé, Raul Hidalgo, was fishing today. As children, we were both bound by a marriage contract arranged by both sets of parents. We needed to discuss the February date set for our wedding. The Philippines was again at war. Shouldn't we cancel?

Gloriana shoved a fishing pole and bamboo basket into my hands, then used dramatic gestures to describe her new love interest. "Santiago is tall. His biceps are hard. His shoulders are wide. His hips are lean. And his buttocks tight. The perfect specimen of a Filipino heartthrob."

"I think you're going to the river with the intention of catching more than fish, Glory."

"I, Gloriana Consuelo Cruz Ugale, have snared him like a tilapia. Tonight, I'm going to reel him in and eat him up."

Gloriana giggled and pirouetted ahead.

Mamang leaned out of the unglazed window to call after us. "Liling, I'm trusting you to cook dinner for your father. I have a Bible study, remember? Oh, and following that, I will be attending another meeting."

"*Another* meeting, Mamang?"

"Sponsored by the Philippine army. In the church hall." Being an extrovert, Mamang signed up for assemblies, gatherings, and classes, not for the information necessarily but to escape the tension in our home. After spats with Papang, she needed to socialize to lift her spirits.

Mamang continued, "It is about village security. A Mr. Agapito

Macadangdang is speaking."

"A-ga-pi-to?" A long-ago memory came of a third grader whose parents withdrew him from school, presumably to work on the family pig farm.

"Yes, I think you and your sister are acquainted with him. He goes by Pitong. Perfect for Glory. He does not tolerate nonsense. Seems a hard worker. Superior husband material."

"Mamang!" Glory sounded exasperated. "Stop trying to couple me. I love someone else."

"Love? What is love? Love is not a thing." Mamang muttered something about the errant, rule-breaking younger generation. "How I wish your father didn't get into a drunken argument with... Well, never mind, you've heard the story."

The story went like this: Our parents arranged a marriage for baby Gloriana with a boy from a barrio in the valley. Years later, after spending an evening at the saloon, Papang said regretful things to the child's father, who subsequently rescinded the contract, leaving my sister with no betrothed. Glory was actually thrilled. The boy turned out to be dark-skinned, overweight, and pimply. No, she was determined to fall in love and marry someone of her own choosing.

"Well, I hope you are lucky and catch a *big* one."

"Oh, I will, Mamang. A big one." Glory giggled.

"Be safe. The Japon. Yes? And Ligaya, keep an eye on your sister. Make sure she doesn't get into trouble—*again*." I glanced at Glory. Had she heard what our mother had just said? I hated it when Mamang said things that implied I was more mature than my older sister.

The large fishing basket thumped against my thighs. It annoyed me, but not more than the thought that my sweetly manipulative sister was just using me as a ready-made chaperone. I did not feel useful; I felt used.

• • •

"Last one in the water gets to wash the carabao," Gloriana's voice rang out. Water buffalo, too, loved to plod through the gentle waves. The river was where the farmers often rinsed off their worker beasts crusted with the black mud of rice terraces. Human beings and animals necessarily shared the river. We laundered our clothing on the shallow edges, hoping to God no bovid was defecating upstream.

Gloriana waded into the shallow end to cool her sweaty feet. "Remember when Papang used to meet us here after school?"

"I do remember. The weather was so hot that the air hurt my lungs."

"I ran so fast; faster than you, Liling, and I always jumped into the river first."

"Oh, no, sister. *I* ran faster and jumped into the river first."

"No. I needed to get into the cool water before I collapsed from heat stroke."

"Yes. You became sluggish in the heat."

"No."

"Yes."

"You win this time, Glory."

"Remember when Papang taught us how to fish for tilapia?" Glory was being nostalgic.

"And milkfish and catfish."

"We ate a lot of fish." Glory laughed.

"Yes! Would you say he was sweet back then?"

"He was kinder back then."

"I guess so. That was a long, long time ago," I lamented and tried to change the subject. "Glory, I'll make ready the fishing lines while you scan the surroundings for—What's His Name?"

"Goodness, Liling! His name is Santiago. San-ti-ah-go. There he is." Gloriana pointed to a bend in the river where a striking male specimen stood studying the horizon. I followed the direction of his stare but could see nothing worthy of such intense examination.

Movement soon startled me. A Japanese soldier stepped out from the wooded area onto the shore. Santiago earnestly motioned for us to hide.

"Move to the monkeypod tree, Glory," I mumbled. "Quickly. Hide!"

"But why?"

"Japon. Now, Glory. *Now.*"

I tilted my head some small degree toward the opposite shore where Santiago and now the Japanese man stood. I peered from behind the thick trunk and saw the soldier remove his khaki shirt to reveal a chest like a shaggy rug. Hair sprouted from his navel. Curly, black "pubics" completely veiled one-third of his shaft.

He turned briefly away from the river. I gasped. His back was hairy, reminding me of a gorilla. The Japon pulled down his olive-green trousers. Short bristles thick upon his buttocks and legs, and fringes peeked from his crack. He turned to face the river again, carefully folded his uniform, and laid it on the rocks.

The soldier immersed himself in the river; I guess he was eager to cleanse layers of muck his skin had absorbed from sewage-filled trenches. I had heard of the Japanese habit of daily bathing. They scrubbed themselves with firm pressure to exfoliate the body. Rinsed. Then submerged themselves in new, clear, steaming water. Clean water was a luxury that Filipino peasants had little access to.

Gorilla seemed to scrutinize Santiago with his creepy eyes.

Loud rustling, louder than the river's rippling, sent a warning. I signaled Glory to duck even lower. Another Japanese man walked to the pebbled margin, slowly undressed, and waded into the river. He was far less hirsute; in fact, this soldier was bald, clean-shaven. What a contrast to the hairy one!

Baldy gestured as if making an offer, "Want me to wash your back?"

"He looks as if he is petting a gorilla," observed Gloriana.

"Shh!" I scolded.

The bald soldier playfully punched the river's surface, causing a splash that sprayed Japanese Gorilla in the eyes. Gorilla delivered a threatening stream of what sounded like expletives and shoved the other. Baldy, the minion, fell backwards. When at last he found his footing, he sputtered and coughed. Seemingly remorseful, he bowed multiple times in deference to Gorilla.

"I want to take a better look." Gloriana stepped out a bit. A twig snapped. She hurried back to her hiding place. Both soldiers and Santiago scanned the landscape.

"Shh." I grabbed Gloriana's palm to keep her from straying.

Gorilla jerked around. His expressive eyebrows moved in undulating waves resembling fuzzy caterpillars. He locked his close-set, crescent eyes upon me. I stared at him, knowing instinctively that he had condemned hundreds of my countrymen to be killed.

I drew in a ragged breath and rubbed my temples. The band around my skull tightened.

We waited and watched an overlong time. The soldiers finally departed and, at last, Santiago indicated it was safe for us to emerge from behind the tree.

Gloriana giggled and snatched the fishing rod.

I shook my head. "We should go home, Glory. It is not safe here."

"Santiago is protecting us. Nothing feels safer than that."

"But the Japon."

Glory stuck out her lower lip. "Oh Liling, why are you always afraid of foreigners? They are just people like us. You have to trust your instincts."

"I'm not afraid of Dr. Billet."

"Oh, goodness. Of course not, Americans are allies of the Philippines; they helped to free us from Spanish rule."

"Yes, but after winning the Spanish-American War, the Americans kept our country. They're just as bad as the Spaniards for colonizing us. They promised independence but betrayed the Filipinos."

"Never mind that. The Americano doctor's son is sweet on you."

"Glory, why do you persist in calling Dr. Billet 'the Americano doctor'? He has a name. It's disrespectful."

"Because I can't say Dr. Bill-ET without laughing."

"It's pronounced BILL-et. Accent on the first syllable, not Bill-ET."

"I know. I know. I'm pronouncing it the Filipino way. And Bill-ET means 'bird.'"

"Yeah, but in Filipino—"

My sister snorted when she laughed hysterically; sometimes there was even a light spray of spittle.

"Glory, you have a dirty mind."

"Bird is Filipino slang for penis. Poor Americano doctor. Remember he told us he thought the villagers were especially friendly? They grit their teeth when smiling, afraid they will collapse with laughter." Glory pantomimed greeting the physician. "Good evening, Dr. Penis. I mean, Dr. Bird. Oops, Dr. Bill-ET. I mean, Dr. BILL-et." There was that snort again.

"I will be polite and address him properly as Dr. BILL-et. And I decided I would call him Dr. B outside of his presence so as not to give those within earshot a reason to snicker."

"Liling, call him what you wish. The rest of us will refer to him as the Americano doctor."

I felt sad for Dr. Billet, the same way I felt sad for a Chinese author I had read, last name Dung.

"By the way, Liling, how is Berto?"

"I haven't seen him in a while. He's at the university but plans to return a week before our nuptials. Raul will be thrilled to see his best friend again."

World War II. I felt a sense of foreboding. Our wedding may have to be postponed.

. . .

Did the man across the river just wink at my sister? I wanted to stay, to meet Santiago formally, but then I remembered Mamang's earlier instructions.

"Glory, my instincts tell me we are in danger from the Japon most of all, but also from Papang if he learns of this incident and your decision to remain here—unchaperoned."

"Well, he doesn't know about Santiago. And he will be grateful when I come home with dinner."

A swell on the surface signaled an underwater struggle. "Liling. Liling! I caught a tilapia!" With a broad smile, Gloriana tugged hard on the pole.

"Looks like a fighter."

I paid attention to the powerful, silvery, fusiform body writhing and pulling. The homemade hook was lodged in the tilapia's lip, and with every exertion, I could see the lip tore a little. This battle between two forces metaphorically conceptualized the ravages of war, its violence, its suffering. Who would be the victor? Who would be the loser?

"Watch out, Glory; the rocks are slippery."

The fish won, wrenching so hard that Gloriana's brittle bamboo pole snapped in two. She tumbled into the water.

"Glory!"

The wild splashing caused Santiago to spin around. Thinking Gloriana was drowning, he yanked off his shirt and jumped into the river to rescue her. While cautiously towing my sister by his side, he swam back to the opposite beach. The broken bamboo was swept away along with our dinner.

Air and water were getting colder as the sun set.

"We must go, Glory!" I shouted across the narrowest expanse of water. "It will be dark soon."

"Not yet, Liling—please."

"I'm sorry, Glory. My headache is excruciating. Papang will be upset because I'm late starting dinner. The Japon are nearby. Come *now*."

"Stop being so bossy, Liling. I'm your elder."

"*You're* the bossy one, Glory—the stubborn one." I wanted to say what was really on my mind. *The stupid one.* I pressed my lips together instead. We sisters occasionally bantered like that; one wisecrack was followed by the other's goading.

A distant Japon conversation floated from the woods. Japanese, not Filipino. Filipinos are able to pronounce the L sound. The Japanese people articulate a slightly rolled R when reading the letter L. "Hehrroh, rraydee. I weerr keerr yew." *Hello, lady. I will kill you.*

. . .

Santiago wrapped his arms around my sister as I turned to leave. Gloriana pressed into him. Was my heart racing because I was frightened by the Japon soldiers, because Glory had nearly drowned, or because she was enfolded in a strange man's embrace—something a good, unmarried, Catholic *Pinay* would never do? I witnessed their affection and huffed as I returned home.

What could I do? Gloriana was twenty-seven years old, two years my senior. She should be able to take care of herself, but her critical thinking skills and common sense were absent sometimes. My sister was fun to be around—most of the time. She could be silly, charismatic, and carefree, qualities that made her popular. But she could also be impulsive, reckless, and immature.

Was Papang drunk by now? I felt uneasy.

. . .

I focused on washing three large handfuls of rice kernels and set the pot on the clay stove. I cut some Asian string beans and small eggplants and sautéed them with fermented shrimp paste. Papang returned from the beer hall and was not at all in a jovial mood; he had a craving for fish this evening. Unlike Gloriana, I was not skilled at catching tilapia to bring home for frying. Instead, our humble meal would consist of salted balls of rice, a meager serving of cooked vegetables, and over-ripe bananas, the fare of financially strapped families.

I dared not initiate conversation lest Papang ask the whereabouts of my sister. Darn, Glory. Should I feel guilty for having to leave you? What excuses will I give Papang for you this time? Yet again, you place me in a dangerous predicament.

I had not yet had a chance to be formally introduced to Gloriana's most recent infatuation. He struck me as being handsome enough from afar, but I would have liked to assess his personality. Gloriana tended to attract bad boys—she said she liked bad boys.

. . .

Papang's aggressions had begun when we were very young, Mamang tells us, after the serial deaths of four of his six sons.

At that time, my little girl brain could not comprehend what was so naughty about such behaviors as Gloriana accidentally spilling her juice and why it warranted such forceful physical punishment. "Papang hates me," she used to confide to me.

"No, Papang hates *me*," I countered.

Young Glory used to escape outside and race away from Papang. It was comedic the way she ran 'round and 'round the hut with our then healthy and hefty father an increasing distance away. She contrived to fling herself out of the orbit and then hid in a deep, dried-up ditch.

"Where is Gloriana Consuelo Cruz Ugale?" Papang bellowed.

"I don't know." Mamang put a finger to her lips while looking sideways at four-year-old me.

Gloriana had once asked me why I was so stupid as to stand like statuary in a musty museum. All the years of abuse, I would suck on my lower lip and wince, trying hard not to whimper. My stoicism only compelled Papang to strike more forcefully until long ghastly welts appeared on my buttocks and thighs. I eventually discovered that crying had the power to soften Papang's heart. I would remain erect and silently allow the cascading of many tears. It felt manipulative to be able to control my emotions like that, but Papang relaxed his blows, and corporal punishment was discontinued shortly thereafter.

Papang moved his rancor to the beer hall where I knew he was in the habit of demanding three, four, and five refills. Drunk and exhausted, he returned home, where he crashed asleep with his cane, his belt, or a bamboo switch in hand.

. . .

I flashed back to that time when I was four and had shown my friend, Raul, the welts on my thighs.

"Oh, Liling." His eyes revealed his shock. "Your papang did this? Why?"

"I didn't do anything. Glory's fault. She spilled her coconut water. Then she spilled rice. Is that naughty, Raul?"

He shook his head.

"Papang made two hills of hard rice kernels on the floor. He made my sister kneel on them until dinnertime."

"Ouch! Your papang is *mean*." Raul puffed out his chest. "But I'm not scared of him."

"You're braver than me, Raul."

"It was Glory's fault, Liling. Why did he hit *you*? I don't understand."

I shrugged. "I don't know. Maybe because I tried to clean up the rice. Maybe because I cried. Maybe his back hurt. Maybe he owed money. No money, no beer." I've been told I was a precocious child back then.

"That's a hundred reasons, Liling."

"My papang is a madman."

Raul confided, "My father punished me when I fell out of the mango tree."

"*Our* big mango tree?"

"Don't know why he beat me. I had blood on my skin."

"You already hurt, but he still hit you?"

Raul nodded.

"*My* papang would do that. But not your father, Raul. I never saw him be mad."

"He's not now. Afterwards, my father cried. Told me over, and over, and over he was sorry." Raul paused as if reliving the memory. "He *never* hit me again."

Raul pulled up his right pant leg and showed me a tiny scar on his knee. "This is from the fall." Then he traced an old, wider, three-inch-long, keloid-covered injury. "This is from my father."

. . .

My sister could not avoid a confrontation. The floor creaked as she stepped inside our one-room hut. Tonight, despite an injured back, Papang leaped to his feet, holding his cane high above his head.

Our father screamed Filipino obscenities. "You dirty, dirty, dumb-dumb!" *WHACK.* He beat Glory like a man gone crazy. I attempted to rescue her, but Papang shoved me violently. I tripped over a stalk of brown bananas.

All of my senses were painfully aroused. The smell of Papang's foul liquor breath. The whoosh and crack of his cane. The sight of our desperate mother and my defiant sister. The pain of the tear on my lip and the taste of blood in my mouth. The drama was familiar. The trauma felt "normal."

"Please, Respicio, stop. The neighbors can hear," begged Mamang.

"You think I give a damn about other people's opinions?"

"Mr. and Mrs. Hidalgo. Think of Liling," cautioned Mamang, referring to our neighbors, also my future in-laws. "And our daughter, Glory. You are going to kill her."

Papang screamed the most terrible profanity a Filipino could say, literally translated into "Your mother's cunt."

He whacked Mamang too. "You raised this filthy daughter. This whore! What kind of dirty, dirty, dumb-dumb mother are you?"

He turned the stick to me. "This is for not telling me. You're supposed to be the *good one*." The remark stung me more than the physical punishment. I think surely those words must have hurt Glory.

Gloriana fought back. She pushed Papang. I knew full well she may have caused more damage to his spine. This launched Papang into a higher stratosphere of rage.

As usual, I froze, stoically accepting punishment.

Papang stopped as suddenly as he started, whacked the cane against the table, and stomped to the opposite side of the room, where he dumped a cocoa powder can's contents onto the bench. I willed him to extinguish the flames of his fury at the beer hall.

Only a few centavos fell out of the makeshift bank.

"Shit!" He'd get but a trickle of beer.

Hearing his continued vitriol, Mamang fervently prayed aloud for her husband's soul. On Sundays, she lit many votive candles, believing her supplications were delivered to God upon the smoke that wafted toward heaven. She often claimed that without her intercessions, Papang could go to hell, Glory might end up single and pregnant, and I would be left single and suffering agonizing headaches.

My mother talked of separation every time Papang went on a drunken rampage, but our largely Catholic country legislated divorce as illegal. It was considered immoral; she would be refused the sacraments for desecrating the sanctity of marriage. It took years for annulments to be granted, and Mamang had decided the cost in time and money wasn't worth it.

"God of Loving Fathers, I beg Thee, please make Papang gentle and kind." I pressed the back of my neck and rolled my shoulders. I uttered a painful "Amen."

Mamang clasped her rosary in her hands, turned to Papang, and started praying, "...and forgive us our trespasses as we forgive those who *trespass against us*—and lead us not into temptation but deliver us from evil."

Did I hear Mamang say, "Forgive me, Father, for I am going to kill that bastard husband of mine?"

Though not directly to the punisher, Gloriana spit out the venomous words, "Go to hell."

. . .

At last, "River Day," stacked with seismic events, was coming to an end—a migraine, a Japon sighting, a near-drowning, a sister's reckless liaison, a dismal dinner, and a father's drunken tirade. I could not have borne another catastrophe. After the fracas, my sister and I lay beside each other on our floor mats as we had since we were children.

We had a history of waiting in the darkness until Papang's snoring and Mamang's huffing were deep and rhythmic. We only exchanged sisterly secrets when safety was ascertained.

"What does Santiago do?" I whispered.

"He kisses me."

"I know that." I think I must have sounded annoyed. "I mean, what does he do for a living?"

"I'm not sure exactly. He is a skilled fisherman. He's good with his hands." Gloriana chuckled.

"Be serious," was my rebuke.

"I am serious. He is clever at fashioning new bamboo poles and fishnets. And he is patient. One has to be patient when waiting for fish to bite. Besides, he has a smooth chest and bulging muscles."

"Oh, good. Not like that Japon gorilla. I myself do not like a man with a hairy chest. And my man, his hands; I require that fingernails are clean."

"Even if he is a mechanic, or farmer, or plumber?"

"*Especially* if he is a mechanic, or farmer, or plumber."

From Papang's corner came a long, uncomfortable break in the series of grunts, sounding an alarm for us both. Gloriana gripped my hand until we heard a forceful snort that signaled we were no longer at risk.

I asked, "Is he a laborer?"

"I don't know what he does for a living."

"What? You don't know?"

"Not yet. His hands are smooth, not those of a farmer. Santiago is very generous; he shares his catch. He recites passages from the Bible. I think Mamang will love him for that."

"Hmm."

"It doesn't sound as if you like him, Liling."

"Well, he and I have not yet officially met. Let me vet him."

"You mean interrogate him."

"Then I shall say whether he is worthy of you."

"Liling, I think it's the other way around. I may not be worthy of him. I am plain, uneducated. Truly, who would want me, particularly a man as good-looking and protective?"

Gloriana waited. "Today, I purposely fell into the river."

"What? You did what?" I was unprepared for the revelation.

Gloriana giggled softly. "It was a test, dear Liling. I was testing to see whether my Santiago would rescue me. Me, the damsel in distress, and him like a knight in shining armor."

"You're crazy, Glory. I thought you were going to drown. Don't do that again; you scared me to death." A short while later, curiosity caused my exasperation to subside.

"So, did he pass your test?"

"He earned many, many stars."

I struggled to stay awake. My eyelids were heavy. With my tongue, I touched the small wound on my lip.

On this night, Glory finally revealed the contents of her heart, but I had long suspected she had fallen in love. I was astute in noticing that Glory and Santiago exchanged subtle gestures and glances even across long expanses of land and flowing water.

Although I had entered the period of light sleep, I definitely heard Glory disclose that she and Santiago had *made love* on the river shore until the full moon rose. I gasped and my eyes snapped open.

"What? Say again?"

"We made love."

Both of us were taught the unwritten, but oft-spoken, expectation of guarding one's virginity.

"Once you give it, you can never get it back." Mamang's Mantra, we called it.

Papang frequently admonished, "I will disown you. I will find the bastard, butcher his *bayag* with my machete and feed his shriveled balls to the dogs." Papang would have wanted to castrate everybody—naughty boys, criminals, rapists, cheaters, liars, the insane, and most of all, any man who dared to have sex with his daughters outside of marriage.

Consummation may only take place after the wedding. It is the Filipino way. It is the Catholic way.

Gloriana was quiet too long a time. Did she regret disclosing so much detail to me?

"I love him like you love Raul."

I sighed. I understood. My love for Raul was growing.

"Keep my secret. Please." Gloriana sounded anxious, even though I had told her on multiple occasions that I was utterly trustworthy.

"I promise."

Chapter 4

LIGAYA "LILING" UGALE

December 10, 1941

"Auntie Liling, is this how I crochet the fancy stitch?"

"Yes! Perfect! Pacencia, dear, in time you will be able to make lace to sell to the Chinese merchant."

"Show me another crochet trick, Auntie."

"Let's just sit for a while, dear, so I may rest my eyes."

"Headache brewing?" asked Glory while putting pastries on a plate for our afternoon repast.

"I can't wait until your wedding," said Pacencia. "I'm so excited about being your flower girl."

"Oh, you will be the prettiest flower girl, ever." I pushed her bangs away from her eyes.

"Auntie, do you think I'll marry someday?"

"Of course, smart girl like you."

Mamang joined us with freshly squeezed orange juice for all. "Not for a while. And no play-ing before marriage."

"Huh?" Pacencia looked at her lola for answers. "Don't play?"

Glory gestured sharply at Mamang. "I believe your grandmother is referring to adult play."

"I don't think Mommy and Papang made me a marriage contract."

"No, your father is a modern-thinking man," said Glory.

I added, "He married the love of his life, your mother. He would want you to marry someone you love too."

"How long have you and Raul known each other, Auntie Liling?"

Mamang interrupted, "I remember that little boy Raul had wavy hair. His mother thought perhaps he had inherited his curls from a European ancestor, a Spanish king or queen, at least a duke or duchess. Raul's last name is Hidalgo. It means 'royalty.'"

I have to smile. As usual, Mamang exaggerated—a bit of wishful thinking on her part. In Spanish, Hidalgo actually translates to the lower nobility or simply a gentleman property owner. I would have corrected her, but it would have been disrespectful.

"I was maybe four years old. Mamang made me wear a nice hand-me-down from Glory's old dresses. Marched me to our next-door neighbors. Yes, and Papang made a toast. 'May our children be joined for life, blah, blah, blah. Here is to my daughter and her new husband-to-be. *Mabuhay*! Mabuhay! Mabuhay!'" I laughed. "Of course, I didn't understand back then what husband-to-be meant until Raul told me all he knew—that we were supposed to kiss in church."

"You said, 'Yuck.' Remember? Made Raul promise to never kiss you." Mamang laughed.

"I climbed on his back, and we 'horsied' away to play under our mango tree. And then, our stomachs rumbled. I was too little to reach any of the ripe mangoes."

" 'I can climb,' Raul said. He scrambled so high it made me nervous. I prayed—"

"I know what you prayed," Glory said. " 'God of Mango Trees, I pray Thee make Raul come down. Now. AAA-MEN.' " Everybody laughed.

Mamang pointed at me. "A bossy child way back." Mamang clearly enjoyed the memory.

"Not as bossy as Glory," I retorted. "He tossed a mango. I scooped my hands to catch it. Sweet mango juice dribbled down my chin, chest, and arms. Raul said that mangoes are luscious."

Mamang laughed some more. "Yes, that's when you learned the word luscious. Except you pronounced it, 'Lush-shush. Lush-shush.'"

I turned back to Pacencia. "In middle school, my friends and I prayed for handsome boyfriends. Every once in a while, your lola would have to remind me I had an obligation to meet my marriage contract. No one was as thrilled as me. Raul and I had fun together wrestling, swimming, and climbing our mango tree. Until I was about twelve, nobody said we couldn't play rough. Soon, I had to wear a bra and Raul's voice deepened, and we weren't allowed to horse around anymore."

"Did you say, 'I love you'?" asked Pacencia. "I mean to each other."

"Well, your lola thinks there is no such thing as love, at least not romantic love. Ask your grandma."

Mamang shook her head. "Especially no love before marriage." She shook her finger at Pacencia, or maybe at Glory who sat behind the child.

Glory whispered in Pacencia's ear and laughed. "She means no sex before marriage."

"Eww."

"Raul is generous, kind, ambitious, patient, and best of all, fun-loving; he has the impeccable manners of a benevolent aristocrat. He is an industrious rice farmer who is well-groomed."

"Ask your auntie Liling how clean his fingernails are. It disgusts her that most farmers do not scrub well after field work."

Filipino custom makes it acceptable to eat with our hands. "A man must have clean fingernails," I replied.

Chapter 5

LIGAYA "LILING" UGALE

April 1942

The red, white, and blue-edged envelope I held in my hands had traveled eight thousand kilometers over the Pacific Ocean. We had all been worried sick about Boy ever since the Pearl Harbor bombing. More than two thousand people had died in Hawaii that December day—sixty-some were civilians—we had prayed fervently that Boy wasn't one of them.

"Everybody! Mamang! Papang! Where's Glory? A letter from Boy!" I had not yet opened the envelope and we were all crying. In a moment, we would assign joy or grief to our tears.

"I refuse to wait for your sister." Papang shook his head.

"Shush, Respicio!" Mamang brought her index finger to her lips.

Glory appeared suddenly with a large tilapia. "What's going on?"

Holding my breath, I tore the paper flap. My eyes focused upon the date the letter was written; a good four months ago.

December 14, 1941

Dear Mamang, Papang, Bartolome, Glory, and Liling, I tried desperately to reach you. I am alive! I was at Mass when the bombing started. (Yes, Mamang, I do go to Church every Sunday.) I ran outside and saw dozens of airplanes with red circles painted on their wings. I almost panicked. If I didn't die in an explosion, I thought I might die from a heart attack.

I could not reach you by phone. Communication between the USA and the Philippines is restricted. Civilian concerns and distress were dismissed—military matters come first.

One of the college professors keeps a residence in Hawaii. He returned to the US because there was no more work for him; the university in Manila was destroyed. Liling, he taught your friend, Gilberto Abueg, who asked the professor to seek me and convey an important message. "Your village still stands. Nothing has happened to your family." I fell to my knees with relief.

There is a lot of hate and fear here. My Japanese friends and I don't speak to each other anymore. Some of them were sent to internment camps. Good riddance. How dare they attack my homeland!

How is everybody? I worry that you are starving. Here is a money order to make your Christmas a little easier. I wish I could send more. Please take care of yourselves. Watch out for the Japanese; they are sneaky.

Aloha,
Boy

"What does *aloha* mean?" Mamang asked through her tears.

"I don't know," Glory said. "Maybe it's Hawaiian for 'Yours truly.' "

God of Hope and Faith, we thank Thee for keeping Boy safe. Hallelujah! He is alive! Amen and aloha.

• • •

I refused to return to the river for fishing, so fearful was I of the Japon. My anxiety manifested somatically as frequent and severe tension headaches.

The next day, my sister begged me to accompany her. Glory dug through farm soil, searching for earthworms, and threaded them onto nails she had hammered into hooks. She admitted sneaking to the river often in hopes of meeting with Santiago, but lately he was absent more often than not.

"It is lonely on the bank. Come with me, Liling."

"Are you going to trick me into being a convenient chaperone? Risking my skin for your lust is not an option, Gloriana Consuelo Cruz Ugale."

"It is not the same without you. Please?" Glory could persuade anyone to buy tickets to purgatory.

I reluctantly followed Glory to the river. We both put our lines into the water, and together, we joyfully pulled out three medium-sized tilapias. Within my peripheral sight, I saw Santiago struggle with his line. Gloriana smiled broadly, then waved. He did not wave back. She dropped her hand to automatically cover her mouth. His lack of response bewildered me; I'm sure it confused my sister. What was going on? I would hate it if he purposely deflowered my sister, only to abandon her for being too loose. Many Pinoys hold to a double standard.

I could read the desperation in Glory's face. She would have called out to him, but there were others on the bank washing laundry, bathing, filling barrels with water. Another flirtatious, let alone sexual, encounter was an impossibility in the presence of so many villagers. A single woman meeting a man unchaperoned—she would be the evening's gossip confabulated by old Filipinos who were stuck on stupid, meaningless cultural values. Had Glory known that she would never again hear Santiago's voice or feel his warmth, never again connect with her lover, she would have discarded all caution and run into his arms—tradition be damned.

Santiago, at five feet, nine inches, stood tall for a Filipino. He had unbuttoned his shirt today while fishing under the tropical sun. Like many Filipino men, he had a hairless torso with only baby fuzz on his arms and legs. Throughout their night of passion, Glory said, she had become familiar with his body.

During our special time that night, Glory asked, "Liling, did you see what Santiago wore around his neck?"

"No, sister," I whispered.

"I noticed something new and glistening hanging around his neck. On a thin leather strap was a beautiful silver cross that shone bright and prominently on his golden-brown chest."

"Were you born with eagle eyes?"

"I pay attention to those kinds of things."

"A crucifix, you say?"

"The unusual relief of the Jesus figure was not upright. Instead, I think it was a cast of a man stooped in suffering, like Papang, as if bearing the weight of the sins of the world."

"Papang, like Jesus?" An absurd thought.

"The most unusual feature about his pendant was the prominent size of the thorns embedded into Christ's forehead."

. . .

Papang stumbled into the bamboo hut. With eyes glazed and without light, he kicked me with his booted foot. Intentional? I wondered. I involuntarily whimpered, but I kept my eyes closed, pretending to be asleep.

I breathed slowly, shallowly, so as not to make any sound that might trigger Papang's wrath. He crashed into a stool, which fell onto

Gloriana's mat. For some reason, Gloriana curled into a fetal position and the stool just rolled into the space where her legs would have been.

Papang lay next to his wife. I heard rustling, a small groan of protest, a hard slap, the rhythmic grating of the slatted bamboo floor, and a drunken grunt. Papang's shadowy figure rolled onto its side. Shortly after, he snored like the devil himself, descending into an eternal inferno.

I thought I heard Mamang—or was it Glory—hiss, then say, "Go to hell."

• • •

"Liling?"

"Yes, sister?" Snoring signaled the time was right for sharing secrets.

"I have missed four lunar cycles since the last time Papang beat us." She had counted the days since her last bleeding. Long overdue. "Make it not be so. I cannot be. I simply cannot be with child." Gloriana cried.

"Gaunt but glowing" was how I described my sister these days.

We continued to fish for the family's supper, but Santiago was never seen again. Glory's description of the moon on their night of intimacy, a golden coin she had interpreted as an auspicious omen, stuck with me. It was time for some good luck in this family.

"Liling, I close my eyes and imagine the weight of his body upon mine. Not too heavy; he propped himself on his elbows so as not to crush me. The scent of musk on his skin. The melody of his voice. My senses are full of Santiago, Liling. I cannot get him out of my mind."

She sobbed softly and caressed her own arms. "I pretend I am sometimes the giver, sometimes the receiver. In my dreams, I search his eyes for confirmation of his love. They confuse me. Are his eyes reflecting God's love or man's love?"

"Crying is healing, sister." I did not know what else to say. Where are you, Santiago? Why are you ignoring Glory?

My sister wore loose clothing. She went about her chores so as not to attract unwanted attention from Papang. I caught our mother studying Gloriana, specifically her abdomen. Mamang said nothing;

she only made the sign of the cross.

Almost five months after their joining at the river, Glory informed me it was time to confess. She could no longer hide her pregnancy.

. . .

"Glory, when are you going to tell Papang?" I asked. "You're beginning to show a bump." I worked quickly, picking lima beans from the bushes while Glory groaned every time she bent to pull a pod.

"I'm bracing myself for Papang's reaction."

"It is certain he will yell."

"He will be violent."

"Or he may not." I tried to sound optimistic. "Have you informed Mamang?"

"Liling, our mother guessed. I suspected she knew because every time our eyes met, Mamang looked utterly displeased."

"I'm sorry you are going through this, sister."

"I'm not. I'm not sorry, Liling. I love Santiago."

"Yes, but he absconded, who knows where?"

"I fear the Japon have murdered him." Gloriana was tearful.

We continued working for a while, listening only to the sounds of bean pods tossed into a large steel container.

"Glory, you must resist the urge to yell back at Papang. I am so afraid he will react violently and endanger your baby."

Gloriana sniffled.

"I am here for you, sister. And I am here for your baby."

. . .

I carried one of the filled containers into the hut where I found Papang standing ominously at the window that overlooked his fields.

"Why is Glory moving like a sloth?" Papang scrutinized his eldest daughter as she trudged through the lima bean patch, a look of exhaustion on her face. She paused frequently while harvesting the legumes.

He was impatient; lima beans needed to be boiled for at least thirty minutes before they were tender enough to eat. He barked at Mamang. "What kind of dirty, dirty, dumb-dumb mother are you to have raised such a good-for-nothing daughter?"

I had heard him deride Mamang's maternal skills a thousand times in regard to Gloriana's qualities. But, in fact, Mamang had always said she judged her eldest daughter to be a fine young woman.

"You, Liling, are reserved, demure, and courteous, concealing a strength you don't even know exists."

"Oh? Thank you, Mamang."

"Whereas Glory is confident in herself as a woman. She is assertive, vocal, passionate, and self-sufficient. And yes, she can be brash and foolish."

"I tend to agree."

Mamang and I pretended everything was satisfactory and hid behind a veneer of silence lest the already irritated patriarch be further aggravated.

Papang observed, "Glory is more absent-minded than ever. Her face is swollen, and the pigment in her skin is darker. She can barely lift the container of produce. Look at Gloriana. She's out of breath."

My palpitations and respirations increased. Papang was not stupid.

"Glory's ankles are thick, and her step is heavy. If I didn't know better—"

Gloriana placed her hand upon the small of her back as she stooped to harvest more of the pods. Then she placed her hand on the round of her abdomen. Suddenly agitated, Papang spit out, "If I didn't know better, I would think she is—she is—"

"Pregnant," Mamang blurted, completing Papang's thoughts.

"My daughter, a whore!" Our father was furious. He looked like a fuming, horned bull aiming to gore any plant, animal, or man in his way. He picked up a near-empty bottle of his precious beer and hurled it in Mamang's direction. The shatter and commotion caused Glory to burst in from outdoors.

Papang's wholly vehement reaction to the reality that Gloriana would be delivering an illegitimate child jolted me.

"Whore! Who is the father? I shall cut off his *bayag* and feed them to the *carabao*. Who is the father? WHO IS THE DIRTY, DIRTY, DUMB-DUMB FATHER?" Papang raised his cane.

Terrified, we three women bolted away from the madman and galloped next door to the Hidalgo home where Raul and his father provided temporary protection. I knew the Hidalgos were aware of the brutality in our home; nipa huts are thin-walled. I had felt petrified when Raul indicated his father was contemplating breaking our marriage contract. "God of Future In-Laws, please bless Mr. and Mrs. Hidalgo with eyes blind and ears deaf to Papang's fury."

Our neighbors busied themselves with making coffee and putting out morsels of sweet, sticky rice for us.

Mamang turned to Glory and was soft-spoken, I suppose to counteract the effects of Papang's rage and because it was important to her that Gloriana understood the unvarnished truth of her thoughts and feelings.

"Your father is being forced to accept this trouble—that you are no longer *pure and chaste*. Unlike your papang, I will use a gentle tone, but I hope you realize I am absolutely disappointed in you, Gloriana Consuelo Cruz Ugale. Greatly disappointed. I have tried my best to guide you as lovingly as I could, but parents cannot control the choices their adult children make. We had so many dreams for you and your sister—to be blessed with a stable life, a joy-filled life. In this moment, Glory, I cannot comprehend how that will be."

Trying to make myself invisible, I put my head down and stared at the ground, crossing my arms over my chest. The Hidalgos pretended not to listen. If they didn't suspect Glory's pregnancy, they would certainly know now. Besides, my sister made a big show of rubbing the bump on her belly.

Gloriana turned to our mother, sobbing. "I'm sorry, Mamang."

"What a terrible complication! Have we not enough stress? Bartolome's eyes are failing, your father is bent with crookedness, your sister has excruciating headaches, and the Japon are decimating our country. Now, you are unwed and to be a mother. The gossip and rumors. I can hardly accept the predicament you have placed us in. We already do not have much upon which to survive. How can we feed another mouth? I desperately wanted my daughters to have a good life because, in all honesty, I did not have a good life for myself."

Despite Mamang's admonishment, my sister smiled through her tears. She placed her hand on her abdomen. I knew instinctively the fetus must have been kicking.

I loved being in the Hidalgos' home, always so warm and welcoming. I wanted so much for Raul to hold me, but he could not shield me with an embrace. Touching between an unmarried man and woman was not allowed in the rural Philippines of that time—a cultural expectation Gloriana had obviously ignored.

Vicious attacks by my father caused Mr. Hidalgo much consternation. Another round of violence, Raul told me, would be the last straw for his father, who believed that marrying a woman meant marrying her family. Raul's father was tempted to break the marital contract to protect his son from his future father-in-law's abusive behavior.

Mr. Hidalgo sat beside his wife of forty years. "I know the Ugale women are respectful, protective, and compassionate toward each other and toward my kin. I have discerned this for myself. I only want the best for my family, especially for my son, Raul. Respicio's behavior—not the best."

I felt embarrassed.

Raul had a pained look on his face. I tried to appear calm. Was Mr. Hidalgo going to revoke the marriage arrangement? It would not be the first. Glory's engagement had been ruined when Papang had argued with her betrothed's father.

"May I pour you some coffee, Mr. Hidalgo?" I asked, helping Mrs. Hidalgo with the refreshments.

"You have a pretty voice! Matches a pretty disposition."

"Thank you, Tata Hidalgo. I needed to be reminded of something good about me."

"Call me Papa, Liling. You and Raul will be married, and we will be your family. Safe harbor for the two of you."

My heart fluttered and Raul met my eyes. Mr. Hidalgo would not break the marriage contract. My anxiety and despondency had been stuffed and packed tightly into my heart. I could no longer hold back my emotions. I released tears of sadness for Mamang, Glory, and the baby. Tears of relief for myself—Raul's papa was loving and kind—my fiancé and I were still to be married.

Chapter 6

AGAPITO "PITONG" MACADANGDANG

May 1942

I, Agapito Macadangdang—most everybody calls me Pitong—enlisted in the Philippine army after the bombing of Pearl Harbor. Being a combat soldier was supposed to be glamorous: women swooning over my uniform, world travel, free education. But no. I got nothing.

Danger followed me everywhere. I was horrified by the regularity of battle. My constant companions were bullets and bombs—coming and going. The goal of the Jap enemy is to kill men like me. I could also be killed by Americanos or even a Filipino. Hah! "Friendly fire."

I hated that the US occupied the Philippines after it won the Spanish-American War. American teachers came to open public schools and forced us to learn English. Too bad I hadn't paid attention in class. Too bad my flash temper and poor English made military duty risky for me. What if I died because of a simple misunderstanding?

Base life was extremely difficult. Long hours, shitty chores, endless push-ups, bland food. I was hard up. Every type of equipment in short supply. Mosquito nets, blankets, pup tents, trenching tools, gas masks, and helmets. Where is the appeal?

I was ordered into my first battle without orientation; never before had I fired a gun, never even seen an artillery piece. The only thing I was skilled at—jumping to attention to salute the officers. For laughs, my soldier friends blasted, "Attention!" just to watch me snap to. Just teasing I suppose—entertainment for all.

Philippines, one country, thousands of islands. Each district with its own dialect. The enlisted men spoke the words of their home regions. Language barriers made our work slow. We made mistakes that caused many arguments and fist fights. Some soldiers conversed in basic, broken English. Some well-educated Filipinos were lucky to be fluent in English. As a result, they were quick to be promoted, unlike me.

"Private Macadangdang, did you get the drill?" My Americano trainer yelled at me after teaching us bah-yo-net u-tee-lee-zah-shon (bayonet utilization) in hand-to-hand combat.

"Sirrr?" Ay, my heavy accent. My rolling Rs.

"Show me. Did you get the drill?" the Sergeant shouted louder. Was he speaking to me? My toes twitched and my face flushed warm. My buddies at attention only stared straight ahead. One private glanced at me, pity in his eyes, and shrugged his shoulders.

I left the formation, hurried to the mechanics shop and came back with a hand drill, proud of myself for figuring out what the Sergeant had wanted.

"You idiot!" Ay, he blasted my ears.

Amazing that nobody laughed at me afterwards. They seemed relieved the trainer had not picked on them.

Later on, my squad members discussed the incident in the barracks.

"What kind of Americano speak-ed English no one can understand?"

Another soldier slapped his forehead. "Blue means sad. I am blue. What is that? And what means slice bread?"

"Slice bread means *good*...I think," a companion from my village tried to explain.

"Pitong, but the Sergeant said, 'Better than slice bread.' "

I said, "Yeh. Gooder. Is that not so? Gooder?"

"See what I mean? Speak English, Pitong."

"I am con-ju-gay-teeng. Bad. Badder. Baddest. Good. Gooder. Goodest."

"Doesn't sound correct, Pitong."

"One time, when Sergeant asked me, 'Penny for your thoughts?' I searched my pocket for a *centavo*. Why did he scream at me again? Is a centavo not like a penny? Two cents the same as two centavos. I thought I am smart."

My buddies slapped me on the back. "Better you than me."

I felt as if I was back in the third grade when Sister Augustina whack-ed my palms with her wooden ruler. Understanding American sayings, impossible.

Always lacking sleep. Could not sleep more than three hours straight. How could I? Too many flying rockets whistled and *boom, boom, boom*. What was worse? A night of explosion or a night of silence? When quiet, my mind went crazy. I imagined a sneaky Jap coming into my tent, slicing my throat.

Going and going is my brain. What if I caught dysentery? What if I got lost and my squadron left me behind in the jungle? What if this? What if that? My brain like rotten bananas.

Always tired, always hungry, and always ashamed of my English. I prayed for my parents, and my young adult brother and teenaged sister back at my village. To protect my family, I volunteered to serve my country.

I was supposed to marry a woman I had never met. Well, actually, we were in each other's presence as babies, when both sets of parents arranged marriage between little one-year-old Pitong and the infant girl Salome.

Scanning newspapers about my hometown became my hobby. I searched for any stories and photos about my beautiful Salome. All I found were news stories about the Japon and the cruelties they enacted upon the Filipinos.

Salome, I will be home as soon as I can to protect you. Wait for me, darling.

Army work, I hated it. I wished to resign as soon as possible so that I could marry.

. . .

I was forced to stay enlisted. Big battles were planned in strategic areas of the Philippines.

During village check, I patrolled the barrios for safety and security. I heard cries of human hunger. Every night and every morning, the children of the provinces cried, screamed really. The young ones were tired, irritable, unable to concentrate on their studies. Their stomachs were bloated and tight with cramps. Their hair brittle and falling out. Starving, suffering were my people. No food, no energy. No energy, no work. No work, no food.

I hated Japs. I continued to hate the Japs. "Japs," that is what the Americanos call the Japon. To my ear, the word was as insulting as the sharp edge of a bolo knife because the vowel "A" was not pronounced with the warmth of the "ah" in Japon. "Hah-pon—pucking [fucking] Japs."

I tried my best to train in the harshest of army conditions. Becoming a skilled infantryman required hard work, training, and repetition. Finally, I was promoted to Private First Class. Even my buddies were proud of my accomplishment.

I studied English, but I still have a thick accent. My instructor recognized my difficulties with rolling Rs. My tongue kept disobeying. Sometimes I confused F with P and V with B. "I um bery froud to be Fribate Pirst Class." [I am very proud to be Private First Class.] I was lucky I did not stand out—we all sounded the same—other Pinoys mispronounced English words, too.

I often tried to improve my English to fulfill my dream of making a new life for myself and my bride in the United States.

...

One day, on temporary leave, I sat on a bench under the shade of bamboo. I observed a thin woman making her way through my cousin's barrio. The woman looked to be in her sixties, but she had jet black hair. I was grateful to be able to speak Filipino again. If the stranger approached me, I would not have to struggle with English. As a former sergeant-at-arms, I felt it my duty to follow her, well hidden, of course.

She called out to everyone who came near her, knocked on many doors, and shouted her questions through open windows. Her determination was sure to get her whatever she was seeking. At the sun's highest point, her energy began to wane; the woman must have traveled a long way, but she had a look of sheer determination on her face. She asked many people about a man named Santiago.

A shopkeeper wearing a dirty white apron severely interrogated this stranger. "What is his last name?"

"Sir, I do not recall his surname."

"What? You do not know his full name? Well, then how can you expect us to help you?"

Answering another villager's questions, the lady admitted, "Ma'am, he frequently goes freshwater fishing."

"Is he employed as a fisherman? Or is fishing his hobby?"

She shrugged. "I don't know."

"If you don't know, I don't know." The villager waved her away.

The stranger approached yet another person. "Where might I find Santiago? He owns a sizable silver crucifix on a leather cord."

The man ignored her.

She stepped toward the recreational field at the small high school. "What does this person look like, *Nana*?" My niece, an adolescent, addressed her politely by addressing an elder with an honorific. It is the Filipino way.

"I am told that he is tall for a Filipino. He has smooth, brown skin. No hair on his chest, or arms, or legs. His shoulders are broad, and his hips are narrow."

The teen smiled. "When you find this man, please introduce him to me, Nana." And she ran to join her clique. The students, still in uniform, looked in the woman's direction and snickered. Such silly girls. My niece came over and whispered to me.

"What is your business here?" I asked the old woman. "I am told you are seeking Santiago. Well, my cousin is a neighbor of Santiago's family."

She studied my face. "Tell me, have we met?"

"I was the Sergeant-at-Arms of our village. But I enlisted in the Philippine army. I am here only a brief time, and I am transferring back out tomorrow."

"Ah, yes. I remember you now. After the Japon invasion, you delivered a talk at our village about safety and security."

"Hurrah! My speech made an impression on at least one member of my audience." I smiled. "My name is Agapito Macadangdang. Private First Class. Pitong is my nickname."

"Ah, yes. Pitong. At last." She clapped her hands and placed her palms on her cheeks. "A sergeant-at-arms would surely be acquainted with most, if not all, the citizens of this barrio. I am Maria Cruz Ugale."

"I am happy to make your acquaintance, Nana Ugale. Tell me, is there a Salome in your village?"

Mrs. Ugale paused to think. "I'm afraid not. At least, not that I know of."

I shrugged. "My parents are trying to be matchmakers. An arranged marriage. But they lost track of Salome since her parents passed away. Would you be able to help me find her, Nana?"

"I'm sorry, Pitong. I have not heard of a Salome in our village. Pitong, like you, I am trying to locate someone. I am looking for a Santiago."

"I am acquainted with two Santiagos who live on the outskirts of this barrio."

"Tell me what you know of Santiago who hails from this side of the river. At the border, you say?"

"Junior or senior?"

"I think he is about twenty-six. Twenty-seven. Maybe twenty-eight."

"Then you are looking for Junior. He is a good man, that one."

The woman lifted her eyebrows and her eyes narrowed. "Ha! A 'good man'?"

"He was a fisherman. In his village he was acknowledged as a generous man who shared his catch with the rectory."

"Pitong, may I speak with him?"

I shook my head. Mrs. Ugale tried to steady herself. "Nana Ugale, please forgive me for my lack of hospitality. Here, sit down, please." I pointed to the wooden stool under the bamboo, then offered a drink of fresh coconut water and a banana. "Santiago departed five months ago for Manila—"

The woman gasped, an indication that five months is a significant number.

"Will he be returning soon?"

I finished my statement, "—to join the priesthood."

I thought the woman was going to faint. "Ay, Apo Dios. He, he what?"

Was the old woman hard of hearing? "Santiago departed five months ago for Manila to join the priesthood."

Mrs. Ugale threw her head back and downed the coconut water as if it were a strong whiskey.

I refilled her cup. "He came home one night when the moon was full. I remember it well because I was visiting my cousin. We took a walk, and we both noticed that Santiago's apartment remained dark far past the time he usually returns from fishing. When he finally returned, we noticed he had a strange look on his face, as if bewitched. I can only describe it as a pain, uh, mixed with, uh, pleasure. We all questioned him about his health for he seemed sick in some way.

"One of our barrio mates guessed, rightly or wrongly, that Santiago had killed a Japon. 'A hairy bugger,' he said. Who knows? This man likes to exaggerate. If true, then Junior is a hero for saving us from the Japs. Nevertheless, it was obvious to us that Santiago was conscience-stricken about taking a life."

I thought I heard my visitor say, "Or *making* a life."

"Pardon me?" I asked.

There was a long pause before she continued. "Pitong, is he acquainted with my daughter, Gloriana Consuelo Cruz Ugale? Perhaps he spoke of her?"

I shook my head. "Did Santiago speak of your daughter? I doubt it. Santiago was a quiet man. Prone to solitude. As far as I am aware, he rarely socialized. I should say that the maidens in our barrio still found him appealing.

"He dreamed of someday leading his own parish ever since he was an altar boy at our church. A good Catholic, that one."

"Did you say he is a good Catholic?" Mrs. Ugale raised her eyebrows again. "Pitong, do you think he will return?"

"To be a good Catholic is a requirement to join the priesthood, wouldn't you say, Nana Ugale? He was accepted into the seminary, ma'am. Only God knows."

"Tragic. Ay, Apo Dios. What have *you* done?" the lady said quietly, but I heard. I was unable to determine whether you meant Santiago, or her daughter. "What have you done?" might also have been directed to God.

"What? Tell me, why do you inquire?"

She made a stirring motion with her hand in her pocket. I heard the rattle of wooden beads. She pulled out her rosary. "Thank you, Pitong. I mean, Private First Class Macadangdang. You have been very helpful." Then she stood abruptly to leave.

"Please, Nana, call me Pitong. Uh, I hope you find Santiago. He is a good man."

She turned around and walked backward. "Pitong, please do not inform anyone of my visit."

She made the sign of the cross.

"Nana Ugale, please let me know if you come across a woman named Salome. I am supposed to marry her." She nodded and waved.

An hour later, I realized she had forgotten to ask Santiago's last name.

. . .

I imagined my betrothed to be gorgeous. Black hair in a chignon. A laugh like a morning warbler greeting the day. In my daydreams, I returned to adolescence, a teenaged Pitong at the barrio fiesta, watching Salome perform the *tinikling*, a Filipino folk dance using bamboo poles that were rhythmically slapped together.

Her feet had to move fast and high in intricate precision or risk the moving bamboos ensnaring her ankles. Salome's movements were agile and precise. Her captivating smile and flirtatious eyes were beautiful to behold. I imagined her perky breasts and how they bounced every time she hopped between the long sticks. I was greatly satisfied. My parents had picked well.

I pictured myself releasing the frangipani blossoms that were pinned to the bun at the nape of her slender neck. In my fantasies, I feasted upon her sensualities. She shook loose her long hair so that it draped over her shoulders and covered her breasts. I saw myself naked, leaning down to kiss her forehead, her eyelids, then swept away her tresses to kiss her brown nipples.

I must have moaned because through the daze of my sleep, I heard my bunkmate ask, "Is he in pain?"

"Hell, no. He's having himself a hell of a wet dream. I should say *heaven* of a wet dream."

"Da-amn."

Suddenly, a rocket burst, signaling the start of another battle against the Japs. It shattered my screen of slumber.

"Shit!" I yelled.

My bunkmates laughed. "Pitong, what goes up must come down."

Chapter 7
SANTIAGO

May 1942

Mama elevated the priesthood, talked about no other vocation for me my entire life. Even when I had become good at commercial fishing, my mother still envisioned me a priest. Why? I do not quite know except that Mama believed if she sacrificed her only son to God, she deserved a pass directly to heaven.

Mama was an extremely devout Catholic, superstitious at times. She spoke to statues, made the sign of the cross prior to any task, and sprinkled holy water upon me every time I went to sea. Our residence looked like a tacky chapel with candles, crucifixes, a velvet painting of the Last Supper, and a giant wooden rosary as part of the décor.

Our house was a place for silence and stillness. Mama and I whispered to each other all of the time. Like in a church, there was to be no running, no playing, no joyful dancing or singing; therefore, I had no friends. Prayers before meals and before bedtime were required, and attendance at daily Mass was expected, even when I was a boy. No one except Father Benito visited. The priest encouraged me to be an altar boy, an answer to my mama's prayers.

The priesthood fascinated me, and I especially admired Father Benito, who was everything I was not. He had a commanding presence—something I needed to develop. He had a terrific memory for people's names and Bible passages. There was a beautiful resonance in his speaking. People closed their eyes when he sang the parts of the Mass so they could more fully appreciate the tone of his voice—smooth, sweet, and dark like raw sugar. He was more likely to preach about God as just and stern than loving and merciful.

I suppose I selected fishing as a line of work because I could be in solitude. I was never lonely; a bird or sea creature always came along. I felt closest to God while outdoors, marveling at the magnificence of the world He created. The earth and universe were my church.

Father Benito was to be my mentor, helping me to pursue my sacred calling. As a child and teenager, I had served almost weekly as an altar boy at the satellite church across the river. He was certain that I, his neophyte, was being called by God to join the clergy. Father nominated me and welcomed me into the seminary. The priest remarked often that he was proud to have someone from his district become a candidate for priesthood, especially a fisherman like Jesus' disciple Simon Peter.

Pastor of a Catholic church was my end goal. I never paid attention to any woman. Never had plans to marry.

And then Gloriana came into my life. We met frequently at the river on opposite banks where the waterway was narrow. She was a strong and confident woman. Fun. Funny. Hard-working. And a great river fisher. I had never been captivated by such beauty.

Why did she show her body to me? I was weak. I went astray. I wanted to.

The secret of my one-night tryst with Glory will go with me to my grave. Unmarried sex was a grievous sin. I deserved to be scourged. I reviled myself.

My decision to join the priesthood was not taken lightly. I agonized for an entire sleepless night over the choice between two entirely different roads. Life with a woman I had fallen in love with, or my lifelong commitment to God with the Catholic Church as my bride.

I chose the life of a priest.

I tried in the privacy of my dormitory cell to forget my Gloriana, but the more I resisted, the more my genitals disobeyed. I had vivid pornographic dreams, and I chastised myself for experiencing such pleasure.

My anxiety increased as ordination drew near. I am not a virtuous man. How in God's name will I be able to comply with the vow of celibacy?

The nuns who laundered the seminarians' linens simply went about their tasks. I hoped the sisters did not blather among themselves nor find it necessary to report "spilled milk" to Father Benito. Thank God, the other novitiates assured me that pleasuring was the ticket to a man's sanity and survival. Even though masturbation was considered breaking the vow of chastity, it was not uncommon to find semen in the beddings at the seminary house.

I rubbed the now-healed scars on my arms and chest, feeling fortunate they went unnoticed. My injuries were well-covered under my cassock's sleeves. What happened at the river between me and the hairy Japanese would also forever remain a secret. Still, the people in my hometown regarded me as a hero, an honor I knew I did not deserve.

Father Benito would have never deduced that the reason I, his recruit, had entered the seminary was nothing holy, just cowardice.

Chapter 8

GLORIANA "GLORY" UGALE

Late May 1942

My father, who normally balked at theological dogma and refused to attend Mass, forced me, Gloriana Consuelo Cruz Ugale, to go to church to make confession. To Papang, I was the biggest sinner of all.

I waited in the closet-like structure situated in a recessed wall within the sanctuary. The priest sits in the middle part and confessors wait on either side. The wood grain was stained dark. I wondered if it was built in the time of the Spanish conquerors. It smelled of old incense mixed with mold. The sliding screen between the pastor and parishioner opened with a slam.

"Bless me, Father, for I have sinned." My voice trembled. The usual steady, deep timbre in my voice betrayed me so that I sounded like a frightened little girl.

I had not liked Father Benito since he had lectured me when I was in the first grade. I was going to hell for not being a good girl, he said. His words had stayed with me all these years. If I'm not such a good Catholic, Padre, put me in a Bible recitation contest. I can spew many more verses than you.

"I, um, have been impure with a man, Father. We are not married. Not married." Damn, Papang. Confession is not a machine that washes away your sins. On the other side of this screen is a man who, I'm willing to bet, is a sinner himself.

"How many times, my, my, my...?" I thought he was going to say, "My child." I'm not childlike. I'm not an innocent. Papang calls me childish. Still, it hurts that I am not worthy of the priest's paternal regard.

My jaw tensed. *You mean how many times did we fuck, Father?*

I coughed. Sputtered. "Only one time, Father."

"Whether you have been intimate one time or a thousand times, if it was previous to marriage, it is a mortal sin," the priest admonished me. "Intimacy belongs only within the bonds of matrimony."

Are priests not allowed to utter the word *sex*?

"Gloriana Consuelo Cruz Ugale, you have sinned against God."

I jerked. My pocketbook fell from my lap to the floor, spilling its contents. I watched my lipstick roll away in slow motion. The priest had identified me. My defiant nature arose. "Shall I rid my womb of the baby, Father?"

The priest's voice grew louder, as if he were evangelizing to a crowd. " 'And she committed her fornications and defiled herself.' It is said." Brimstone and fire. Father Benito paused, creating dramatic effect. "Admit your wicked immorality, for it is done."

I shuddered. *I'm going to burn in hell.* But then with righteous indignation, I recited in full voice, yes, in competition with the pastor. "And you think, oh man, that you can judge me, and escape the judgment of God?" I knew the concepts were correct, if not a Bible passage exactly word for word.

Through the screen, I saw Father Benito run his fingers through his salt-and-pepper hair. He straightened his shoulders, lowered his chin, and flattened his palm against his forehead.

Angry thoughts filled my head. *I do dare fight with you, Father. You would be wise not to engage with me.*

I think I may have delivered him an unexpected jab, for he faltered.

"Is the baby's father a Catholic?"

"I don't know."

I opened the door to sneak a look at the clock that hung on the railing below the choir loft. My lipstick rolled out. How I wished I could escape the confines of the confessional to retrieve it. I had saved for weeks to purchase something my mother called frivolous. About a dozen congregants were waiting in the sanctuary for their turn to confess who-knows-what. They craned their necks to see and strained their ears to hear.

I remained silent, counting the seconds until the end of this sacrament.

"*You don't know if he is a Catholic, or you don't know where he is?*" Father Benito was persistent.

"I just don't know, Father." Unintentionally, I reverted to using my little girl voice.

"Anything else before I pronounce a penance? You must be honest."

You mean I must disclose *all* of my sins? I remembered the hot nights when I ached for Santiago. I relived every moment of our rapturous joining, and it electrified me. I often reached down to touch my petals the way Santiago had fondled, then spread them to lightly knead the tiny bud within. One time, I lost myself in masturbatory excitement and cried out, stirring Mamang and Liling from sleep.

"Is something wrong, Glory?" Mamang had turned toward my sleeping mat.

"Just a nightmare, Mamang," I panted.

Ligaya shushed us both. "Go back to sleep."

The priest cleared his throat, which brought me back to the present. He repeated, "Is there anything else before I pronounce a penance?"

None of your business, priest. I took a deep breath before responding. "I have engaged in self-gratification many times," I said tentatively. What is it about this priest that draws me to share the secrets of my body? My heart?

"So?" asked the pastor, encouraging me to disclose all. "You must confess."

Should I keep my transgressions secret? What the hell, our God in heaven is all-knowing. “Well, Father, I have been disrespectful to my father. I do not believe he is a good parent.”

Father Benito responded, “And God’s fourth commandment states, ‘Honor thy father and mother.’ ” He paused. “I have noticed that you have received the Eucharist during this period of sinfulness. And *that* is also a sin.”

I grit my teeth.

The priest was impatient. “Eh? Speak up.”

“Yes. I have sinned, Father.”

“Eh?”

Now, provoked by the pastor’s scolding tone of voice, I shouted, “Yes. I have sinned!”

There now, the rest of the penitents in the sanctuary will not have to wait to find out who emerged from the ornately carved booth. They will already know it’s me.

Damn humiliation! Bastard Benito! I slammed the door as I exited the confessional. I could not complete my penance fast enough. Twenty Hail Marys and twenty Our Fathers.

“—HolyMaryMotherOfGodPrayForUsSinnersNowAndAt-TheHourOfOurDeath—Damn it. Amen!”

I heaved. My anger had turned to tears.

Chapter 9

LIGAYA "LILING" UGALE

Early September 1942

In the four remaining months of her pregnancy, Gloriana mentioned often that she cherished the moments her womb fluttered. The village women freely shared tales of horrible deliveries with bad outcomes. Glory put a stop to that. Fear had begun to consume her. Frightened mothers give birth to fussy babies.

I often found my sister wrapping her hands around her abdomen. "Watermelon" was what she laughingly called her tummy, until Auntie Soledad described her own delivery experience—"like pushing out a constipation the size of a watermelon."

One corner of the hut was assigned to be the nursery. A crate was fashioned into a bassinet. *Apples* was stamped onto the wood. The irony of forbidden fruit was glaring. A rice bag hammock was hung, perfect for rocking. Three baby blankets and three sets of booties—one for using, the second to be ready on the shelf, while the third was being washed—were lovingly crocheted by Pacencia and me and offered as gifts.

I tilted my head to better hear Gloriana whistle brightly; she did so almost all day, every day. She shared her thoughts about being a single mother and imagined long happy years raising her child. She dreamed of escaping to Hawaii with the baby. She could not or would not believe that poverty, illiteracy, and disease existed in the USA. Her hope-filled elation coursed vastly and profoundly. At night, when Glory thought I was already deeply asleep, I sometimes heard her whisper, "Santiago, wherever you are, I am having your baby."

Papang's wrath came in the new, unfamiliar form of brooding silence. Hit Glory? He did not dare. Interesting that he called the child "The Bastard Baby" with such disdain that we were sure he did not want it, yet he avoided dispensing physical damage for fear of being the cause of a miscarriage.

• • •

Pangs of labor came intermittently, Glory said, much like the torture of rounds in a boxing ring. She nudged me, interrupting my dream about mangoes and Raul.

"Liling, it is time."

"Yes, time for sleep." Groaning, I turned away from Glory. My mango and fiancé fantasies must continue.

"Liling, I'm in labor. The baby is finally coming." Gloriana had been impatient. It was two weeks past the expected due date.

"Arrgh. AHH-OOH!"

My sister shoved her palms hard against my upper back until I was fully roused.

Glory rubbed her swollen belly. She paced. Sat. Stood. Paced. Finally, she lay her tensed body down.

The clay stove was lit. A kettle of water was set over the fire. Thank you, God of Readiness; we still had a container of water from the hand pump in the village plaza. Mamang's movements were rushed, yet efficient. She brought out her collection of clean rags; her long ago experience with diapering babies with cholera had led to plenty being saved. Mamang plopped herself between Gloriana's knees. "Now, we wait." Having labored and delivered eight times, our mother deemed herself an expert in childbirth.

I knelt by my sister's side, wiped droplets of glistening moisture from her forehead, and held her trembling hand. "Glory, don't hold your breath. It is better if you inhale and exhale deeply."

"It hurts, Liling."

"Yes, sister, I believe you."

"Ay, Apo Dios!" exclaimed Mamang. She prayed the rosary.

I prayed to the God of Easy Births with worried anticipation. Mamang spoke sadly of her infant son who had died as a result of a bungled breech birth.

Glory cried, "Please don't speak of such things. Now I am even more frightened."

"I'm sorry, Glory. You are right. Of course, I pray that this delivery will progress smoothly." Mamang made the sign of the cross.

I pressed Gloriana's palm. "Sister, I am always here for you. I love you."

The difficult labor progressed slowly. "You can do this, sister. You can. You are strong and courageous, the hardiest and most determined woman I know." I tried to be encouraging, but it was as if she didn't hear me.

Witnessing Gloriana writhe with pain sent Papang into a fit of anxiety, making him especially irritable. Mamang, for once, *encouraged* him to go to the beer hall nearby.

In bouts lasting more than many hours, the baby within tried to wrestle its way out of the womb, causing Gloriana to thrash wildly and shriek with threats to commit suicide.

"I want to die. Let me die." Gloriana looked like a Madonna in the throes of martyrdom. I could tell her contractions were sharp and agonizing.

"You will not die, Glory. You must be concerned for your baby. We cannot have a motherless child. And besides, I'm not ready, in your absence, to take on your responsibility as a parent." My anxious words sounded like a lecture.

For some reason, imagining me as a mother made Gloriana laugh, but only until the next contraction clutched her insides. Gloriana screamed so loudly—sounding like echoes in a cave of screeching bats—that our drunken father must have heard the noise. I knew him well enough to know he would order beer after beer to suffocate his embarrassment.

A few of the neighbors gathered outside the hut. If Mamang regarded the folks as friendly, she labeled them "just curious." But she characterized her enemies as "nosy."

With one final, powerful effort, Gloriana cried out, "Santiago!" just as the infant slid into Mamang's waiting hands. Mamang and I gasped. The bundle was purple, flaccid, and soundless; the cord was wrapped around its neck. Mamang slid her fingers under to loosen it. She delayed cutting the umbilical cord; I surmised she knew instinctively that oxygen-rich blood continued to circulate through the newborn. I tended to Glory until the placenta was delivered. The pulsating stopped, cuing Mamang to finally tie and cut the cord.

Mamang worked quickly with a depth of concentration. She did not panic at first. She wiped the infant vigorously to stimulate it. Nothing. She suspended the baby by its ankles to drain the fluid from its lungs. Nothing. She directed her breath into its face. She placed the limp body in prone position and thumped its back. "Breathe, baby; breathe."

"What's happening, Mamang? Liling?" asked Gloriana.

Mamang and I glanced at each other, awash with alarm. Abruptly, our mother barked at me, "Liling, go and cut a leaf from the papaya tree, *now*. The stem must be long and narrow. Hurry, Liling."

I raced outside and returned with a young, light-green papaya leaf. Mamang deftly cut the top off, leaving the thin stem. Mamang peered through it to ensure the cylindrical opening was patent. One end was inserted into the back of the baby's throat and Mamang sucked upon the other end. She spat out a grayish liquid. My work with the Americano doctor taught me that meconium-stained amniotic fluid was not a good sign. Grandbaby's mouth was suctioned three times in quick succession. Mamang loosely swaddled him in clean rags.

"Ay, Apo Dios," Mamang prayed feverishly. "Apo Dios. Apo Dios."

A miracle breath, and then another and another and another. The baby immediately transformed, abdomen heaving. Purple gave way to pink. He waved his arms and legs as if signaling, *World, here I am! Bright, like the light of the moon.*

"Ay, Apo Dios. I am grateful to you, Father God." Mamang made the sign of the cross on the newborn's forehead and kissed its crown.

"I thank Thee, God of Births. Amen."

High-pitched sounds of stridor stirred Gloriana from her fatigue.

"Glory, it's a *boy*!" Mamang announced with a look of relief and pride in her own midwifery skills.

"A boy?" Gloriana smiled weakly.

From my work in the clinic, I had learned that babies born on time have smooth skin covered by the protective butter of birth. Infants delivered long after their estimated dates of arrival usually looked like ancient desert yogis, their dried-up placentas and shriveled uteruses ensconced in secret chambers. This wasn't the case in this infant's overdue birth.

"Yes, Glory. A handsome son."

Gloriana held out her arms. Mamang placed the infant on her bare chest, skin to skin. Eyes that were wide and wise peered at his mother. Gloriana wept, not so much because of exhaustion and pain, but, I believe, because her soul was filled with a first-time mother's love. Furthermore, the father of her baby remained absent, and somewhere, and nowhere.

"You see? I told you that you could do this, and that I would be here for you." The love I felt for my sister and my nephew abounded.

Glory spoke, "Thank you, Miss Queen of Compassion. I love you."

Mamang tenderly pushed stray strands of hair from my sister's moist forehead.

"Mamang, thank you for sending Papang away. I would not have been able to tolerate his negativity and angst."

"I understand, my dear. I gave birth eight times with Respicio walking and talking like a sulking carabao."

"Papang is too demanding and destructive. I expect him to behave well in front of my boy. I will never tolerate his abuse again, ever." Her tone changed then.

"Santiago, we have a son," a whisper came forth. Glory looked past the thatched ceiling. Did she think Santiago was dead? My sister had not heard from or about him. Though I had never met the man, I would forever think of him as an irresponsible betrayer.

Glory looked at me. "Santiago means Saint James in Spanish. Did you know that, Liling?" Then she returned her gaze to the heavens. "I shall name our baby Jaime [HI-meh] after you."

"Did you say something, Glory?"

"I said, 'I name him Jaime.' Jaime Luna Ugale."

Gloriana refused to divulge Santiago's last name; therefore, the infant was given her surname, Ugale, which of course, confirmed he was illegitimate—sure to be the subject of more rampant village gossip.

"Jaime *Luna* Ugale," I repeated slowly. "Moon?"

A smile formed on Glory's handsome face. "Yes, like the moon that shone the night of love at the river. A golden coin that brings good luck."

. . .

No neighbor was going to take away my pleasure of being the first to tell Papang of the birth. I raced toward the beer hall to inform my father he now had a grandson.

Papang's response was entirely unexpected; he sobbed! Racking heaves came forth from his body. Perhaps because of anxiety. Perhaps it was the effect of all the alcohol. Remorse and guilt? Trying with all my might, I could not figure out the reason for his intense emotional reaction.

For all these years, Papang's sorrow at the loss of his four young male children must have been locked away behind a smokescreen of viciousness and brutality; the result of embers of hatred toward God, who had dared to steal his sons. And now, it was as if God had shown him the hope of a new day, a new generation, his legacy—in the form of a baby. My father hung down his head. In shame? In thanksgiving? With relief?

All rancor toward Gloriana seemed to have been replaced by forgiveness. Over his beer, Papang talked about the time he had whipped little girl Glory, after which she had asked plaintively, "Why do you hate me, Papang?" The memory broke him, and he cried some more.

Papang's grief and remorse were purged in streams of tears. So unnerved was the bartender that he offered his customer a complimentary glass of a premium beer.

Papang pushed the drink away and said politely, "Thank you for the drink, but I do not need it anymore."

The bartender, the other patrons, and I were flabbergasted. "Huh? What just happened? This is not the Respicio we know," said one patron.

• • •

Gloriana held her baby against her breast. She nuzzled her lips against the folds of Jaime's neck, then upon the convex curve of Jaime's cheek, and upon the tiny, creased soles of Jaime's feet. Her baby had a mass of thick, jet-black hair. His features were symmetrical, and he had no birthmarks. No flaw like the one on her face. I am positive my sister searched carefully.

My nephew looked as striking and perfect as the cherub statues at Father Benito's church.

Glory was a natural caregiver. With ease and pleasure, she diapered, bathed, and breastfed baby Jaime. Her expressed wish was to be a modern mother, using baby bottles with formula, and pristine white cloth diapers, not the frayed, roughly textured rags she and Mamang had collected. To be old-fashioned was despicable. Unlike me, she longed to immigrate to the United States, a place she believed was up-to-date, sanitary, and safe for her child.

Jaime was an alert, happy baby. Naturally, his grandmother Maria and I, *Auntie* Ligaya, helped care for the boy, rocking him in our arms, changing his soiled diapers, singing lullabies, and soothing him to sleep. Astonishingly, Papang also participated in nurturing his grandson with clumsy attempts to tend to his care.

"Have you noticed that Papang has softened considerably since Jaime was born?" I asked in a private mother-daughter moment. "I don't know why he has changed, but I wholeheartedly welcome it. My prayer is for continued improvement of his disposition."

Soon after, I overheard Mamang say to her sister, "Last night, Respicio reached across his sleep mat and stroked my arm. He was gentle."

Auntie Soledad responded, "Hmph!" I don't think Auntie respects Papang at all.

For Mamang's sake, I hope Papang transforms into the husband she deserves.

"Let us pray," said Mamang as she knelt before our home altar.

"God, the Father of all Fathers," I said, "grant my papang wisdom and patience."

"Forgive him his sins," Mamang interjected aloud.

I continued, "Grant him tolerance, and kindness, and understanding."

"Forgive him his sins," repeated Mamang. I looked at my mother with displeasure.

"We praise you for my nephew, baby Jaime, whom Thou hath sent as our angel to bless all of us. Help my mamang—"

"Bring the baby his father," Mamang interrupted.

I gave her another look of exasperation. "*Help my mamang*, Glory, and me to be *patient* and strong," I finished.

"Amen," added Mamang.

"AMEN!" shouted Gloriana from the nursery corner.

I pushed open the awning to let in fresh air. I observed Papang rocking Jaime in his arms while sitting on the bench under our mango tree. Was this the same grandfather caring for the "bastard baby?" Something had changed about the man.

Chapter 10

LIGAYA "LILING" UGALE

December 1942

The baby smoothed all of Gloriana's rough edges; the tenderness she felt for her newborn had erased most of her memories of trials past.

In the beginning, Gloriana could be found nursing according to her son's internal clock. Jaime was not a demanding baby who shrieked when hungry. He simply whimpered a little to alert his mother—*I am ready to be fed.* Then he cooed before falling back to sleep in his mother's arms.

Three to four months after the delivery, Gloriana could be found gushing over her baby with maternal devotion one moment, and in the next, she would devolve into a disconsolate, weepy wreck. Her jumbled emotions disturbed us; her excitement at being a new mother was not long-lasting.

Mamang was the first to suspect a problem existed. We could hear the infant crying. "Glory, Jaime needs to be fed." When left unattended for prolonged periods, the starving infant would scream uncontrollably. "Glory, it is time to feed your baby," Mamang would direct more firmly. She gently touched her indolent daughter, who could muster only enough energy to jerk away her arm.

Gloriana failed to rouse herself to nurse Jaime, even when Papang intervened. "What do I need to do to get you to take care of your baby?" he shouted. It frightened everyone in the house. No sadistic sounds had emanated from Papang since Jaime's birth sixteen weeks earlier. But now he threatened, "Do I need to hit you?"

"You threw the bamboo switch away, remember?" retorted Gloriana.

"You dirty, dirty, dumb-dumb girl. I have my cane. I have my belt."

Gloriana merely grunted.

"You are a dirty, dirty, dumb-dumb." Taunted, Papang's wrath had been rekindled. So pronounced was the heat that I was surprised our hut did not incinerate.

Mamang wrung the skirt of her apron. "Your prayer didn't work, Liling."

"Prayer works in mysterious ways, Mamang. I am confident God is in the midst of this."

"Well, our prayers need to work *now*."

"God of abusive Grandfathers," I began intoning.

Mamang hissed. "What are you doing? You want your father to go berserk because we are pessimistic about his behavior?"

"But you said *now*, Mamang."

My mother rolled her eyes and placed her index finger to her lips to shush me.

Papang picked up his precious grandson and handed Jaime to Mamang, who placed him at his mother's breast and inserted the engorged nipple into his mouth. The baby latched on and gulped her milk greedily while Gloriana lay inert, staring into space.

I started a new prayer. "God of Weary Women—"

• • •

"Liling, please schedule a medical consultation for me with the Americano doctor."

"You mean Dr. Billet?"

Gloriana almost snickered. "Yes. Dr. B, the Americano doctor."

"Glory, you're annoying."

I accompanied my sister and carried baby Jaime.

"Why, hello, Miss Ligaya, Miss Gloriana. Mighty fine-looking lad ya got there. Delivered at home, I heard."

After the usual niceties, Glory listed her symptoms. "Doctor, I cannot sleep. I cannot eat. I cannot concentrate."

"Caring for a newborn is exhausting, Miss Gloriana. Your sister can help you, yes?" I nodded. "Your parents, are they able to assist? I prescribe rest. I must insist on it."

"But, Doctor, how can I rest? I must breastfeed my baby. He needs milk every three to four hours."

Gloriana stated she felt less bonded to her child, leading to confusion and consternation about her performance as a mother.

"Shouldn't I be filled with joy and nurturing emotions? I am not. I'm a wicked mother."

"Wicked? No," I chimed in. My poor sister.

"Now, hold on there, Miss Gloriana. Talk to every new mother in the Philippines and she'll tell ya she's mighty blue. Mighty blue, indeed, and mighty tired. Take comfort that you're not the only one."

"Mighty blue?" Gloriana did not seem to understand. I shifted Jaime from one arm to the other. "Statistics don't help me, Doctor. If it's normal to feel like this, then all of us new mothers are normally abnormal."

Using a teaching voice, Dr. Billet continued, "We have hormones, ya see, and they are going crazy, mighty crazy, I'd say, in our bloodstream. Sleep deprivation diminishes our reserve. Anxiety seizes us."

"Us? Our? We?" Gloriana showed her irritation.

Uh oh, here we go. My pulse quickened. Was Glory going to give in to her impatience and rant at the physician?

"I need medicine, Doctor, not information." Gloriana caught

herself. "I'm sorry, Doctor." Minding our manners and respecting a professional is a cultural expectation.

"It's fine, Miss Gloriana. It's not you. As I said, and I'll say it again, it's the hormones."

While Glory glared, I cast my eyes downward and sighed.

. . .

One month after the unimpressive clinical session, Gloriana still could not drag herself out of bed. Often listless and lethargic, she drifted throughout the day, weepy, scarcely able to muster the strength needed to care for Jaime. The baby's cry elicited none of the gentleness she had demonstrated in the early days after his birth. Instead, she exuded a sense of dread and emptiness. Sometimes, Glory confessed that she thought she heard the baby crying and Papang scolding, but when she looked in their direction, both were snuggling and murmuring to each other. Delusions? Auditory hallucinations? I wondered.

One day, Gloriana announced that she felt exceedingly ill and again too weak to feed baby Jaime. I dropped my crochet project and touched her forehead. No fever detected.

"Auntie Liling, is Auntie Glory sick?" Pacencia had been visiting to help create the Christmas parols that Mamang wanted to hang inside and outside our hut.

"She doesn't have a fever. But your auntie Glory has been complaining of discomfort for several weeks now."

"Lola? Want me to fetch the Americano doctor?"

"No, dear Pacencia, and you must be respectful. It's Dr. Bill-ET." Mamang used the Filipino pronunciation. Glory did not chuckle about the physician's unfortunate name, confirming to me that she was seriously ill. "Auntie Glory already visited him; his advice did not work. We must look for help elsewhere."

Even though Papang did not regularly attend Mass, he did depend on the Church to help his family heal and prosper. At Papang's insistence, Father Benito arrived to perform an exorcism.

"I cast thee out, Devil's spawn." A mocking look passed from his eyes onto Jaime. Confusion filled me.

"I drive away the satanic powers that assemble in dirty girls who birth bastards." Papang nodded. Mamang's eyes were closed, indicating that she was not paying attention to what the priest was saying but praying on her own. No alarm had registered on my parents' faces; both seemed to accept the derisive wording. They allowed the padre's statement to pass.

The parish priest sprinkled holy water upon Gloriana, who then stumbled around the hut as if stung by acid, and tumbled down the wooden steps like a rag doll thrown by a child having a tantrum.

"Ay, Apo Dios!" Mamang made the sign of the cross. "Oh, Glory. Glory!" We rushed outside. Glory lay at the bottom of the stairs, curled into a fetal position. Although she was incoherent, I was able to pick out the sounds of "Santi—"

Papang held the child while Mamang and I tried in vain to lift Gloriana. The priest kept praying and sprinkling holy water upon the limp body on the ground.

"Pacencia, run to the neighbors and ask Raul for help. Use your big girl voice. Hurry dear. Hurry!"

Thankfully, Raul came in haste. He carried Gloriana back into our hut and laid her slackened body upon the mat. She slept for hours and must have dreamt the saddest of dreams, for rivers of tears flowed down, down into the ridges of both ears. Fear and loneliness must have frayed her nerves.

Papang quietly sang a Filipino folk tune, a song I recognized, one he used to sing to Glory and me when we were children. Unfazed by the crisis involving his mother, Jaime smiled and babbled. I could not help but watch Mamang's face change as my father kissed the boy's cheek and then sang some more.

"You are different, my dear spouse." Mamang gave him a smile instead of her usual sad smirk.

"Different?" asked Papang.

"The nicer version of you. The you I met long ago. The lost you now is found." Love is not a word in my parents' lexicon.

For the first time in a very long time, I saw Papang reach for his wife's hand. She intertwined her fingers through his. It lasted only a few seconds, but the love in my heart was expanded by that rare display of affection I had the privilege to witness.

Glory's recovery continued to plateau. That sleep deprivation contributed to her malady was a given, but Father Benito continued to claim credit for exorcising the devil. It was sad that our priest and Mussolini, Italy's Fascist dictator, shared the same name. Benito means *blessing*.

Chapter 11

GLORIANA "GLORY" UGALE

January 1943

"You should go to Bible study with your mamang." Another of our father's *You have tos.*

"I hope you do join me, Glory," said Mamang. "I take much comfort in the Word of the Lord. Plus, I have a mind to show off my grandson to the other attendees."

"The priest will be there?" Hesitation was in my voice.

"Do not worry; he is rarely at Bible study."

"Come with us, Liling. I can't bear being in the church without you, Miss Sure-I-Would-Do-Anything-for-My-Favorite-Sister." I attempted a smile.

My sister and I reacted with absolute shock and trepidation when Father Benito made a stately entrance and sat on a hefty chair, a throne really, more befitting for a king than a countryside priest. He opened his Douay-Rheims Bible and began reading.

> "Go not after thy lusts but turn away from thy own will." [Ecclesiasticus (Sirach) 18:30]

One of the parishioners coughed and then others followed. Though the priest did not use identifying information, I assumed the message was meant for me. The participants turned to stare. I wrapped my thumb and index finger around my wrist; skinny bones. Were they concerned about how much weight I had lost?

Most of the villagers derided me for having had unmarried sex and bearing a bastard baby. I had heard that they had placed bets on the identity of Jaime's father. Never would they find out—for I vowed to take my secret with me to heaven—if I should go to heaven, where I was certain I would rejoin Santiago.

The gossip mongers reportedly also wondered what other terrible deed I had committed to now be so sickly, as though patients were to be blamed for their illnesses.

Other women in the same predicament must feel stuck like me. According to the Church, you couldn't birth a bastard. Abortion? Considered sinful. Adoption was frowned upon. The standard answer—Don't open your legs—wasn't an answer. The so-called Christians shook their heads, saying I should not have behaved like a whore in the first place.

The priest resumed reading.

> "As Sodom and Gomorrah, and the neighboring cities, in like manner, having given themselves to fornication, and going after other flesh, were made an example, suffering the punishment of eternal fire." [Jude 1:7]

I held my breath. The priest continued.

> "And the field, is the world. And the good seed are the children of the Kingdom. And the cockle are the children of the wicked one." [Matthew 13:38]

Mamang thumped her breast three times, the Catholic act of true contrition. Then she said, "Mercy."

Father Benito formed a steeple with his hands and relentlessly continued. "Turn to Deuteronomy 23:2. 'A mamzer, that is to say, one born of a prostitute, shall not enter into the church of the Lord, until the tenth generation.'"

The people sitting in the pews shifted. The priest had crossed an invisible line that I, Gloriana Consuelo Cruz Ugale, must have subconsciously drawn around my son and me.

Liling had warned me about possible moments like this. I was weary of being the subject of so much contempt and refused to hang my head in shame. I rejected the idea of giving power to anyone in the Catholic Church who would further humiliate me and my family. Shaking, I sprung up and trumpeted emphatically, confidently.

> "But Jesus, calling them together, said: Suffer children to come to me, and forbid them not: for of such is the kingdom of God." [Luke 18:16]

A pair of congregants stood and applauded but stopped soon after; no one else had joined their ovation.

An extended period of absolute silence was followed by a distinctive sound—Jaime's cooing.

I kissed my baby's face. He smiled. I overheard a parishioner say, "Glory looks like the Madonna." My palpitations subsided.

"Hurrah," Liling said to me. We whispered back and forth.

"I love you, sister."

"Our God is forgiving."

"Our God is compassionate."

"Our God is loving."

Father Benito held his mouth agape, stupefied by my daring retort. Appearing flustered, he continued the lesson.

Was it a sin to love? I stroked Jaime's cheek with my finger. He resembled his father so much that I knew deep in my heart it was fitting that I had named my baby Jaime after Santiago, and after the moon—like the planet that had shone its light upon us that fateful night.

Santiago and Jaime Luna. I didn't believe the two would ever come to know each other. I sniffled. Turning to my sister, I asked softly, "It is not a sin to love, is it? The product of our love is our baby. Our baby was not born of sin." I repeated my thoughts, trying to convince myself. "It is not a sin to love. My baby was not born of sin. My baby was conceived in love."

The priest's eyes reflected the golden glow of the votive candles. I was frightened; tongues of fire appeared to lick his shiny face. What other devilish deeds will Father Benito contrive to burn me with?

Chapter 12

LIGAYA "LILING" UGALE

February 1943

Everyone thought Gloriana was on her way to recovery. However, after a plateau of two weeks, she continued to deteriorate. She behaved even more strangely after that Bible study class; some might have claimed she had lost her mind. *Loco*. Crazy. Others even blathered that the devil had raped her.

Five months after Jaime's birth, the rice yield was nil, and the vegetables were hit with a type of fungus propagated by the recent rains. The baby was constantly hungry and Gloriana, in semi-starvation, could not produce enough milk. In desperation, I went to the only palm tree close by and searched frantically for a coconut in the tall grass. I could not scale the tree, and there was no one close by to climb its slender trunk. I then noticed an old coconut nestled in the grass like a hidden Easter egg. I anxiously hacked open its husk with a bolo knife and struck the blade across the brown, speckled shell. Dry. No milk for Jaime. I choked on my tears as Jaime's piteous screams of hunger filled my ears. We searched for a wet nurse to no avail; no villager had recently given birth.

Despite copious prayers from Mamang and me, Gloriana's postpartum symptoms exacerbated. She continued to have difficulty sleeping. It didn't help that the infant now cried incessantly. We all tried to step in to take care of the child, but we also had other responsibilities—Mamang as co-manager of our rice farm, and me as maid for Dr. Billet's family. I also took over some of Glory's clinic obligations. Our duties became overwhelming and could no longer be ignored.

Papang offered to help, but Gloriana did not trust him. He was stooped and memories of the torture of his temper still stung her. "Aunties and Nanas," related by blood or not, gave temporary respite, but they also had their own families to attend to.

Gloriana refused to eat.

Thankfully, Jaime was soon introduced to solid foods like mashed bananas and rice gruel, which he ate with gusto. We saved the water from washing our rice kernels and added sugar to satisfy his thirst and need for calories. While Glory became thinner, Jaime grew healthier and gained weight. His skin was a robust golden beige. He smiled almost all of the time now. He was active and energetic, loving to crawl away and "hide" in the hut, to Papang's delight, and he always returned to his grandfather as if he were the steadfast home base.

Glory mumbled, "Santi, Santi, Santi, Santi, Santi—"

"Liling," said Mamang, "she is praying to the saints."

"No, she is not. Listen carefully."

Mamang caressed Gloriana's forehead. "Santi, Santi, Santi, Santi, Santi—"

"Oh, Liling, she is asking for Santiago. My heart is breaking."

I held my sister in my arms; really, there were now two "infants" in the house. Gloriana stared without blinking, having abandoned all motherly duties. Her eyes were swollen. Every few days, she shouted gibberish, conversing with a being no one else could see or hear.

The Americano doctor was reluctantly summoned. First, he examined the baby boy. Following that, he reviewed Gloriana's medical history and evaluated her condition.

Dr. Billet shook his head as he replaced his stethoscope in his medical bag. "Mr. and Mrs. Ugale, I'm afraid I have good news and bad news, mighty bad news. The good news is Jaime is fine."

Mamang sucked in her breath. Papang leaned heavily on his cane. I bounced the happy baby in my arms.

Dr. B said, "Gloriana has an eye infection. I will prescribe an antibiotic ointment for both eyes. The affliction is highly contagious, especially for babies. Make sure you wash your hands frequently."

No water; the clay pot was empty of water.

Dr. Billet gave another diagnosis. "Miss Gloriana has postpartum psychosis. She is seeing things that are not real, hearing things that are not real. We call them hallucinations. Hah-loo-sin-nay-tions." The doctor sometimes spoke at a slow pace, thinking that would assist the farmers in understanding. "No medicines are available in the village for that. I can only recommend that she be admitted to the psychiatric hospital in the city."

Predictably, Mamang clutched her rosary. Papang slumped onto the bench. Jaime started to cry, and I bounced him harder.

"Doctor, are you certain that nothing more can be done? What about the baby?"

"I know of a patient who just gave birth to a stillborn. She lives a distance away. I can ask if she is willing to help with nursing." The doctor said this knowing full well that feeding another's child prolongs the grief in both new mothers. The wet nurse would likely decline to help.

"The only thing that can alleviate Miss Gloriana's suffering is rest in a stress-free environment where she can sleep without disturbance or fear." The doctor glanced knowingly at Papang.

Sidelong glances. Ever so slightly, Mamang shook her head.

"We need time to think about it, Doctor."

"I see. I'm so sorry. Miss Gloriana was a fine janitor. Though, unlike you," he turned to face me, "she tended to flirt with the male patients."

After the doctor left, my parents chose not to get back to him.

• • •

When I went to the market the next day, I could not help overhearing scraps of conversation I would have preferred not to have heard. I detest gossip.

"She is possessed by Satan. Did you see? One of Glory's eyes is red, and the other yellow with pus," declared one townsperson.

"She is cursed by a vengeful neighbor," said another.

"A malevolent ghost has haunted their hut," offered yet another villager.

Meanwhile, we all tried to help Glory. Pacencia's mother, Cora, performed an old Filipino ritual wherein small bowls of food are put out to feed the spirits. Papang killed a chicken for another shamanic ceremony, and placed some of its blood, its heart, and its liver on a makeshift altar.

Auntie Soledad, a staunch Catholic matron, laid a crudely carved crucifix upon Gloriana's chest. She prayed, invoking the intercessions of the Blessed Virgin Mary, mother of God, mother of all mothers. She proceeded to call upon Mary Magdalene, patron saint of prostitutes, and San Jose, patron saint of an attended death. In other words, a happy death.

"Hold it there, Soledad." Mamang shoved her hand in front of her sister's face to interrupt the ridiculous prayers. "My Glory is *not* a prostitute and she is *not* dying."

"I am interceding on my beloved niece's behalf. Just in case."

"Ay, Apo Dios." Mamang slapped Auntie Soledad's shoulder.

Gloriana stank; she had not washed in days. Hallucinating, she urinated in the rice bin, wasting a week's work of husking and milling the grains. Papang was beside himself with frustration and worry. To his credit, he did not bellow or beat her.

The reluctant pastor stopped by, presumably to perform the next in a series of exorcisms. He glanced at his wristwatch, seemingly having another more important place to go. The priest announced he saw little to no evidence of demonic possession. Instead, he sped through the rosary in a mechanical way.

Had Glory known the priest was there, she probably would have spat on him. But no, she was nearly comatose.

Father Benito added, "In the past, within our parish community, we have experienced miracles with illness. Trust that your maladies will abate with prayer. You might faint, death might overcome you, but that is the devil punishing your body. Believe and repent. For unbelievers who doubt will continue to be possessed." He sprinkled holy water, but this time Gloriana did not go stumbling down the stairs.

Days later, in desperation, my parents implored an indigenous shaman to administer ceremonial rites, channeling the ancestors for sacred healing. Gloriana was placed in a trance as he chanted, asking the angry animas to leave. Near the mat upon which Gloriana lay still and gray, he knelt, then pointed up and down and left to right. He looked out the window far past the horizon, seeking guidance from an invisible presence. A stick of incense was lit; waves of smoke drifted toward Gloriana's body. She coughed, and coughed again, and coughed again.

A monkey monologue of hoots, and clicks, and grunts emanated from Gloriana's lips. They were beyond understanding but flowed; the streams of utterances carried with them the foulness that had poisoned her body. She then wailed for a period, an eradication of a deeply seated depression—her grief over the loss of Santiago, her anger at his betrayal, and her fears for their son—exploded like a long-awaited propulsion of steam from a dormant volcano.

The shaman warned, "Expect excessive sweating, which will dampen her mat. Some people experience involuntary urination and sometimes defecation, but likely not in her case." Gloriana's system had been absent of food and drink.

The healer then synchronized his breathing with Gloriana's ragged respirations. In a few minutes, Glory began to slow her inhalations in rhythm with his, gentle but deep. Before my eyes, the shaman was transfigured into a seraph—emanating white, warm light. There was silence, a sacred silence.

The treatment itself only took a short time, though it must have seemed like an eternity to the handful of onlookers. Bartolome, Cora,

Pacencia, and Raul and his parents gave their support.

Gloriana's taut face had metamorphosed into a look that was relaxed, rested.

A stalk of green bananas, a half-dozen eggs, and a basket of vegetables unaffected by the blight of fungus were set at the shaman's feet as payment. In these times, poor Pinoy peasants like us were often forced to choose between feeding our families or paying for healing services; we could not afford both. These food stuffs did not come from a pantry of supplementary stock, but the Ugales gratefully sacrificed two days of meals to save our beloved Gloriana, and in so doing, save dear Jaime.

Papang was found cuddling the baby, and clumsily wiping away his own tears, which had fallen onto his grandson's face. Little Jaime smiled and babbled, and this made my father breathy with happiness.

One day after the shaman's sacrament, Gloriana awoke. Her eyes were clearing with the help of both Western medicine and indigenous sacraments. The infection was washed away by copious tears.

Gloriana begged forgiveness for bringing trouble to the family. Papang kissed his daughter's forehead. "Forgive me, too." The interaction affected me deeply; I was overcome with relief and happiness.

"Where is the baby, Mamang? Is he hungry? He must be hungry," Glory said in a matter-of-fact way, as if no drama had taken place over the last month.

What had cured Gloriana? Was it the Americano doctor? The priest's rite of exorcism? Sacrifice of the chicken? The offerings of special foods? The intercessions of the saints? The ministrations of the shaman?

No one knew exactly. I strongly believed it was *my prayers*.

Miraculously, Gloriana's breasts were engorged with milk for her baby.

Chapter 13

LIGAYA "LILING" UGALE

March 1943

The hike to the tobacco farm was long but picturesque. Pacencia's presence made my walk truly enjoyable. Conversations with this ten-year-old were easy; I did not have to work at firing questions that elicited only one-word answers.

After Gloriana's breakdown, I often visited upon my brother's invitation to update him on her condition.

"Has she relapsed? What of Jaime—is he healthy?" He also asked after our father. "Is Papang less agitated than usual? When I was at the hut, I did not hear one threat or insult. An aberration, I'm sure." Surprisingly, Bartolome actually perceived a personality change in our father.

My brother and I were close, despite the ten years between us, and he depended on me to perform tasks that required attention to detail. Today, I would be poring over his accounting books.

I believe Bartolome asked me over sometimes so I could be his eyes. The family worried about my brother's deteriorating eyesight. Since our papang was disabled, Bartolome, as the eldest son, confided that he felt a duty to take care of the Ugales. Machismo was one of his values, leading to a determination that he should be responsible, strong, and courageous—the new self-assumed head of the family. But with poor vision, he did not feel capable of being completely effective.

Glory had been so ill that we had stopped holding our nightly encounters. A substitute confidante was what I needed, and Cora sustained me through her listening abilities and wise words. My sister-in-law also shared her secrets with me.

One day, Cora whispered that although she no longer smoked, she encouraged Bartolome's habit; she associated the scent of burning tobacco with the afterglow of lovemaking. Her conversations with me rivaled the reading of any romance novels from Mrs. Billet's collection. They made me blush. Pinays don't "experiment" or develop sexual prowess through multiple partners. I wanted, needed to remain chaste, yes, but I also had a great desire to learn the art of pleasuring. When the time of consummation came, I did not want to be an idiotic prude in bed. Without even a hint of vulgarity, Corazon educated me on many sweetly exotic matters.

Cora was gathering the farm's bookkeeping records when we arrived. She smiled. "Pacencia?"

"She is outside playing with little Vicente. Maybe not for long; he was placed on restriction by Auntie Soledad."

"Ah, perfect. She will be out of our way then as you help me with these accounts."

Putting her pencil down slowly and turning toward Bartolome, Cora said, "Darling, our hard labor is not reaping benefits. Is cultivating and curing tobacco worth our sacrifices?" She used her fingers to flatten the furrowed bump between her brows, believing it to be a maneuver that prevented permanent wrinkles.

"Did we not make money this season?" Bartolome picked up the cash book and tried to study the figures. "My eyes are getting worse, Cora. Where are my glasses?"

"Here they are, darling, right in front of you." Thicker lenses were prescribed almost every other year. Was there a dull, opaque film forming behind Bartolome's pupils?

"I distributed free cigars to the Americano troops. Mostly, they choose my cigarettes. Lately, they request my chewing tobacco because the soldiers are ordered not to light up during a blackout."

Pregnant, Cora waddled toward her worktable. "That's why we're not making a profit. I'm not surprised the whites prefer the cigarettes." She rubbed her abdomen. "My darling, I think the Japanese are stealing our tobacco."

"The Japon? Why do you say that? No one has seen any slant eyes around here." I did not dare tell my brother about the sightings of Japanese soldiers at the river.

"A huge batch of leaves was hung on the drying racks, and today I discovered they are gone. To take uncured tobacco, still yellow, not yet brown. Stupido! What villager would steal from us? They know we are struggling. They know I am pregnant. Bartolome, I say it must be the Japon."

My brother's jaw tensed. "So, less revenue. Poof." He gestured a flareup with his hands. "The Americanos will guard the fields; they owe me."

I moved to the window and kept an eye on some Americano soldiers. Wielding rifles, they had stopped to check out the contracted women's work.

Outside the curing shed, Auntie Soledad had congregated with other village women, their grandchildren screeching while playing *bati-cobra*, a poor peasant children's game similar to American baseball, in which a small bamboo stick is hit with a longer bamboo stick.

Occasionally, I heard Auntie Soledad berate her grandson, Vicente, and the other kids. She had been struggling to grasp the latest gossip. "Children, quiet down please; we old ladies are hard of hearing." Later, she would scold the youngsters for something contradictory. "You're too quiet; you children must be making trouble."

Vicente could be quite mischievous. His grandmother instructed him not to play with matches, but he found the nub of a used cigar, lit the end, and pinched it the way he had seen Auntie Soledad do a hundred times.

He burned the webbed space between his index and middle fingers. No words of comfort came from his grandmother. "You *must listen* to me at all times, Vicente. Now be a good boy and *sit beside me*." It was the worst punishment the grandmother could have meted out.

The workers sat in a circle, squatting upon their haunches, tying tobacco leaves in piles, which they then arranged inside an extremely large container. They gossiped about the barrio across the river; it seemed a Japon soldier, a hairy bugger, had stolen a high-priced, high-performance carabao, and some bananas and eggs. The Japon had challenged a fisherman, who fought to take the water buffalo back and was now considered the village hero.

"Who was the fisherman?" Auntie Soledad asked. "Maybe we have met."

"You are acquainted with a lot of people, Soledad. His name is something like Santiago." Santiago! My ears perked.

"No, no. The Santiago I met was a seminarian, not a fisherman." Ah, not Glory's Santiago.

"Well, the Japon had better not steal my eggs," remarked one matriarch.

"No manly soldier would want them," Auntie Soledad teased. "Yours are flat like they were fried, over-easy. Only, the aureoles are not as big as yolks."

"I'm going to stick a banana in your mouth," came a sassy retort.

"Ooh, I hope it is a *big* banana." Auntie Soledad and the other women howled. Inside the hut, hearing all of this caused us to laugh, too.

Auntie Soledad's eyes were expressive, accented with wrinkles so deep a person could bury her fingertips within the crevices. Her surprisingly soft skin looked like grainy, tanned leather. The grandmother's smile revealed tobacco-stained teeth the color of sepia. She had bony cheeks, bony arms, bony legs, and unbound breasts that swung like a pair of weighted plumb bobs. Unlike my mother, who had jet-black tresses, Soledad had silvery-white hair slicked back with coconut oil and secured with tortoise shell combs. She was the very image of a retired flamenco dancer.

"Ya seen that?" asked one soldier to another, pointing to a woman near Auntie Soledad.

"Yeah, that old lady put the red-hot end of her cigarillo into her mouth. Not carefully. Casual-like."

"What the hell? Don't it burn her throat? Blister her tongue? Lawd!"

"Do she look like she in pain, buddy?"

"Hell, no. Seem like she enjoyin' the heat, or smokin' her insides, or somethin', I guess."

The Filipino grandmothers preferred buying only the cheaper, cured whole tobacco leaves, not the manufactured products.

"Hey. That other granny, she lightin' up the same way, too. I dare ya to do that, brother."

"Oh, hell, no. I ain't doin' no such-a thing. Hot enough on the outside in this stinkin' country. Why anyone want to be hot on the inside o' they bodies, I just do *not* get it."

They studied Auntie Soledad rolling her leaf into a small cigar, placing it between her lips, and lighting it with a match. Then they saw her take the cigarillo out, flip it around, and put the lighted end into her mouth.

"Don't that scorch your palate, ma'am?"

Auntie Soledad answered, "Yes, sir."

"You mean you like smokin' like that?"

"Yes, sir." Her friends seemed impressed that Auntie Soledad conversed easily with the Americanos.

"They're chatting with Auntie Soledad," Bartolome said. We all snickered knowingly.

"You sellin' that tobacco?"

"Yes, sir."

"How much?"

"Yes, sir."

"How much?"

"Yes, sir."

. . .

Bartolome reported that Japon soldiers had encroached upon his land and helped themselves to his harvests. This infuriated my brother, whose incipient hatred for the Japanese hardened him, making him hawk-eyed and overprotective.

"Hey, Bart!"

An Americano soldier appeared at the door. "Came to pick up those dips and cigarettes for the troops. Personally, I love chew. Thank you so much."

"You're welcome."

"Yeah, well, point me in the direction, Bart, and I'll load the cases into the truck."

"Didn't you already pick up the crate?" Bartolome looked at Cora and me. "Left it for you last night. It was gone when I checked at sunrise."

"Fuckin' Japs!" The soldier slapped his thigh.

Bartolome rammed his fist into the nearest wall, making a hole in the thatch. "Japon!"

. . .

The door slammed and a whoosh of cheerful energy filled the home.

"Hi, Auntie Liling—again." Pacencia waved at me. "Papa, Mommy." She kissed her parents on their cheeks. "This is the valance I crocheted. Auntie Liling said I am smart with nimble fingers." I winked at my dear niece. She held out her work.

"Lola is making me learn to pray the rosary. It takes *ten* hours."

Bartolome laughed. "Yes, well, my mamang, your grandmother, forced me to pray the rosary, too; what a struggle for a boy! A fact. It is painful."

"I learned a lot in school today. I hate math, but I love reading in English. The Americano boy taught me hopscotch. He said he likes me—eww. Don't tell, okay? He's gonna kill me. He has hair the color of corn. Not black, like mine. Yellow. Auntie Glory is fine. And oh, Jaime is so cute, cute, cute. The Americano lady gave me crayons. She and the doctor are rich. Can we be rich someday? Jaime drew too. Just cat scratches." Pacencia giggled. "I wish I could have a baby brother like Jaime."

Bartolome glanced at his wife. He smiled and gently tugged Pacencia's pigtails.

Without being reminded, my niece put her schoolbooks away and started to wash the rice for the evening meal. Filipino children learned how to cook rice from a young age.

Bartolome told me he was grateful every day for the privilege of parenting such a dutiful and respectful child. Much credit should be given to his wife, for my brother and I believed that babies are born with the same qualities their mothers embodied during pregnancy. An irate mother will produce a colicky baby. A despondent mother will bear a gloomy baby. Happy mother—happy baby. Cora was happy. Pacencia was happy. Cora was obedient. Pacencia was obedient. Was Cora very talkative during her pregnancy?

"Mommy, you're getting e-*nor*-mous." The girl clasped her hands far in front of her belly. "Remember, Mommy and Papang, you said I can help name my baby brother or sister."

Cora nodded. "Yes, we promised."

"If a boy is born, I will name him Rosario. If a girl, Rosa, after my favorite flower."

Her father chuckled. "Rosa does mean rose, but Rosario means rosary."

Pacencia shrugged. "I don't like praying the rosary, but I still like the name."

. . .

"May I go back outside to play, Mommy and Papang? Vicente is organizing a game."

"No," Pacencia's father said in a gentle but firm way.

"But...but..." Like children are wont to do, Pacencia tried to reason with her father.

"It will be dark in a while, and who knows what dangers lurk outside."

His daughter submitted.

• • •

Auntie Soledad's Vicente and other farm kids contrived to play hide-and-seek. They neglected Auntie Soledad's admonitions about straying too far.

Vicente was determined to win. A happy-go-lucky boy, he ventured a distance into Bartolome's tobacco field. He walked quietly on the balls of his feet along an irrigation line as a playmate counted. "One, two, three…"

He slid down an incline and stumbled into the ditch.

"Ten, eleven, twelve, thirteen... Ready or not, here I come!"

BOOM! A small mine blast caused the children to scream in their hiding places.

Shrapnel, cakes of dirt, and small stones rained on Vicente. He glanced around, frightened that his Grandmother Soledad would punish him severely for having disobeyed.

The explosion and children's shrieking propelled me into action. The adults ran toward a stunned child who pointed in Vicente's direction.

One pebble, perfectly round, wet, and shiny, like a glass marble, lay on a patch of grass. The boy bent to pick it up. He screamed and dropped his eyeball.

I tried to stay calm while assessing the situation. Cora attended to Auntie Soledad, who sat in shock. Bartolome checked on the other children. I'm certain he felt relieved about keeping Pacencia from playing hide-and-seek. I wrapped Vicente's nucleated eye in a damp handkerchief, covered the cavity in his face, picked up the panicked boy, and carried him to the clinic.

I panted. "Oh, God of Eyes. God of Eyes. God of Eyes. Help. Help Vicente. Amen."

The bleeding had subsided by the time we arrived at the clinic. My apron was soaked with blood. Fluid was oozing from Vicente's ear.

I waited nervously in the waiting area, pacing, then moving from one seat to another. I tried to read a magazine but couldn't concentrate. At last, Dr. Billet emerged with Vicente. The boy's empty eye socket was packed with gauze and bandaged.

"Vicente." I quickly discarded my bloodied apron, then ran to hug him. He shuffled back and forth on his feet and then held on to me. "How incredibly brave you are!"

"Auntie Liling, I stepped on my headless shadow."

"What?"

"Grandma Soledad warned me never to step on a headless shadow or someone will die."

"Oh, good grief, dearest Vicente. It is an old lady's superstition. No one is going to die, right, Doctor?"

The Americano doctor winked at me. "Indeed, Miss Ligaya. Son, you must listen to your auntie. There is no science supporting the misfortune of stepping on shadows."

"Miss Ligaya, please inform Vicente's parents and grandmother that there was not much I could do to save the child's eye."

Auntie Soledad will be furious with Vicente.

Dr. Billet handed me a specimen cup containing a small eyeball staring at me, lens opaque, floating in chloroform, bits of dirt and grass still adhering to it. Bile rose to my mouth.

I abhorred the use of obscenities. I was too cultured or too Catholic to curse, but today in my head I *damned* the Japon. *Wait a minute....* I took time to ponder theology, a dialectical debate in my head. Dear God of All People, do you *love* the Japanese?

"Of course, our little patient here will still be able to see from his other eye. Might have a little trouble with depth perception, mind you. He won't be sharp at sports, I'm afraid. Aesthetically, they may want to consider having him wear an eye patch. Might someday get a prosthesis. Glass eyes are mighty expensive, though. I'm mighty sorry to say he may have lost some hearing."

I sank into an armchair, filled with despair and unnecessary guilt.

The Americano doctor became paternal in his approach. "You do not have to hold any remorse, Miss Ligaya. You did a mighty fine job, mighty fine. Your quick thinking, how you dressed his wound and responded to this emergency, is commendable. I mean, you could someday make a mighty fine nurse. Miss Ligaya, you *saved* the boy's life."

• • •

"Now that we got Vicente squared away…." The Americano doctor sounded more jovial.

"Doctor, what does 'squared away' mean?"

"Fixed and settled." The physician smiled.

These American sayings exasperated me.

"By the way, I examined your father the other day. Mighty nice man. Mighty nice."

He's not always all nice, but he's nicer.

"Well, I noticed he loves to lift little Jaime and hold him on his lap. Mighty cute lad, that one. Respicio's kyphosis is severe; his back is curved more than ever."

"Yes, we worry about Papang's mobility. Jaime is his joy. They're very close, and that makes Papang happy."

"Well, let me tell you, the missus is mighty tired of the décor here. She has a grand desire to redo the waiting room. In my mind, the place is not pretty, but it's practical—I chose the old furniture." The doctor laughed. "Utilitarian, you know what I mean? I know, I know, she wants pretty. In fact—" the doctor went searching in his desk "—my wife brought in this swatch of cloth."

I recognized the fabric that Mrs. Billet gave me just before the

Japanese invasion. "Extra yardage," she had said. I had never got around to sewing Pacencia's dress.

"I've decided just to let the missus redesign the interior or there will be no end to it. So, I am *giving* the mahogany armchairs to *you*, my dear Ugales. That should help your father with sitting and standing."

I flashed back to the time I tried to sell my crocheted curtains to the Chinese merchant. He was stingy and I refused to sell them for less than their worth. As a result, the purchase of an armchair as prescribed for my ailing father, had been postponed indefinitely.

"Thank you, Doctor. You are kind."

"Now mind you, there are scratches here and there from normal wear and tear."

He howled with laughter. "Here and there. Wear and tear. It rhymes."

"You look *mighty* proud of yourself, Doctor. *Mighty* proud." I imitated the physician, and that made Dr. Billet guffaw some more.

"The chairs are mighty sturdy. Mighty sturdy indeed," he added.

"Indeed," I echoed. Employer and employee smiled at each other, sharing a jovial moment in such trying times.

I took Vicente's hand and kissed the bandage on his eye. Then I prayed, "God of Sight, I ask Thee humbly for healing. Please preserve this boy's hearing. Help him to see sharply with his good eye. Amen. Oh, and another thing, please calm Auntie Soledad so she doesn't cause drama. Now, Amen."

"A *mighty* Amen." With that, the Americano doctor patted the child and me on our heads and sent us on our way.

Praise be to you, God of Mahogany Armchairs…God of Eyes… God of Miracles.

• • •

"Can I carry my eye? I want to bring it to school and show my friends."

"What? Oh, dear. Well, I'll let you carry the container for now, but your grandma Soledad will have to be the one to decide what you do with it."

"I'm sorry, Auntie Liling." I smiled. Vicente is my aunt's grandchild, making him my cousin once removed. In the Philippines, children almost always call an elder woman Auntie or Nana; and an elder man Uncle or Tata.

"Yes, my dear?" He looked pitiable with one eye downcast and bandages around his head, holding in place the bulging wad of gauze in his empty socket. "Sorry? Why, sorry?"

"I stepped on my shadow; it's bad luck."

"Oh, dear one, you did not step on your shadow, you stepped on a mine."

"What is a mine, Auntie Liling?"

"Well, it's a bomb that's buried in the ground and explodes when somebody disturbs it."

"Oh." Vicente squeezed my hand tighter as we walked in the direction of Auntie Soledad's house. I was in a pensive mood. The sun will be setting soon and all of Asia will be in shadow. Bad luck?

After a period of silence, Vicente broke away and bolted ahead of me.

I called out. "Stay on the path! Be careful where you step. Vicente don't go near the tall grass. Slow down! Wait for me. Vicente, wait for me." The little boy stopped suddenly and stood still. He cupped his hand around his "good" ear and stared deeply into the woods that line our route.

"Auntie Liling?" I had finally caught up to him. He looked anxious.

"Stay with me, Vicente. I don't want you to get hurt. You lost an eye. You were lucky you didn't lose your life."

"Auntie Liling?"

"Yes?" I reached for the child's hand.

"The fucking Japs are all over."

"Vicente! Where did you learn that bad word?" I was shocked to hear a six-year-old utter it.

"I hear-ed the Americano soldiers say, 'fucking Japs' all the time."

Oh, God of Language. I sighed.

"Auntie Liling, the fff—I mean the Japs are all over."

"Yes, I know, they're all over the Philippines."

"I mean, Auntie Liling, they're all over…here. Near here. Just now. I saw them. I hear-ed them. Auntie Liling, I'm scared."

"I haven't seen or heard anyone, Vicente. You might have heard a carabao. Could it have been a monkey?"

He insisted. "I know what I saw and hear-ed."

"Right." Six-year-old kid with one eye and poor hearing detecting the presence of stealthy Japanese.

"Auntie Liling, I'm Superkid!"

I smiled. "Vicente, you *are* a super kid."

"I have superpowers and someday I'm going to kill the fucking Japs."

"Vicente!"

PART II

MAELSTROM

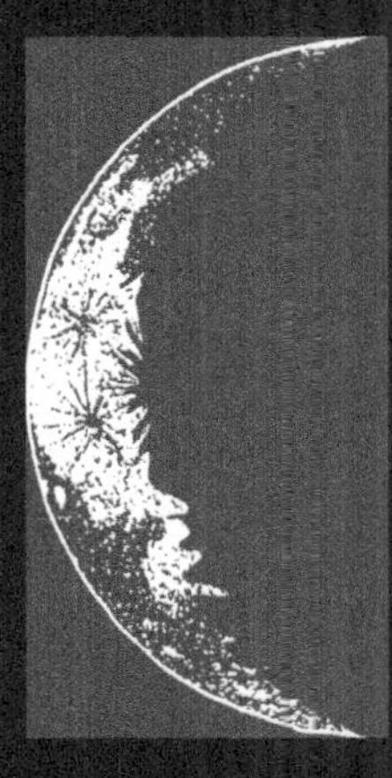

Chapter 14

LIGAYA "LILING" UGALE

September 1944

"VIRGINS ONLY."

My nightmare was so vivid, I heard a rough voice and felt rough hands shackle my wrists and yank me off my mat. I screamed and kept screaming. A slap stung my cheek, hard, like an exasperation-powered whack to a pesky mosquito. My eyelids were too heavy with sleep. My knees buckled. Another slap and my eyes flew open. I was not dreaming!

Six inches from my face was the Japanese version of our water buffalo, the one that turns violent around cows in heat. He spewed sounds of hate-like bullets from a machine gun, stuttering, "*Kuso. Kuso…Ku-ku-ku-ku-ku-ku-soh!* Shit!" What was the water buffalo trying to convey? Heaving lungs full of fear caused me to freeze—I stood stoic—the way I had coped when Papang beat me.

Glory fought with another Japon who took orders from the Oriental Bull. She shouted Filipino curse words—"Your mother's cunt!" She walked forward to steer the Private away from Jaime, who clutched his chest. Not an asthma attack; please, not now.

"You're not a virgin." The third Japon kicked Mamang on the hip.

"Ay, Apo Dios!" Mamang needed to be rescued. Papang struggled to stand, but he tipped over when the Japon pushed him lightly. Papang poked his cane at him. The Japon kicked Mamang again. Papang pounded him on the back of the leg with the walking stick. The soldier pointed his gun at the old man. The earth stopped rotating, and out of the quiescence, a little boy's voice rang out, "Lolong!" Jaime ran to his grandfather, who held him and rocked him. Who was the shield for whom?

Forced outside under the mango-colored moon, I counted nine elderly women who must have been spinsters; they asked for virgins only. One dozen adolescents, seven school-aged girls (*No, please, not Pacencia*!), and one female infant (*Why Baby Rosa*?). Numerous younger adult women joined them, corralled in an inner circle within the plaza.

Used and used-up females were positioned in an outer circle; mothers, grandmothers, like Mamang, Glory, and Cora. How did the Japanese know which women were no longer virginal? I surmised the others were exotic dancers or street walkers. The Japon were choosing virgins over the hookers who were learned in eroticism.

Women in the outer circle had been tied with their hands behind their necks in such fashion that struggling to escape resulted in choking. Mercifully, matrons, like Mamang and Auntie Soledad, stood tethered more loosely. The Japon probably thought the elderly didn't have the strength or guts to run away.

The enraged men were held captive in the courtyard of Father Benito's church, near the cemetery where the bones of Spanish conquerors lay buried. Camouflage nets and chicken-wire fencing contained dozens of Pinoys, but they failed to contain the village men's savage fury.

Gorilla from the river! I recognized the very hairy Japon soldier with a smoker's gravelly voice, who stood at the top of the church stairs, shouting orders in a thick accent. "Hurry the fuck up. Hoist it up. Up! Now over. Not that way. Hurry up. They're like freaking mad monkeys. *Kuso*!"

"Let us go. Bastards!" said the Filipino men, their red-hot anger like exploding lava.

"Shut the fuck up, Monkey!" Only one stripe. No badges. Must be a Japanese private. He whacked somebody's head like a bat to a ball. Agonizing punishment was meted out to men who attempted to defend and deliver their women.

The hairy one ordered a farmer to salute him. When the Pinoy refused, he was ordered again. Still, he refused. Gorilla motioned soldiers to pull down the Pinoy's pants. Without warning, the Gorilla sliced off the man's penis. "Now you will never salute." He laughed and the other soldiers howled.

"Tiny dick." The Private wiggled his little finger.

The farmer dropped to the ground in a fetal position and used his shaking hands to staunch the bleeding. A sustained, high-pitched screech shot out.

"Shut up. Shut up!" Gorilla picked up the cork-shaped appendage and shoved it into the suffering man's mouth. Nobody refused to salute after that.

Little Jaime clutched his grandfather's hand. "Mama. Mama!"

Papang tried unsuccessfully to cover the child's eyes. I followed my nephew's gaze and turned to look at Glory. She was not crying. Just angry. "You bastards! Untie me, now!"

Careful, sister, I thought. *They will punish you for your defiance.* Gloriana kept yelling, showing her fists.

Papang let go of Jaime's hand to help the castrated Pinoy. I watched nervously as my nephew waddled toward the chicken-wire fencing, then crawled through a tight opening. Jaime located his grandmother. He slipped beneath Mamang's long skirt. He was trying to hide. Mamang adjusted her clothing to fully conceal the little boy.

The Oriental Bull shoved me on my back. I glanced over at Raul, crazed, screaming my name, "Liling! Liling!" He was assaulted with the butt of the Private's rifle. He staggered. The captain mounted me, and Raul fell backwards, as if kicked by a wild animal. Shame consumed me. My dear parents and beloved fiancé would see me stripped, naked, raped. I closed my eyes and tried to seal the entrance to my secret place by holding my knees together tightly. A maiden's first experience of love should be gentle and sweet, not like this. "Oh, God of Loving, not like this."

The soldiers just stood watching. One of them said, "Captain Fuku, pretty one there. Lucky you got first pick."

Mamang's voice floated above the others. "My daughter is to be married. Do not defile her." Raul watched, helpless; he wiped blood from his neck.

"Shut up, old woman," rebuked Captain Fuku.

I willed Mamang to quit begging. *Stop drawing attention to yourself.* You will compromise Jaime's safety. Was it possible for a two-year-old to remain motionless under her skirt?

"Good you stopping screaming. Nobody want those chichis." Oriental Bull seemed amused—or perhaps not.

. . .

I expected all rapists to smell like putrid rot; instead, I found a faint scent of clean, like fresh pine, underlying the sticky sweat of the Japanese. The Oriental Bull, with nostrils flaring, pinned my arms above my head. He used his knees to force my knees apart. His slanted eyes pierced me, his fingers pierced me, his tongue pierced me, his cock pierced me. I was stabbed multiple times but not cut. No lacerations, but my soul bled.

My flesh dissected, the rapist opened me and sucked my juices until there was no more to slurp. I lost my sweetness that day. Became tainted. Rotten. Raul had called me "Luscious." I would never want to hear that word again for I am spoiled fruit.

The church bells sang, heralding the midnight as the Oriental Bull thrust exactly thirteen times. I counted, matching the rhythm of his rocking to twelve peals plus one. My cheeks felt wet—a mixture of my tears, his drool, and our sweat. And down—between—oh, God of Tears, there was wetness.

When will the real nightmare be over?

. . .

"It's unfair that we entry-class soldiers can't enjoy the plunder." The Private was eyeing Gloriana. The soldier shrugged. "Her face is plain-looking, but all women are pleasing 'down there.' " The other guards laughed.

"Go! Go! Go! Go!" They spurred him on.

He abandoned his post and attempted to grab Glory. Corazon responded by pulling Gloriana's arm, resulting in a vicious tug-of-war. The Japanese Private won. Gloriana protested, "I have a son."

"I have daughters," Cora said. The soldier ignored the young mother.

"You're not virgin?" the soldier asked Gloriana.

Chin up, arms crossed, my sister replied, "You cannot take me. I'm not a virgin. I'm not. I have a son!" Gloriana was willful as always.

The Private was already hard. He fumbled with the buttons on his khaki trousers. Before long, I heard whimpering to my immediate right. Oh, Glory. I recognized my sister's voice; her utterances were melodious. They say that during a rape, victims cannot experience orgasms. Was Gloriana moaning? Did she moan in her joining with Santiago? A disturbing thought—I must not think that way.

I forced myself to watch Gloriana's skinny rapist jerk like a patient with a movement disorder. He mauled her and laughed; no, it was really a shriek. "Again. Again."

My sister tried to bite his lip, but he whacked her across her face so hard that Glory went momentarily limp. This must have excited the Japanese man all the more. In one final orgasmic thrust, he yelled out his country's battle cry, "*Banzai!*"

God of Mercy do not let Jaime witness his mother being violated.

Gloriana, ever defiant, hissed. "Bastard Japon."

Maelstrom. Groans of pleasure and groans of pain. Shrieks of ecstasy and shrieks of terror. Japanese and Filipino languages don't mix. Volleys of verbal arrows assaulted my ears.

. . .

The Oriental Bull continued his assault, but I disengaged from my body. As if anesthetized, I floated above the sea of red-trimmed, drab ochre uniforms, punctuated by the pastels of bras and undies. Between the waves of women's clothing, I saw victims writhing and attackers attacking.

The Gorilla took his place in the inner circle, having shoved a petite woman before him. "You are too ugly. Lie on stomach. I take you behind." A slender woman got on all fours; her hair was disheveled, covering her front. When the woman looked up, I beheld the face of a princess, a very beautiful princess. Why did the Gorilla call her ugly? And then I noticed a flaw so slight that most people would disregard it. She had a cleft lip.

. . .

The cacophony of screaming, crying, wailing, and raging was disorienting. Every ugly human utterance formed a disharmonious symphony composed by the Japon and sung by a choir of frantic Filipinos. Piercing this cyclone of sound was an infant's howling. It could only have been Bartolome and Cora's baby daughter, Rosa. Five months old, and cute and pudgy, and sweet and innocent. Innocent.

Corazon begged the Japanese not to hurt her baby. "Sir, take me. Take me instead. Take me instead!" The infantophile did not seem interested. The young mother ripped off her blouse to reveal her breasts, huge and hard with milk. "Look at me. Take me." My sister-in-law looked desperate.

I searched for Pacencia, who had been thrown into the inner circle. A young, prized virgin. Several soldiers held the schoolgirl down, groping her hairless pre-pubertal mound. She screamed, "The bad, bad, bad, bad, bad mans!"

"Quiet down, or we will kill you!" yelled the most vicious-looking Japon of the group.

She screamed again. "Papang! The bad, bad, bad, bad, bad mans."

Her father could not rescue her.

"Papang. PAPANG!"

Darling Pacencia, only ten, had been raped by, not one, but five Japanese. They poked her belly button, and then poked her little flower. She lay supine; her silence showed me that she had surrendered. I glanced at Bartolome, who used his hands, elbows, feet, and head as weapons against any Japon who stood between him and his daughters. He heaved in agony and fell to his knees.

"Stand up," a Japanese private ordered.

My brother would not or could not move.

"I said, 'Stand up!' " Bartolome remained on the ground. The guard yanked him up so forcefully that his spectacles flew off his face. The soldier stomped on them, destroying the frame and mashing the glass lenses into crystal dust. I knew that rendered blind, Bartolome could see only a blurred mass of undulating, writhing figures.

One of the guards grabbed Bartolome's wife by her hair. He shoved Cora to the ground, slamming her head on a hardened dirt path. The soldier squeezed and clawed her chest until bruises appeared on her fragile skin. He voraciously sucked her breasts, one and then the other, slurping like a greedy newborn. The Japon did not stop until her milk supply was drained.

The Private screamed a litany of F-words in a baritone voice. He ordered her to sit on him. She refused; he spanked her bottom. He impaled her. Like a circus animal trainer, he held his victim firmly by her pelvis and commanded her to move her hips side to side, front to back, circle round, figure-eights. When she leaned forward, her breasts hung over his face, and he chewed her nipples.

"God of Mercy, please, this is hell. Let it be over."

. . .

Dawn erased darkness. The serial rapes had continued for more than five hours until the Japon's hunger for sex and power was finally satiated. The Japs celebrated with the random shooting of bullets, rounds of saké, and hoopla.

I did not have the energy to gather my clothing. I rolled into a ball; my arms and legs shielded my nakedness. The men were released. Raul rushed to me. He covered and then lifted me; I clung to him and sobbed freely in his embrace; my safe place, my sacred space.

The label "pure and chaste" is given to Pinays starting from pubescence, with the expectation they remain celibate until marriage. "Pure and chaste" could no longer apply to any female in our village; not a single virgin was left. The pall of humiliation stupefied the women, emasculated the men. Papang, Bartolome, and Raul had lost something else too—their power, their pride, their peace.

Our barrio had been persecuted, poisoned. Those least debilitated gathered the dead, injured, and newly insane.

• • •

"*My* attacker."

My use of the possessive sickened me as I attempted to document the assault. There was no other descriptor for the Oriental Bull. I refused to label him *the* attacker or *the* monster as if he were The Omnipotent One, the Only One. I settled upon the simple truth: Rapist.

I refrained from combining the honorific Japanese suffix, *san*, with his surname, Fuku. Still, Fuku-san snagged my brain. Fuku-san. I knew that saying his name aloud would cause my spit to fly; the spray of my hate was vehement and toxic. Each time I wrote "Fuku," the pressure of pen to paper increased, deeply excoriating the page. Fuku. Fuku. Fuku!

I handed the completed form to the Sergeant. In his Texas drawl, the American mispronounced the rapist's name, "Captain Fuck-*Yoo*. Captain Fuck-You. These freakin' foreign names. Don't they just make you laugh? Give me Smith, Brown, or Johnson. F-U-K-U. Hell, even the spellin' is hilarious."

I myself could not say the word "rape." The Japon called it "comfort."

"Yup, you gals are lucky you weren't forced into sex slavery in one of them comfort stations."

"Comfort stations?"

"Yes, ma'am! Brothels that service Jap soldiers."

I wanted to vomit.

The criminal debauchery was too horrific to speak of, so the villagers referred to it only as The Event—forever more—The Event.

Baby Rosa had died.

"Tell us what happened, brother."

Bartolome seethed. "Her flower was ripped open. *Ripped open* I tell you. But that was not what killed her."

All the women in our hut sobbed during the telling.

Cora cried loudest. "Our baby suffocated."

"The Americano doctor did not know how. Maybe the rapist pressed his whole weight against her body. Maybe he smashed her nose and mouth to stop her crying. Rosa's insides—damaged beyond..." Bartolome made a fist and punched the palm of his opposite hand. "This is what the doctor said, 'She would not be able to enjoy intimacy or bear children as an adult.' "

I coughed. "What else did the physician say?"

" 'Mr. Ugale, it is better your baby is dead.' "

Chapter 15

LIGAYA "LILING" UGALE

September 1944

Papang clasped his cane, breathless from the hike to the graveyard. My heart filled with love for the old man, and also pity, for how he had wasted years of his life immersed in misery and aggravation.

"Where is everybody?" asked Mamang. I glanced around the cemetery, old headstones standing like forlorn guards protecting the dead. The grounds were empty of people except for the Ugales.

I had covered my head with a lace mantilla. Except for Gloriana, we all held rosaries, fingering the beads as we prayed. We dabbed our moist eyes with handkerchiefs edged in crocheted lace—gifts from me for this solemn occasion.

Bartolome was stiff like bamboo, and Papang was bent like bamboo. Rosa's father and grandfather inspected her gravesite carefully.

"Stay away from the hole, Jaime," scolded his uncle.

"If you fall in, I'll bury you alive with your dead baby cousin," teased Papang.

This time, Bartolome scolded our father. "Papang, what a thing to say to a child! You will add to his nightmares."

Pacencia's bruises had turned from indigo to yellow, so she looked the worst, like a jaundiced, hairless puppy. She had been quiet in thought ever since the funeral procession started. Come to think of it, she barely spoke after The Event.

"It's sad that no one cares for the baby or us." Gloriana arranged sprigs of jasmine, hibiscus, and pink frangipani flowers in a glass jar.

I countered, "Glory, don't say that. People are tired. They have no more capacity to grieve."

Father Benito, the villagers discovered, had kept himself hidden beneath the white linen-covered altar during the hours of The Event. "I was praying for you," he said, trying to justify his cowardice. Papang had sworn under his breath, "Go to hell!"

The priest blessed the tiny coffin with holy water. Then he startled the family by shouting like a Southern Baptist Bible thumper.

> "The house of the wicked shall be destroyed: but the tabernacles of the just shall flourish." [Proverbs 14:11]

"My baby was not wicked. Flourish? Father, what does it mean to flourish? My soul is dy-ing," Cora wailed.

The priest brought the volume of his voice down about two notches.

> "And the Lord who is your leader, he himself will be with thee: he will not leave thee, nor forsake thee: fear not, neither be dismayed." [Deuteronomy 31:8]

He then spoke slowly, as if Cora were in the first grade.

"God. Will. Not. Forsake you. He. Will. Give. You life. Corazon Meili Gotiangco Ugale, a vibrant life."

"Stupido! Never. Never!" She pawed at the rough-hewn box. "Ay. My child. My baby. My Rosa." It was a cry no one ever gets used to hearing. The anguish and depth of pain was so intense that I felt disoriented.

I imagined Rosa's soul exploding into the universe. Where the pieces fell, no one would know. I only knew my brother and his wife were part of that explosion.

Bartolome tried to hold Cora back with a vise-like grip, afraid she would hurl herself into the grave.

"Sweetheart, please," he begged. We watched helplessly.

Auntie Soledad, with Vicente in hand, had finally completed the trek to the cemetery. "I'm sorry for your loss, my dear." She extended her hand to Cora.

"Don't be sorry, Auntie. I am lost, too," Cora replied.

The priest continued loudly in competition with the commotion. He at least tried to give comfort with words from the Bible.

> "Behold, I have given you power to tread upon serpents and scorpions, and upon all the power of the enemy: and nothing shall hurt you." [Luke 10:19]

"Nothing hurts us. And everything hurts us. God is the great betrayer." Mamang's rosary hung slackly in her brown, wrinkled hand. "Ay, Apo Dios. Father God, where are you? Have you abandoned me and my family?" Mamang appeared weary, with red-rimmed eyes. She had been well-bonded with the baby, having been present at Rosa's birth and baptism.

Gloriana could not keep her thoughts to herself. She whispered so those nearest her could hear. "Bastard Benito; not one ounce of empathy for human frailty. Not one ounce of compassion. Not one ounce of being Christ-like."

I stood beside Bartolome and Corazon. I surveyed my surroundings and studied the people. My family and I had shared an experience so heinous we would scarcely speak of it again. I tried to forgive the Oriental Bull and chastised myself for being unable to do so. All I ruminated about was being the Dirty, Dirty, Dumb-Dumb.

God of Happily Ever After, I don't believe you. Amen.

Cora struck a match and ignited one of Bartolome's cigars, going against her vow not to smoke. She placed the lit end into her mouth.

Pacencia did not say a word. Come to think of it, not a whisper or a whimper has escaped her mouth since The Event.

...

My brother and his wife not only mourned the death of their infant; they mourned the death of Pacencia's voice.

"Pacencia? Did I teach you the block stitch already?"

My niece simply stared at me.

"Pacencia?"

Irritation made my neck stiff. I pulled my shoulders up to relieve tension lest it migrate and exacerbate as a headache. Mamang tried to intervene. "Pacencia, your auntie asked you a question. You must be polite and answer." Not a sound came out of her once chatty mouth.

"Girl, come here," demanded Papang. She stood before her grandfather. He raised his cane as if to hit her.

I yelped in alarm. "Papang, what are you doing?"

"Stop, Respicio!" Mamang laid a hand on Papang's raised arm.

He shook his head. "It was a test. She flinches but does not cry out. Does not speak in anger or in anguish."

The girl lost the capacity to speak; was struck dumb immediately after The Event. "Gang rape," the *policia* labeled it.

Pacencia had used silence as a means to survive; now silence had developed as a coping strategy to protect her psyche.

I accompanied Bartolome's family to the specialists to have my niece evaluated and treated.

"Maybe Pacencia doesn't know the basics of the different dialects she is being taught. Perhaps, since she was excelling in English, she now refuses to speak in Filipino," opined the Americano school specialist appointed to teach English to students from the remote countryside.

Bartolome shook his head. "But, ma'am, now my daughter does not converse with us in our own rural dialect."

The school mandated that Pacencia be further examined at the city clinic. We all traveled the long way by jeepney.

Pacencia sat on the wooden examination table. The physician peered into her ears.

"Do you have evidence that she hears?"

"Well, *Doctora*, she follows directions. So, I believe she can hear. Except, she does not listen to us when we ask her to use her voice."

Pacencia's tongue, teeth, palate, lips, vocal cords, and the joints of her jaw were checked.

"Was she ever in an accident where she was injured on the mouth?"

I gagged as I recalled fellatio being forced upon the child.

Cora replied, "No, Doctora."

She was injured, only it wasn't by accident. I thought it but didn't speak.

"Does she converse with her friends?"

"No, Doctora," Bartolome answered this time. "She stopped speaking to them. They no longer come by to play."

"Does she speak with family members?"

I shook my head. "No, Doctora, not even to her lola, or lolong, or her cousin Jaime, whom she loves dearly."

"Does she whisper?"

"No, Doctora."

"Does she sing?"

"No, Doctora."

"It is hopeless, Doctora," said Bartolome. "We have coaxed her to speak, using compassion and reason. We have tempted her with rewards; sweets she likes and toys she has wished for. We thought perhaps punishment would work. We have removed privileges. Cora and I have spanked her, scolded her."

I added, "We tried everything, Doctora. My sister and I, her aunties, intervened and tried to reason with her. My father even threatened her with lickings. What else can we do?"

"Please, I ask you to cure our daughter." Cora looked in her handbag and pulled out a handkerchief.

"It appears that Pacencia is—*dumb*—I'm sorry; that's the lay term," the pediatrician explained and then gave her diagnosis. "Conversion

Disorder. That is what it is, Mr. and Mrs. Ugale. Her vocal mechanics are normal, but she has an anxiety disorder."

"Please, Doctora, your words—too hard—I am not understand." Cora sat beside her daughter and held her hand.

"It means your daughter is sick, in her head."

"No," her father vehemently disagreed. "She is merely a very *disobedient* daughter. Please, just talk to her, Doctora, so she will obey. She will listen to your authority."

Cora wept.

"Did a trauma occur recently?" asked the pediatrician.

"No, Doctora," Cora insisted, even though she had witnessed The Event.

"No physical abuse? No sexual molestation?"

A tightness attacked my jaw. The beginning of a headache, I was sure. "Cora, speak the truth; it is important."

Cora responded, "No. I said, '*No.*' "

Was it humiliation that prevented Bartolome and Cora from recounting the truth about their daughter's gang rape? I think Cora realized she had raised her voice because she said demurely, "I am sorry, Doctora."

"Nothing can be done, I'm afraid. There are no medicines for this. I encourage you to take her to the psychiatric clinic in Manila where therapists might be able to help. But it is far away and expensive, and they offer no guarantees. The disorder is involuntary."

The doctor caught herself when she saw Cora's quizzical look. "That means your daughter did not *choose*—to *not* speak. I surmise that something happened, so atrocious, so vile, that she was frightened and embarrassed beyond our comprehension. Only time can heal, Mr. and Mrs. Ugale. I'm sorry."

Pacencia, young victim of war rape, had brought shame upon Cora and Bartolome, and now she further shamed the family by refusing to speak. The child could not scream to save herself. Poor Pacencia could not even whisper "Fire" or "Help" or "Rape!"—words she needed for survival, especially in wartime.

Chapter 16

LIGAYA "LILING" UGALE

October 1944

All of the villagers now had dead eyes.

Once a thriving, lively, carefree community, our village had become a dreary and desolate place, surrounded by fallowed fields. *Depressed* and *dispassionate* described the peasants.

Noise came almost strictly from the animals: the braying of the carabao, the cackling of hens, and the crowing of roosters. Starving villagers abandoned their starving pet dogs who wandered, howling for any tiny morsel. Occasionally, the shriek of a jungle monkey would interrupt the nothing of night. I tried unsuccessfully to overcome the insomnia that was so often initiated by flashbacks of trauma. The animal caterwauling did not help my sleep. Neither did my fear of attacks by the Japanese.

The Event compelled the population of males to naturally congregate into three groups. In the first, the young, earnest, and fit hurriedly enlisted in the Philippine army. The second group consisted of Filipinos determined to fight but who had failed their physical exams or bore criminal histories. My almost blind brother, Bartolome, fell into this category. He joined the rogue guerrilla militia. The last third of the men were commanded by the first two-thirds to remain behind. They were the elder and/or infirm, like Papang, and males too young—all unable to participate in active combat. However, the third group was assigned to still noble causes—to run the farms and protect the women and children. These three very diverse packs were united by two characteristics: their fierce loyalty to the Philippines and their fulminating hatred for the Japanese.

General Douglas MacArthur kept the promise he made in 1942 when he and his troops were ordered by President Franklin D. Roosevelt to leave the Japanese-occupied Philippines. "I have returned!" he said, and the Filipinos were relieved once again to have his protection.

The villagers depended heavily on the American soldiers for safety and psychological strength. The American men conveyed an air of authority with their booming baritone voices. Their tall height, huskiness, and brawn made the petite Filipino men look like backward pygmies. Their United States-manufactured weapons were accurate and modern, not like the motley collection of bolo knives, leather horse whips, booby traps, rusted firearms, and machetes used by the Filipino guerrillas.

"Mamang, Papang," Gloriana asked, "may I go out with my friends this evening?"

"No," said Papang bluntly.

"I am sure you will at least allow me a chaperone with scrutinizing eyes."

"No."

"We do not want a repeat of The Event," Mamang said. "You will be safer at home."

"But Mamang, we not only have physical wounds, we have emotional wounds. I need to be with friends, to laugh, to dance, to play."

Papang grunted. "To drink."

"No, Glory. It is out of concern for your safety. Agapito Macadangdang recommended we remain in our homes, lights out, not even a lit cigarillo."

"All right then, if you do not allow me to socialize with my girlfriends, perhaps you will permit me a visit with my boyfriends." Gloriana took a risk in using sarcasm.

"No." Papang bristled at her teasing and remained firm.

"Liling will chaperone me. I'm sure of it. Won't you, Liling?" she pleaded with me.

"No." The sternness of my voice surprised me. Glory was used to getting her way, especially with me, her younger sister. "You don't listen, Glory. You're selfish. You think only of yourself, not Mamang, not Papang, not me. You put me in danger." I glanced at Papang. "And I'm the one who gets punished."

"Please?"

"No, Glory. I said, 'No.'"

"Well, I'm going anyway. I'm an adult and I can decide for myself." Gloriana stormed out of the hut. I'm sure she was lonely, bored, and had to be with other people besides her family. She wanted to, needed to find a new partner, perhaps a father for Jaime.

Papang hurled the infamous Filipino curse at her back. "Your mother's cunt!"

Mamang hurled her rosary at him. He deserved to be struck.

• • •

"Liling!" Raul called out as he walked by our hut.

No answer. He knocked on our unpainted plywood door. Still, no response.

Raul climbed up "our" mango tree, gathered the ripened drupes, and delivered baskets of the fruit to my family—every day.

"Your beloved Raul came by *again*. He left some mangoes for you *again*." Gloriana showed me the most beautiful fruit.

I shook my head.

"You can't sulk all day. It's been two months since The Event, and you are still moping."

"Yes, well, I'm not like you, Glory. I can't bounce back that easily.

I can't defy Father like you do."

"What is it? You are different, Liling, and I don't like it. You used to be kind to me, no matter what." Gloriana paused. "You've allowed your rapist to conquer you. Fight back, Liling. You need to get out of this rotten old hut into the sunshine. In nature."

"I would, but—the Japanese." I was consumed with foreboding.

"Oh, Japanese-zee. Crapanese-zee. They're war criminals, terrorists, sadists. They've gone from our village, but look at you, still imprisoned by them. That fucking Fuku raped your body, not your mind, and certainly, not your heart. Go to Raul, Liling. Let him soothe your pain."

"I am polluted, Glory, in body, mind, and heart. No man will ever want me." Gloriana seemed to listen intently. "I ought to spare him the pain of obligation to marry me according to the contract."

Gloriana sighed. "Nonsense. He *wants* to marry you."

Nothing my sister said could convince me to live a full life—with Raul. I cried, "I am a dirty, dirty..."

Jaime finished quietly, "Dumb-Dumb."

. . .

My perception that Raul had rejected me because of The Event was far from the truth. Pinoy men, I thought, only wanted to marry pure and chaste women, not raped, dirty ones.

I had not realized that during The Event, Raul had witnessed a strength and courage that caused him to love me even more. In truth, I wanted him to hold me, comfort me; and in so doing, release me from the bondage of my anguish.

I allowed weeks to go by without contact or communication. I rarely exited the hut, careful to emerge only when I could assure myself that our paths would not cross.

Chapter 17

LIGAYA "LILING" UGALE

October 1944

Sprinkles of water fell on my newest crochet project. I didn't care. No one caused me to laugh as easily as Jaime, a playful boy who delighted in occasionally splashing his mother and me. A quick soap and shampoo with a Pure Brand soap bar. Quick rinse. Gloriana bathed her toddler in the Filipino way, using a half coconut shell to scoop water from our galvanized steel tub as Jaime stood in it. Mothers tended to wash their children while the air was still warm in the afternoons. Midday, when the sun was hottest, was not the best time for soaking, even though the water was warm—like pee. You'd sweat and just have to bathe again.

"Stand still, Jaime," his mother scolded mildly.

"Mama. Owee." Jaime rubbed his eyes, which only made the sting worse.

"Stand still, Jaime. Please." Gloriana used the hem of her cotton dress to gently wipe her son's eyes.

A second rinse of his hair with the now cold water. Tiny chill bumps formed across Jaime's skin. Dr. Billet labels the phenomenon "goose pimples." "Chicken skin" is what Filipinos call it. My sister wiped down the shivering child with a stiff, sun-dried towel.

Jaime raised his arms. "Towel hug, Mama. Towel hug." Gloriana wrapped the cloth around the toddler's torso and squeezed him. "Your turn, Auntie." He waddled to me, trying to keep the towel in place. I enfolded my nephew in my arms; we hugged each other tightly. I sniffed his hair.

"Jaime, you don't smell like fish anymore. You smell fresh and pure."

"Like you, Auntie Liling—fresh and pure." I flinched.

"Now, you need to brush your teeth," his mama said.

Jaime made a face.

"Do you want brown teeth like old Auntie Soledad?"

"No, Mama."

"Or," I added, "no teeth at all like Lolong Respicio?"

"No, Auntie Liling. He try bite me, but him no teeth." His laughter reminded me of soprano wind chimes. "I love my lolong."

• • •

"I'm going to make dinner." Gloriana scaled and cleaned the fish that Jaime had "helped" her catch.

"Jaime," Mamang said, "go ask your lolong what he wants to eat."

We were already prepping *pinakbet*, vegetable stew, with produce from our garden. Pork fat sizzled in the frying pan. Mamang added to the mounds of sliced eggplants and cut string beans. I chopped the tomatoes.

"Okay, Lola!" What a cooperative child!

"Lolong, what eat?" Jaime yelled. No answer.

"Go closer, Jaime."

"Lolong? What eat?" He cocked his head to listen.

Gloriana turned to Mamang and me. "I think Papang's hearing is going."

"Maybe that is a good thing." Mamang chuckled.

"Lolong. His ears. Owee."

Papang's climbing age and infirmities drew pity from me.

"Auntie, Lolong not hearing. I know what he say."

"What will your grandfather say, Son?" Gloriana now cut the bitter melon.

"He will say 'begetables.' But I no like begetables."

"Do you want to be blind like Uncle Bartolome? Or a hunchback like your lolong?"

"No, Mama."

"Then you must eat vegetables."

"No like bitter melon."

"We will ask Auntie Liling to put less bitter melon in the pinakbet."

"If I make the vegetable stew," I said, "and I add a little bit of pork, and less bitter melon, then will you eat your vegetables, Jaime?"

The boy nodded, but not enthusiastically.

As usual, Jaime climbed onto his grandfather's lap and Papang held him close, guarding a precious, priceless package.

"Lolong eat soon. You like begetables. I no like begetables. I eat begetable stew so I no crooked like you, Lolong."

Gloriana gasped and covered her mouth with her hand. Indirect criticisms used to extract outrage. Jaime had hopped off his grandfather's lap and was playing with his cane, pretending to be an old man, hunched over, and walking slowly. In the past, such teasing, no matter how innocent the remark or behavior, would have aroused Papang's rancor.

Papang laughed. I had never heard him laugh so heartily. A collective sigh of relief emanated from the women.

"Come here, little boy. It will be a long, long time before you begin to walk like that. And that's why you must eat your vegetables."

"Yes, Lolong."

Papang took Jaime by the hand and led him to the table for dinner.

"Will you pray, Jaime?" I winked at my nephew.

In a clear voice, Jaime said, "God of Food, bless our food. Amen."

"Ay, Apo Dios." Mamang sounded cheerful. She made the sign

of the cross enthusiastically; Jaime tried to follow her, but he missed touching one shoulder.

"A very nice prayer, Jaime." We all clapped.

"God hear me?"

"Oh, yes, God was certainly listening."

"I think I know who taught you to pray," Gloriana said.

Jaime pointed at me, but in doing so, he knocked over a jar of coconut water. The liquid spilled onto his grandfather's lap.

Papang raised his arm, raised his voice, and started to swear, "Dirty, dirty—"

Jaime finished in a neutral voice, "—dumb-dumb."

Mamang snapped at my father. "You will hit your grandson? What is the matter with you?"

"Jaime! What did you say?" The little boy appeared bewildered. Glory rarely showed anger in her son's presence.

Mamang scowled.

"Son, those are bad words." Glory shook her index finger. I had never before seen her gesture like that with a child.

Jaime bit his lower lip. "But Lolong say it. And I love Lolong."

"I know, Jaime."

"Lolong say, 'Dirty, dirty'—when he mad. He mad I spill my coconut water. So, I mad. So, I say 'Dumb-dumb.' Oops."

Gloriana sighed. She glared at Papang. "How do I 'unteach' my child?" She softened her face and turned to her son. "Enough, Jaime. You don't have to say it. In fact, I never want those words to come from your mouth again. Do you understand?"

"And Lolong?"

Mamang nodded. "And Lolong, too." She gave her husband one of her angry looks worth a peso.

Jaime turned to his grandfather. "Lolong, no mad. You mad so, so, so, so fast. Then I mad so, so, so, so fast. Then I sad."

Papang and his grandson looked at each other. Papang said, "Today, you are my teacher. A two-year-old child teaching a very old man. I am sorry, Jaime."

"I love you, Lolong. You are not dirty, dirty, dumb-dumb. Oops."

Had a magician stopped by our dinner table and performed a trick? Papang had stopped himself from swiping. He did not scold. He did not hit.

• • •

"Where's Papang?" Gloriana asked. "I noticed he left in a bit of a huff right after dinner."

"Maybe he's tending to the carabao. He'll be home soon," said Mamang.

A clapping game with Jaime filled the rest of the evening with merriment.

"Time for bed, Son," said Gloriana. Jaime usually shared his mother's mat, but tonight he wanted to be at his grandfather's side.

"No, I wait Lolong."

"Where is that fool husband?" Mamang moved to the window. Too dark to see.

"One more game of clap-clap and then it will be sleepy time."

The tapping of Papang's cane signaled his return. Jaime ran to the door. "Hi, Lolong!"

Papang did not respond, just proceeded to his mat and reclined. Jaime snuggled by his side; Papang did not object. After the flames in the oil lanterns were extinguished, Papang began to snore immediately. Soon, the child was asleep with his head upon the crook of his grandfather's arm.

I can sharply remember the day when Glory, as a talkative toddler, accidentally spilled her juice, just like Jaime. I flinched, recalling how she had suffered the stings from Papang's cane. My siblings and I had all endured such torment at one time or another. I rubbed the places where my skin retained its memories of welts, bruises, and bleeding.

Although Papang had begun to soften two years ago, it was a while before I could fully trust my father. His outbursts had been sudden and unexpected, and though they were tempered now, I still saw glimpses of his underlying anger, as demonstrated tonight, quick to react with swearing. I had not been terrified in our home for months now. But tonight, we had to be cautious about making mistakes or speaking the truth. Had Papang snuck out for a drink? The hut was filled with unease.

* * *

The sounds of the night were soothing most of the time, but tonight they stirred me. Papang's rhythmic guttural snoring. A dog yelping in the distance. The breezes blowing through the banana grove.

A cough. And another. A little boy's cough. A wheeze. A cough. More wheezing. I opened my eyes, rolled to my side, and saw Jaime weakly shake his grandfather. Jaime seemed short of breath. "Lolong? Lolong?"

Gloriana sprung into a sitting position and rushed to Jaime. "Mamang! Something is wrong."

"Wake up, Respicio. Jaime is wheezing." Mamang stood over her snoring husband, an intoxicated mass, inert and non-responsive.

"Jaime? Papang?" I called out sleepily.

Upset, Mamang spit out her words. "Your fool papang is dead drunk, Liling."

Jaime's wheezing had intensified, and the child started to cry. "Mama. Lolong." His weak voice carried across the room. "Lola. Auntie." Sitting up and gasping for air, he rubbed his chest. A two-year-old would not have had the words to describe his malady, but I observed flaring of his nostrils; wide, frightened eyes; and sharp, sibilant sounds emanating through his open mouth.

"God of Good Health, I pray to Thee. Help Jaime, *please*. Amen."

Gloriana picked Jaime up.

"Come with me, Liling. We have to take Jaime to the Americano doctor."

We both ran as fast as we could to get help. Glory wept the entire way. My insistent knocking on the door of the clinic, which was annexed to the residence, roused Dr. Billet.

"What do we have here? Miss Gloriana? Miss Ligaya? What's the matter? Your boy, what's his name? Come in. Come in."

The physician listened to Jaime's lungs. I now noted a slight bluish-gray tinge to his skin. Jaime's shoulders lifted and dropped, lifted and dropped like twin bellows. He pursed his lips to exhale, after which he gulped to fill his lungs. The little boy looked like a tilapia out of water—dying. Was Jaime dying?

"The diagnosis is asthma. Acute. Your boy is mighty sick. Mighty sick, indeed. Don't worry, Miss Gloriana. We're gonna sort this out and your boy will be up and runnin' before ya know it. Up and runnin'. Ha-ha." The Americano doctor was a little too jolly.

Gloriana did not laugh.

Dr. B rushed to administer oxygen. He broke an ampule of clear liquid and drew the medication into a glass syringe.

"Now, this might hurt a bit, little man. Be brave."

I whispered to myself, "Be brave."

* * *

"Why crying, Lolong?" Jaime asked weakly. The boy had been released from the clinic after his breathing had improved, his heart rate stabilized, and the bluish-gray pallor of his skin faded substantially.

Papang dabbed his eyes. He stared at the ground, too ashamed to look at his grandson, perhaps feeling guilty, believing his emotional flareup had caused Jaime's respiratory distress.

Hands on her hips, Mamang stomped her foot for emphasis. "Jaime, your grandfather is crying because *he* got drunk last night. Because you were sick. Because *he* didn't wake to help you. Because, because you almost died." My mother's irritation must have been blocking the release of her disappointment, fear, sadness, and now, immense relief. Suddenly, her feelings poured out in a torrent of sobs.

The little boy wheezed. "Why crying, Lola?"

Chapter 18

GILBERTO "BERTO" ABUEG

Late October – Early November 1944

"Raul!" I shouted from a short distance. "Raul? There you are." I looked down the road to find the glum face of my old schoolmate. "I was at your house, and your mother, sweet as usual, said I would find you here. Jesus, you look awful. Too much beer last night?"

Raul shook his head and wept.

I was taken aback. "Jesus, Raul, what's wrong?" I sat on the ground next to my friend. "Ta da! Your best man is here." I laughed a little. Raul seemed unaffected.

"Did you argue? Is it Liling? Something happen to Liling?"

I was used to seeing Raul fun-loving, happy, strong—but morose like this was disturbing. His appearance and behavior bothered me. "Raul, tell me what's wrong."

Raul broke into sobs—racking heaves. He must have been holding in a tidal wave of feelings that were only now being unleashed, surge after surge of intense feelings—I'm guessing of horror, hate, and helplessness—pounding in my ears until I, too, became teary. Raul finally spoke but in staccato. "Liling—raped. Japon. Me—me—could not save her." No one likes to see a grown man cry. Raul described something he called The Event with such vehemence and regret that I was dumbfounded.

I heard someone else sobbing nearby and glanced up at the neighbor's window. Was that Liling I saw stepping away from the opening?

"Jesus," I said. "You need money? Medication?" Raul sniffled. "Here, take my handkerchief."

"Liling—hates me. Japon. Liling—no see. No talk. Me—army."

"Oh, Raul. Jesus. She does not hate you," I replied. "How could you believe that?"

I paused. It was too much for me to take in. I sat quietly and Raul continued his soliloquy, describing the details of The Event.

"Raul, I didn't know." I put my arm around his shoulders. We were best friends, more like brothers really.

Disgust must have helped me find my voice. "The Event. Is that what you called it? It's not a fiesta. The Event makes it sound like a damn celebration. It's horrific. Violent. Jesus, Raul. It was rape. It was torture. It was psychological warfare. Call it what it is."

I picked up a rotten mango and hurled it into the banana grove. "Bastards!"

"Berto, my friend." Raul tried to smile. The tsunami had calmed; now only small swells of expressed sorrow arose. "Tell me the reason you're here. I didn't expect you until the wedding."

"I heard it was postponed, although I didn't know the exact reason. You must give me the new date and I'll clear my calendar. I'm your best buddy and best man." I gave Raul a light and friendly slap on the back.

"You came all the way here for just that? I was going to write to you in the city."

"No, not just that. I'm joining the army, and I thought I would visit my aunties and uncles, and you, of course, to say goodbye."

"It's been quite a long time, Berto. Good to see you."

"I should have come sooner, but I could not take a break from my studies."

"How's the university? Liling and I plan to leave this shit-hole life.

Education is the only way out. Her mother, Maria, remember her?"

"Of course I recall. She still got that long, black-as-a-crow hair? I've never seen an elder, especially someone who has suffered a lot of trauma, with hair so dark and shiny."

"My future mother-in-law is pushing for us to immigrate to America. She thinks the streets are lined with gold." At last, Raul lifted the corners of his lips in somewhat of a smile.

"You going?"

"No. Wedding first. Then education. Then job. Then babies. By then, we'll be too old and too broke to go to the USA."

Finally, a chuckle.

"Her sister, Gloriana, remember her? She dreams of going to Hawaii."

"Come on; let's rouse Liling. Surely she'll want to see me. I'm her friend and best man, too."

Just as we started on our way toward the Ugale hut, I spied a bald Japon soldier perched high above in the mango tree. Raul must have seen him too.

"You go ahead, Berto. I have something to take care of."

I held my breath. He picked up a mango. Oh Jesus, Raul! A mango against a gun? Thankfully, the Japanese man jumped down and ran as if fire ants had sandpapered his skin. I looked up at the Ugales' window. This time, I was sure I saw Liling recede into darkness.

* * *

So that was how I got to know Gloriana Consuelo Cruz Ugale better. I hadn't seen her or the rest of the Ugales since I left for the university on a diocesan scholarship. My studies were rigorous, and I had little time for courting. I studied Glory's face. Ah, yes, the beauty spot—college students from the city think it signifies sensuality, if not sexual wantonness. She was more attractive than I remembered, but sadness lay behind her beautiful eyes.

A little boy peered from behind one of the wooden benches, holding a black mongrel pup in his hands. "Oh, Mama, who is here?"

"Berto," said Gloriana, "meet my son. And this black dog is Benedicto. Benny, for short."

"Jaime and Benny," the wee voice said.

"Jaime, this is my friend, Berto."

I brought myself down to the child's level. Gloriana paid attention. I must admit I was disappointed to find she had a child, a bastard child.

"Hello, son! My, what a strong and handsome little man you are!"

"Hello, Tata."

"A polite young man, too!"

Respicio entered the hut. "This my lolong." Still holding the puppy in one arm, he took his grandfather's hand. "Come, Lolong; meet Mama friend."

The old man remembered me. We talked about the beer hall turning into a dump since the start of the war. He had stopped going altogether to the saloon, and he no longer brought beer into the house.

Jaime thrust the puppy toward me, but it snarled. I sprang back up. "Hey!"

Gloriana laughed. "Benny is very protective of the Ugales. He pretends he's a bully and growls at strangers. Don't worry; he'll learn to like you."

• • •

I visited Raul every day. And every day he sent me on a mission to the Ugales' house to check on Ligaya. I came at all hours, but Liling was never there—Glory said she worked at the Americano doctor's clinic. I think she was avoiding me.

On the other hand, Glory was always at home. She and I took walks by the river. We would sit under a monkeypod tree or on a large rock on the opposite shore. She spoke often of her dreams of taking Jaime to the USA. She asked if I would come with her.

I laughed. "Come with you? To Hawaii?"

"Why not?"

"Jesus, Glory. I have university. I don't know you. And there is a war."

"Yes, that's right. There is a war. One must be urgent in wartime because we never know when life as we know it will end. I am the sculptor of my destiny. I refuse to give my power to the war."

"Said with such passion, Glory." I smiled.

"I'm a passionate person."

Glory snuggled against me. Thankfully, no other villagers were nearby. She would certainly be ostracized for being with a man, unchaperoned. Me, I didn't care so much about Filipino tradition, having become liberated at the university. I am a modern man and have fought against the bondage of social customs, hard-fast rules, and superstition.

"Come on," I said. "Let's bring dinner home to your parents."

Glory threaded a worm onto the homemade hook. She smiled.

* * *

In a hushed voice, I said, "I knew you had a child, Glory." One thing about living a village life, you hear everything. My auntie gossips.

"You have a tattler of an auntie, too?" Glory sighed. "Um, you do mind?"

"Mind? Jesus."

"I'm a single mother. And—and—The Event." Gloriana stammered. "You must think I am a whore, a slut." There was shame in her voice.

I did not know what to say.

Finally, noise broke the silence. Benny barked. I looked up to see Jaime chasing his dog. Glory watched her son for a while.

"You haven't met a Santiago at the university or during your travels, have you?"

"Well, I know of two. Why?"

"He is Jaime's father, and I have been searching for him. Yes?"

"One is an infant and the other is in a sanatorium."

Glory burst into laughter.

. . .

Two weeks came and went. My visits with Glory became more frequent. We spent a lot of time together, much of it unchaperoned. I think the villagers were too distressed about the war to care about Filipino social mores.

I saw Liling occasionally, and we greeted each other politely. She and many townspeople isolated themselves. What was it about this village? Everyone seemed exhausted, extinguished.

On this day, I arrived later than usual for one of our rendezvous.

"I'm sorry, Glory. I had to sign documents at the army recruitment office. We leave for basics camp next week."

Gloriana sucked in her breath. "So soon, Berto."

"Yes—and Raul, too."

"Oh, no." She shot a peek at her sister sitting in a dark corner. "Liling will be distraught. Let's talk on the steps. She is nursing a headache."

"Well, encourage her to connect with Raul. To say goodbye at least. He's upset that she has been refusing to see him. But he said he would understand if she's not ready; that's how much he really loves her. It was good to see your mother again. Is she around? I'd like to say goodbye."

"As usual, she's at a Bible study followed by another safety and security meeting. They think more Japon troops are heading this way."

"Your father seems different, somehow. I remember the grand time we had when he joined Raul and me at the beer hall."

"Yes. That was a long time ago. He doesn't drink anymore. Thank goodness."

Glory said that her Mamang and Papang remained wary and weary of blocking her stubborn yearnings. She and I saw each other as much as possible until it was time to leave for basic training.

"Jesus. You are stunning when you smile, Gloriana, and I love your beauty spot." I touched the mole on her face. Gloriana pulled back a little. "I have never felt so relaxed as when I am with you, Glory. These past couple of weeks have been heavenly. Thank you."

"I'm falling in love, Berto. Life is short. The war and all. I will jump into this relationship with both feet and both eyes wide open. Wide open. No man will deceive and abandon me or my son, ever again."

"Then I am your man, Glory. I will never betray you."

"So, you haven't yet answered my question."

"What question, Glory?"

"Will you come to Hawaii with Jaime and me?"

I stammered. It was a very strange question.

"I can't bear a repeat of Papang's scrutiny and wrath," Glory said. "I guess I am asking, Berto…"

"What are you asking?"

"I guess I'm asking you to marry me."

Part of me wanted to flee. Part of me wanted to freeze.

"You are a very unconventional woman, Glory. I love that about you."

"Yes, and you are a very modern, irreverent man."

"Jesus!"

"You see? Irreverent!" We both laughed.

I paused, but only for a short moment. "I am a modern man. Damn tradition. Yes, I will marry you. Yes, I'll go to Hawaii with you and your son."

Jaime and Respicio were petting the dog to calm it while sitting together on the mahogany armchairs. "Lolong, I like Tata Berto. He nice," I overheard Jaime say.

"I like him, too, Jaime. I hope he makes your mother very happy."

Benny, the puppy, escaped from Jaime's lap and growled at me.

Glory drew me close and whispered something cryptic in my ear. "On the eve of your departure."

Chapter 19

LIGAYA "LILING" UGALE

November 1944

I wept when I discovered that Raul had made plans to join the Philippine army. I berated myself; my self-pity had caused me to waste precious time I could have spent with my beloved.

I sprinted to the military central command, the point of departure. Families waved at dark, dusty spirals as truckloads of village men were leaving. Unable to locate Raul at first, my chest tightened.

I scanned the scene, a canvas of commotion and a profusion of tearful goodbyes.

A man knelt to hug a little boy; Gloriana's Gilberto saying goodbye to Jaime. Berto stood and then hugged a woman I recognized as Mrs. Hidalgo, Raul's mother. At last, I spotted Raul nearby, searching, combing the crowds.

"Raul." There was a catch in my voice. Though a bit anxious, I moved to be a respectable distance from him.

"You have come." Raul smiled and stepped toward me. "My *luscious*," he said sweetly.

I winced.

"I'm sorry I said that—uh, my friend," he said. I no longer cared for the word luscious. The Event had changed that. It reminded me too much of the rapist slurping on my soft parts.

I observed the slump in Raul's shoulders. Did his posture indicate fear, or excitement, or relief?

"God of Protection watch over you, Raul."

For the first time since The Event, we acknowledged our incredible, shared pain. "I'm sorry I could not rescue you, Liling. Oh, God." There was so much sorrow in his voice. "I will fight for your honor, my..."

How did we define our relationship? Were we still committed as a couple?

Our eyes locked for a long while. I had one last chance to memorize his face. I wondered if he would still accept me, the adulterated victim. He said he felt like the ineffectual, failed protector.

"I'm sorry, too."

"For what, my love?"

"For...for..." I could not continue; the memory of Fuku was too painful for me to recall.

"Shh. Remember this, Liling. At night when you look at the moon, know that I am also gazing upon it..."

"And thinking of you in love with me?"

Raul nodded.

I murmured, "When you gaze upon the moon, you will be thinking of me in love with you."

The moment of the inevitable departure for basic training arrived. I nodded slightly. Raul lifted his duffel bag to his shoulder. I shook with angst. He paused as if to consider something and seemed to make a decision. He said with such compassion and intimacy, "Be still, my love. I am here." He pressed his hand upon my heart. Then he walked away. Slowly, sadly. He turned back not just once, but three times.

Still single at age twenty-seven, my plans to marry and create a family would be further postponed, thwarted by war. I sighed deeply. Most of the women my age were already bearing their second, third, or even fourth child.

A familiar wailing sound interrupted my pensiveness. It was Gloriana, whose face was red and swollen after many hours of ugly crying.

The driver of the army truck honked impatiently. Gloriana's boyfriend kissed her clutched hand, tried to soothe her with sweet words, then firmly pried her fingers from his. He ran past the slow-walking Raul and disappeared under the canopy-covered truck bed. It did not look like he was one to tolerate histrionics.

Chapter 20

LIGAYA "LILING" UGALE

November 1944

"Be still, my love. I am here." I repeated the last words Raul had whispered to me the day of his departure. I held my palm against my heart just as he did.

Upon our return home, Glory and I found a mango wrapped in a banana leaf on the stoop. Raul must have harvested it for me before he left. I trimmed off its skin. I tried to share the fruit with my sister, but she was too melancholic after the emotional farewells. My tears mingled with its sweet juices; moisture trickled down my chin, reminding me of happier times.

I could not stay home just to cook, clean, and crochet. Could I be close to Raul and fulfill my patriotic duty? Join the women's auxiliary as a clinic and field aide?

World War II made it necessary for the Americans to open a central recruitment office in the village. Almost every able-bodied man was called to war, resulting in the abandonment of the majority of rice fields and farms. No men, no work, no rice, no produce, no money, no nothing. The availability of compensated employment plummeted.

Gloriana and I soon found ourselves standing in a short line at the office, filling out applications.

"Liling, they're only requesting name and residence, no other information. What are we going to write? We don't have formal addresses. No one except the Americano doctor has a telephone. It is pointless for the government to ask us such questions."

I was surprised by the recruiter's cordial manner. I expected a more intimidating voice and posture.

"Mrs. Ugly?" the Sergeant called into the waiting area.

"Miss Ugale," Gloriana corrected.

"I'm also Ugale. Pronounced Oo-GAH-*leh*," I added.

"Ah, *two* Uglies. Tell me, siblings? Cousins? In-laws? Or no relation?"

"We are sisters," Gloriana informed him.

"And best of friends," I couldn't resist sharing.

"Thank you for coming. So, you wish to volunteer?"

A puzzled look crossed Gloriana's face. "We wish to *work*."

"What skills do you bring to the table?" The recruiter picked up a pen.

"To the table?"

"Yes, well, what are you good at doing, Mrs. Ugly?"

"My name is *Miss Ugale*. I can cook. I can crochet. I can sew. I can take care of children."

"Just children?"

"Yes, children," I answered. Adults can take care of themselves.

Gloriana offered, "I work for the Americano doctor. Sterilizing surgical equipment and sharpening needles are my responsibilities at the clinic."

"Do you know how to clean and dress wounds?" asked the recruiter as he shuffled carbon-copied documents from one side of the counter to the other.

I reflected upon the dozens of times Jaime, Vicente, and Pacencia had injured themselves. I was usually the one who swabbed and dressed their wounds.

"Yes, I believe so. Yes, I can do that. Sometimes minor accidents occur on our farm, in the barrio, in the river. I am called to help because

I work with Dr. Billet."

The recruiter looked puzzled.

Glory said, "He's the Americano doctor."

The Sergeant's face was neutral. "And what is your position with the doctor, Mrs. Ugly?" I gave him a stern look.

"I am his maid, and Glory," I tilted my head toward my sister, "is the clinic janitor." The physician really should change her job title.

To be helpful, Gloriana interjected, "Uh, just last week, we restrained a couple of writhing children as the doctor gave them injections."

"And you, Mrs. Ugly?"

"Well, and…and…well—" I stammered, flustered by the Sergeant's continued faux pas. "I know how to bring down a fever even when it is a hundred degrees outside. I make a tea with guava leaves. Pretty soon, the person feels better."

The Sergeant appeared unimpressed. "One moment please, Miss Ugale." Gloriana and I looked at each other, somewhat surprised. He had finally used the correct title and pronounced our surname perfectly. The recruiter took our brief applications and left the front office.

"You think he got it?"

"Let's see how long he'll maintain the proper pronunciation." Gloriana snickered.

I shrugged without much hope of that.

. . .

"Mrs. Ugly? Now, don't you leave. A few more minutes, please," the recruiter called out from behind a file cabinet.

"Why does he persist in mispronouncing our name?" I whispered.

Gloriana replied in her usual frustrated tone, "He doesn't care enough about us Brownies to learn it. Annoying."

"Oh, the way you don't care enough about Dr. Billet to learn his name."

Gloriana laughed. "It's different, and you know it." I shook my head.

"I think it's pointless to try and correct the Sergeant."

"You ought to get used to it; you'll be a missus in due time anyway."

The Sergeant returned. "Yup, I was right. We have two volunteer positions available."

"I'm sorry, sir. Did you say *volunteer*? We are looking for employment."

I wanted this job badly. *Needed* it badly. I had heard rumors that the Americans offered to pay *women*. Almost double the pesos if you were a man. A few centavos per hour was more than a paycheck of zero.

Then, the Sergeant fired questions, barely allowing us breath to answer.

"Do you oppose the Japanese? Do you know any Japanese person or persons? Do you purchase Japanese goods? Is anyone in your family connected to the Japanese? Are you allegiant to the Philippines? Did you assist with the uprising against the Communists? Ma'am, will you give your wholehearted pledge to the flag of the United States of America?"

In this interrogation, I simply nodded while Gloriana quipped, "Yes. Yes. Yes."

"Fine. You both pass. You will work as volunteers for the American hospital."

"No, sir. Not volunteers." Gloriana's eyes widened. "We cannot work for free. Our mamang and papang and my son need food." She sighed a silent scream. "Sir."

The Sergeant looked up sharply. I dared not add anything more to Gloriana's impassioned plea for pay. The recruiter probably detected our distress because he added, "Let me see what I can do, Mrs. Ugly. Sometimes the United States government, in its benevolence, will pay up to five pesos a month for the kind of work you will be assigned to perform."

I frowned, then turned to hide my disappointment. Glory was right; he did not care enough about us Brownies.

• • •

Entering the women's auxiliary meant risking our lives to help dozens of soldiers, mostly Americans. We used our own clean rice bags as dressings. We emptied bedpans of bloody stools and emesis basins of puke.

After a few weeks, Gloriana noted, "We are not receiving our paychecks, Liling."

"Be patient, Glory. You know how slow the postal ships are from the United States to the Philippines."

Weeks later, I remarked to my sister, "The United States of America has not paid us a single *centavo*."

"Bastards!"

* * *

The field hospital was sheltered in a huge general-purpose tent near the jungles where the majority of skirmishes were staged, camouflaged by thick foliage. Gloriana and I joined the other women collecting water, being careful to find areas without stagnation, just rapid flow over rocks worn smooth. I developed a talent for skimming water without collecting any of the river sand. I poured part of the liquid into one pot for drinking. The rest went into another container for cleansing wounds or cooling fevers.

"Glory, I can hear the rockets." I placed my hands over my ears as bomb after bomb burst in the distance. I squeezed my eyes shut when stray bullets zinged by. "I hope not *KIA*."

"K-I-A?" Gloriana tensed.

"Killed in action."

"Oh."

We held each other at the peak of each nearby battle.

"God of Soldier Protection, I ask Thee, please watch over Raul Hidalgo and Gilberto Abueg. Keep them safe so they may return to us. Amen."

In the morning, a senior nurse, a white woman from the USA, abruptly awakened us.

"I am Liling. *Miss* Ligaya Ugale," I said during introductions.

"And my name is *Miss* Gloriana Ugale." The senior nurse didn't seem to care about honorifics.

"I need you to take the other aides into the field. There were casualties. Many casualties."

"Yes, ma'am." She signaled Gloriana to step forward.

"There is an insufficient number of military personnel for body recovery," explained the senior nurse. "You are to go to the edge of the last battlefield and assist with the dead."

The nurse likely noticed my hesitation.

"Don't worry. The enemy has stopped firing missiles and rockets—at least for now."

Near the jungle boundary, Gloriana and I, connected by our gruesome task, needed courage and self-control. The Americans were loath to leave behind any comrades, of any color, but they treated their own white soldiers differently. In a subtle way, there seemed to be more reverence, a sure utterance of prayer, and a respect for the dead fellows' meager belongings.

We field aides located bodies. As quickly as possible, we were tasked with determining that the men, boys really, had definitely expired. Most soldiers were so obviously dead we did not have to check for pulses. We lifted and carried the corpses in silence and with sensitivity into the bed of a truck. It was dangerous work. Sometimes stray bullets shot by us as we traveled through the wilderness or through mazes of rice fields. We received warnings that land mines had been implanted into the soil, well-covered by tropical vegetation or tall rice grasses.

We hurried along the dirt path. On the ground lay a dozen dead in two rows of six, arranged perfectly straight and stiff, as if in military formation for inspection. In life, they had carried the look of aggressors. With brutish behaviors. With piercing eyes that belied their true fear. Glory and I shared the opinion that in death, they appeared more genuine, their faces now fully revealing fright.

Blood mixed with tears had stained their open eyes. I tried to close them, but their eyelids were already set stiff. Some of their tongues protruded, gray, swollen. Had these lads called out for their mothers in their last moments? I coughed, trying to hold back the urge to flee; the dead seemed to be staring at me, in judgment. I imagined them as putrefying zombies grabbing my ankles and clawing my face.

Gloriana and I helped carefully and quietly to lay the soldiers side by side on the bed of the recovery vehicle. It took seven petite *Filipinas* to carry a single, huge, deceased American man. One for each of four limbs, two on either side of the torso, and the last to hold the head. Without stacking, we could fit only six of the corpses in the bed of the truck. I made the sign of the cross upon their foreheads.

"What if they're not Catholic, Liling?"

"I'm blessing them just in case. Besides, there is only one God."

"Not for you, Ligaya. You have a God of this and a God of that."

Later, the makeshift hearse returned empty, and we loaded the next six dead Caucasian Americans. A different recovery truck arrived to transport the other four bodies. I wavered a moment before stepping into the truck.

"Sir, there is no room." I landed on a decedent's thigh.

"Come on, Ligaya. They're dead. They can't feel you. Hurry up."

I held my breath as I glanced at the remaining bodies—Filipinos, all of them, but not Raul or Gilberto. I exhaled with relief and consolation.

"God of Pinoy Soldiers, I thank Thee, for our beloveds are not dead. Oh, God, I thank Thee. Bless the souls of these departed." I waved my arm over the Filipino corpses. "Amen."

"Oh, and furthermore, God of Auxiliary Aides, I ask Thee to please keep Glory and me strong. Relieve her nausea and my headaches. I thank Thee. Amen."

There was talk about bringing a dumpster for the dead Japs.

The infantrymen were reluctant when ordered to retrieve the enemy bodies from the battlegrounds. They wanted nothing to do with the Japs, dead or alive.

"Go get them," their American superiors shouted. "In two days, the stink. The heat. The rot. Better to handle it now. Get going."

At first, the Japs' remains were abandoned and left in the rice fields and jungles. In the heat of night and day, the bodies became bloated with green, gangrenous slime, causing explosions of fetid flesh.

The Pinoy soldiers obeyed, but there was no reverence in their handling of the dead Japs. They yanked the corpses through the mud. Sometimes, limbs got caught on branches, tearing tissue off bones. Sometimes, the skulls cracked when the heads struck rock. The Japanese were treated with contempt and condemnation, dumped into the back of a truck until they were stacked four high.

An army officer ordered, "Ligaya, go check the Jap pockets. Maybe they have some cash or weapons we can use. Never mind their IDs. I don't care who they are."

I returned to checking the pockets of the deceased Japanese. I gingerly pulled out a wallet. While rifling through its contents, a worn photo of a beaming boy fell out. It was creased and cracked as if handled a thousand times. I showed it to Gloriana.

"Liling. He looks Jaime's age!" cried Gloriana.

"Oh, little boy, what have we done?" Though we generalized our hate for the Japon, we felt sympathy for individuals' families.

I flipped to the back of the picture. Under the Japanese characters, English letters spelling the name *Hisao*. "Baby Hee-sah-oh," I enunciated slowly. I then placed it between the dead father's fingers, away from his opened chest.

From another corpse I pulled out a pocket watch. I pressed a tiny latch and the case sprung open. A picture of a beautiful woman in a formal, traditional kimono was revealed. "*Anata*," meaning "darling," was engraved in Japanese characters on the back of the timepiece. I instinctively thought of Raul and placed my hand over my heart. *Be still, my love. I am here.*

Some of the bodies were still soft, some stiff. All were cold. My shoes left imprints upon their skin. I tried not to step on their faces.

That night, I had the most distressing dream—the little baby Japanese boy cried out piteously for its father. His papa rose from the back of the truck with my shoeprint upon his face. A lone Filipino soldier, mortally wounded, had been thrown into the body recovery truck. Eyes wide open. I reached down to close the dead eyes. Raul's eyes.

I was jolted awake and screamed in terror.

Chapter 21

LIGAYA "LILING" UGALE

November 1944

My brother was consumed by hatred.

On one of my visits to Bartolome's tobacco farm, he spoke to me at length about his eagerness to fight the Japon, even though he had not passed the army's eye exam.

He was mad as hell. Mad that his ten-year-old daughter had been gang-raped by five Japon. Mad that she had locked herself into the seeming safety of mutism, or was it preadolescent defiance? Mad that the block letters in the top row of the vision chart were blurry. Was that a P or an F? C or G? O or Q? He guessed wrong. He couldn't afford to buy prescription eyeglasses. Alleviating hunger in his family was far more of a priority than clear vision. What did he need eyeglasses for? He was not good at reading.

A bitter Bartolome joined the guerrilla rebels, a wayward group separate from the Philippine and American armies. He promised to avenge the hell suffered by his wife and daughters.

Unbeknown to Bartolome, American-born citizens of Japanese ancestry were in the US Army as linguists assigned to work as interpreters and translators. Frequently given back-breaking jobs—carrying water and ammo to the frontline, and the most dangerous jobs—finding the safest routes through minefields. "First to go; first to blow," they said.

Late one night, two of the Japanese-Americans were separated from their American counterparts. Bartolome's band of guerrilla fighters happened upon them, lost in the jungle. Each of the two sides did not take the time needed to fully comprehend the other's spoken language.

"Sir, we are Americans. We're on *your* side." The Japanese-Americans spoke English.

Bartolome hissed in Filipino like a venomous cobra. "You raped my Pacencia. Sweet innocence. You took that away from her. You fucking Japon!"

"We work for the Americans in the *American* army. Please understand, sir! We are *not from* Japan!" screamed one soldier.

"You killed my baby girl." Bartolome choked.

"Please!" begged the second soldier. "We. Are. Americans!"

"We were *born* in America." The Hawaii-born men could speak Japanese but with an American accent. They spoke American English perfectly with no Japanese accent. That should have clued in Bartolome, but the pissed-off Pinoy did not pay attention to socio-linguistics.

I joined Bartolome in the plaza where the news that he had single-handedly killed two Japanese soldiers caused boisterous celebration.

However, the victory was short-lived. An officer from Texas, USA, marched into the village square, screaming in a Southern drawl, "Son of a bi-itch! Do you know what you have done? You fucking killed two American soldiers! What do I label this—friendly fire or collateral damage?" He searched the crowd. "Who did this?"

Bartolome told his side of the story. "I'd had enough of the enemy's lies. All I could see was the sallow tinge upon their skin and the squint in their slanted eyes. I used my stolen machine gun to shoot back and forth and back and forth and back and forth across their waists. I had blasted a line of through and through holes. The taller Japanese-American's torso folded over into a bloody explosion of bone and tissue. The other looked down upon his abdomen, ripped open. Guts spilled out. The Jap stumbled deeper into the jungle, carrying his slippery intestines with hooked fingers."

"You fucking annihilated our interpreters! Now who the fuck is going to translate for us? You?" He pointed to Bartolome. "You?" He pointed to the men nearest the bodies. "You?"

The crowd was aghast. Confusion.

An aura of a headache.

"But they're Japon!" Bartolome lost his bravado. "Sir."

Bartolome's demeanor changed from a big-man carabao to a ding-dong goat.

Suddenly, a tiny whisper of a voice wafted through the crowd.

"My *papang*."

I stared at Pacencia.

"My papang..." My niece struggled to complete her message.

"She speaks!" one of our neighbors declared. He crossed himself.

A sympathetic nun encouraged her. "Speak, girl. Go on."

"My papang—cannot see."

"She speaks!" The crowd buzzed excitedly. We all had just witnessed a miracle. For three months, Pacencia had been unable or unwilling to communicate verbally. The big city pediatrician had diagnosed Conversion Disorder. The Americano doctor called it Elective Mutism. "She is mighty anxious, Mr. Ugale. Mighty anxious. Nothing ya can do about it," he had said.

"*Papang!*" Pacencia cried out, arms outstretched.

Bartolome rushed to his daughter and hugged her tightly. This time, it was the father who was speechless.

Chapter 22

RAUL HIDALGO

December 1944

No such thing as ambulances in the old days. We had only one vehicle in the entire village, a station wagon with a manually operated gearshift owned and driven solely by Dr. B. Long before the war, the clinic expanded, and the number of patients increased. The physician no longer had time to complete medicine-related errands himself. So, when I was twenty-three, he employed me as the part-time clinic courier and gave me driving lessons.

Like most auto operators, learning stick-shift was a challenge. I jerked the car as I shifted, grinded the gears, and slammed on the brakes. I used the horn excessively to warn pedestrians to get out of harm's way. However, with practice and the physician's patience, I soon became a competent driver. Dr. B trusted me with his vehicle.

"You need to learn," he said, "so you can drive the specimens to the lab, pick up the medicines from the hospital pharmacy, and deliver the drugs to the homebound patients. Who knows, someday I might need an ambulance, and you will be the one to take me to the emergency room in the city. Yes, sir-ree. I don't trust anyone with my vehicle but you, Raul. You are steady on the wheel. Mighty steady, my boy. Mighty steady, indeed."

I spent hours learning and practicing when Dr. B's clinic schedule was light.

"A mighty fine maneuver there, Raul. Don't forget to press the clutch. Easy now. Easy now. Now, slow down there. Slow down. Slow down! That's right. You'll make a mighty fine driver *someday*, Raul, mighty fine."

I felt proud of my accomplishment.

"Tell you what, son. When you and Miss Ligaya marry, I'll let you drive my car so you can deliver your beautiful bride from the church to the reception. She's a mighty fine gal, that Miss Ligaya of yours."

I was elated, not just at the thought of driving this beauty of a Ford, but of marrying my true love.

...

Blackout—we hoped it was just a rumor. It would turn into an emphatic order because another battle was planned for the uplands. The army assigned me the position of driver. My American lieutenant had apparently been informed that among the hundreds of enlisted Filipinos, I was one of only a dozen individuals in the region who had learned to drive a stick-shift.

At first proud of being in charge of transportation, my eagerness waned when I found it meant maneuvering the narrowest of cliffside roads through the mountains between the steep rice terraces, at night, without headlights. A daunting task. In the blackest hours, I often could not see the darkened dashboard.

I was ordered on a clandestine mission, bringing crates of ammunition to replenish the stockpile for ground assault troops, and to deliver a high-level secret message of vital importance to the soldiers bunkered in the mountains.

I made the sign of the cross, started the engine, and moved through the jungle on narrow paths. Drops of sweat slid down my face. My hands shook on the steering wheel. Land mines—no one knew where. The Japon so savvy that way. In war, they combined their technology with the sadistic nature of the samurai.

Five minutes seemed like five hours. Driving was impossible in the dark. Now, the storm. It was monsoon season. Was that thunder or bombing? Rockets or lightning? My maneuvering was purely instinctual, knowing that at any moment I could trigger a booby-trapped mine. If I was lucky, I would die instantly. If not, one or more of my limbs would be severed by traumatic amputation. I would live as a cripple, a farmer who could not farm. A useless, burdensome nuisance upon Ligaya. No, I'd rather be dead.

I pinched my nose. Decomposition. "Decomp" for short. Somewhere in a rice paddy on the terraces, a rotting body. Must be Japon; Americans always recovered their dead. I trembled and gripped the steering wheel more tightly.

My truck approached the highlands now where the dangers multiplied. It began to rain. The vehicle slipped sideways. I rolled onward with increased pressure to the gas pedal. I must move steadily, or the mud would grope the tires like a lascivious pervert. Being stuck meant I would be a sitting target for the Japon. Turn too far left and I could plummet over one of the eroded cliffs. Ever so slowly, I silently, stealthily made my way toward the mountains.

The lieutenant had instructed me to go to the fourth cave where the army stored supplies, and troops waited for the next inevitable battle. I muttered a prayer of thanksgiving when I arrived.

The soldiers came out to assist. Without talking, we hurriedly lugged the heavy crates into the rear of the cave where they kept expendable ammunition and other artillery. Upon completion, and safe within the soundproofing of the rock formation, we conversed at low volumes.

"Jesus, Raul, I can't believe you're here. Freakin' storm. You are soaked." By happy coincidence, Berto had been assigned to this platoon.

We slapped each other's backs in greeting.

"How am I? How can one be? I'm stuck in a cave with freakin' crazy men." Berto was jovial. I was thrilled; my friend and soon-to-be brother-in-law was here. Two best friends marrying sisters!

After boot camp, we had been assigned different roles and companies. I'd had no idea when we would see each other again.

"Take off your jacket so it can dry a bit."

"Sweating in the storm. Monsoon season already. I am delivering a secret communication from command."

"Come to bring us rice wine, Raul?" A soldier held out his tin cup.

"I came to wish you happy Christmas."

"What's so happy about it?" the soldier asked as he slammed his cup down.

"Never mind the rice wine. I'd rather have beer," said another soldier.

The soldiers, mostly American and Filipino Privates in infantry, maintained their good spirits, despite having recently lost four of their men.

"Smuggled us some Pinay babes in that truck of yours?"

The Event intruded into my mind.

I handed the official document to the highest-ranking soldier there. The Sergeant took it with a flourish, but his lightheartedness soon faded. By the light of a single candle flame, the American platoon Sergeant in charge of the fighters scanned the message.

> For outstanding and unwavering valor, fortitude,
> and meritorious service during the recent battle,
> directly leading to the successful completion of its
> mission with limited loss of life. Congratulations.
> You are a credit to the United States of America.

"That's all? Four men died, damn it. *Fuck* this shit." The Sergeant pitched the paper aside.

That was the "important and vital message" I had risked my life for?

The Sergeant moved on to inspect the crates' contents. He screamed English and Filipino obscenities. Turns out central supply had sent the wrong-sized cartridges.

After the Sergeant's tirade, we tried to recapture the peaceful pleasantries that had started the evening. Gilberto passed around two large mason jars filled with a crude concoction of fermented rice whiskey. The men partook of the dark amber beverage, some with small sips, others with greedy gulps. I drank carefully, conscientiously. The sour-bitter liquid burned my lips and scorched my esophagus.

Of course, Gilberto hoped for news from home.

"Liling continues her recovery from...well." I knew Berto hated labeling the war crime "The Event."

"I know; my Gloriana was raped, too."

"You must miss her terribly, Berto. My Liling, I miss her. My heart aches. My stomach aches. Hell, my entire body aches for her."

"Glory told me Liling believed you had lost desire for her because she was damaged."

I swirled the liquid in my aluminum cup. "Oh, no. *No.* That is furthest from the truth. I love her more and more each day. I wanted to tell her, but she rejected me in the days after The Event."

"Jesus, she did not reject *you*, Raul. She accepted the notion that she was defiled. All Filipinos are conditioned to believe brides must be pure and chaste. I mean, I can count on ten fingers the women I know who secretly are no longer virgins and are planning to marry. They're nice, hardworking women. Why would God, if there is a God, create sex so freakin' great if he didn't mean for us to partake of it?

"Ligaya is irrational in the aftermath of The Event. It's crazy to think every single 'single woman' in the village square that day would be condemned to living life as a spinster. Additionally, Ligaya was suffering and did not want you to witness her pain. If it's any consolation, Raul, Glory said that her sister joined the auxiliary to be closer to you."

"Well, we did say goodbye. I touched her despite not being chaperoned."

"Good for you, touching her. But, Jesus, haven't you listened to a word I've said?"

I tried to understand this man, my future brother-in-law.

"Glory and I made love the night before deployment. She was insatiable, and I could not get enough of her, as if we needed our fill before separating. Life is short, Raul."

"Aren't you afraid you will be discovered being intimate before marriage? You are braver than me."

"Fuck the elders. Fuck tradition. Fuck custom. Fuck Catholics. Fuck mortal sin. I don't know if I'm braver. Maybe I'm stupider."

"Maybe." I took another swig of the crude liquor.

"Life is short, Raul. I pulled out each time, just in time."

"Ay, ay." We laughed. Soon the others joined in and shared stories about their wives and girlfriends.

The drinking and merriment continued for a while. Gilberto and I shared our dreams of life with our darlings after war's end.

Despite the camaraderie between all of the soldiers, the Sergeant remained in a foul mood after reading the useless note of commendation. He made me cut short my stay.

Mission accomplished. Light slaps and punches—males' way of saying goodbye.

"Happy Christmas, everybody!"

"Raul, next year, this war had better end because you're getting married and I'm getting married."

"Berto, happy Christmas and prosperous New Year!"

After exiting the cave, I glanced at the banana moon, which brought an immediate connection with Ligaya.

As was my habit, I made the sign of the cross before starting the engine. Again, in complete darkness, I hunched over the steering wheel with my fingers constricted like a vise. The heavy rains had further loosened the dirt on the rice terrace. I made a sharp turn to the left. Then right. Then left. And right again. The right front tire slipped. The right back tire slid over the ledge. Precipitously, the vehicle stalled at a precarious slant.

"Be still, my love. I am here." I heard Ligaya's voice again. "When I gaze upon the moon, I will be thinking of you in love with me." I closed my eyes to remember my departure from the village and our love-filled moments together. When I opened my eyes, I actually saw and sensed Ligaya, like an angel, placing her palm against my chest as if inscribing her handprint upon my heart. It was not an illusion. The sweet lilt and timbre of her beautiful voice. "Be still, mmm..."

Chapter 23
GILBERTO "BERTO" ABUEG

December 1944

BANG! CRASH! BOOM!

Jesus! What was that? No way anyone could have detected the well-hidden pin and tripped the wires of the booby trap. Fuckin' Japs.

I remained hunkered down in the cave with the other American and Filipino soldiers. A deafening explosion. Strong waves of reverberations. Was that thunder? Had the rains ceased, and the Japs resumed bombing? Sounds of fire crackled. We scrambled to retrieve our weapons, believing the Japs were on the offensive yet again.

The Sergeant ordered us to stand down. "We're safer in this cave than out in the storm."

"But Sergeant, let us get those Jap bastards. We can do it."

The Sergeant glanced at the back of the cave where the wrong ammunition was stored. He used the candle flame to burn the crumpled message Raul had delivered. "For a freakin' letter of commendation? We got no cartridges for the battles scheduled for tomorrow. Bastards! No. Stand down. That's an order."

I have always been a protective friend; I instinctively knew Raul was in danger. Sometimes I'm a rule-breaking rebel; I slung my rifle over my shoulder and sprang into the darkness.

"What the—? Private! Stand down. Stand down. Stop! Stop! Fuck!" Rage in the Sergeant's voice.

I panicked, bolted toward the faraway fire in search of Raul. I stumbled on the dirt road. So many pits full of mud. Water streaming across my path. It took forever. The blaze was large, consuming. I fought my way through the storm. I slid down the almost vertical embankment. Finally, I reached the site. The bottom of a steep cliff. I could not get close. My eyebrows and lashes singed. Smoke and heat. Shell of mangled, melted steel. Despite the rain, the fire ensued, fed by gasoline.

Stray embers and pieces of stuffed leather smoldered. The truck, annihilated, vaporized.

I refused to lose hope. I wanted to believe Raul, the most agile and athletic of my friends, had jumped out of his moving vehicle to save himself. At any moment now. Any moment now—any moment now. I searched around. I wanted Raul to walk toward me, buttoning up his pants. We would laugh, return to the cave, drink some more rice whiskey, and talk about sex.

I cried long before the truth was revealed. At early light, I spied a flock of scavenger birds watching, waiting, circling, and waiting some more to see if I dared intrude upon their territory.

I walked slowly, incrementally, toward the scorched coconut tree. I did not notice the thing at first, only fallen coconuts on the ground, brown speckled husks exposed. The three plugs on the exposed shells, like two eyes and a mouth.

And then I saw it, what looked like a coconut with matted black fiber. A severed head. Raul's head. I gave the most pathetic wail, signifying my immeasurable loss.

. . .

Two soldiers must have been dispatched at dawn to fetch me.

I strode toward my comrades, cradling an object in the fold of my shirt like a kangaroo's pocket.

The soldiers froze in place.

"Fucking Gilberto," muttered the first soldier.

"Asshole," I heard the other one say.

"Going to have hell to pay."

"There he is. Bastard." They laughed. They sounded nervous at the same time. Relieved.

"What the fuck is he carrying?"

I slipped in the mud and flopped to my knees. The contents of my pouch spilled and rolled, landing at the feet of my rescuers.

"What the—?" One soldier bent to examine the thing.

"Oh. No. Oh. No. No! No!"

He collapsed and the other puked.

I convulsed with my crying.

Raul's head. A ragged tear at the neck, scorched edges. A little bruise upon the cheek. Ebony hair matted, from blood, from rain. A placid look upon his face as if he were asleep beside his beloved Ligaya.

I sobbed. I could hardly breathe. Then I mumbled a one-word prayer—*with reverence.* "Jesus."

• • •

The scorched skeleton of the army truck Raul was driving had disappeared within the remote ravine. The storm had washed away the skid marks and extinguished the fires. I ran down to the vehicle to inspect its interior. Raul's body had disintegrated, leaving a thin layer of a charred fatty substance on the ashes that used to be the driver's seat.

We, the three soldiers, in our shock and utter confusion, buried our comrade's head in a secret place. Away from the black birds, away from the Japs. I made the soldiers promise never to divulge the truth of Raul's death.

"Don't you ever tell, or I will kill you."

"It's our duty to inform the Sarge."

I recall raising my fist and speaking through gritted teeth. "I *will* kill you."

It took some time for the three of us to bury Raul's head. I mean, Jesus, we were idiots in slow motion, working in silence. I guess the Sergeant got impatient and ordered three other soldiers to rescue me and the two Privates. You would think kindness and compassion would be part of the countenance of rescuers, but these men treated us like criminals, dragging us back to the cave and depositing us in front of the Sarge. No doubt he had been fuming all night.

In the subsequent Defense Department investigation, the obvious questions were asked about the multiple crates of wrong ammunition and rationale for sending the unnecessary note. Raul had risked his life for the army in a botched errand. The military defended its actions, responding that the letter pertained to the important matter of elevating and maintaining the troops' morale. As for the supply error, the US Army blamed a brown-skinned Filipino, the driver, my best friend. Bastards! As for me, I was reprimanded for disobeying the Sergeant's orders. Right. Jesus, I got criticized for trying to save a fellow military man.

I resisted going into battle after that and showed cowardice on the field and in the jungle. I put my fellow soldiers in danger by not paying attention and allowing my fears to annihilate my confidence as a soldier. The Sergeant sent me to the medic, who then referred me to the military psychiatrist. I was diagnosed with "Battle Fatigue."

My Sergeant scoffed. "Battle? What battle? One fucking small explosion. The guy disobeys my orders and goes out in the freakin' monsoon. I told him not to. Whatever he saw out there—well, entirely his fault. As for Private Raul Hidalgo, who knows where the fuck he is? Absconded with US Army property. Where the hell is the truck? Son of a bitch."

I was given a general discharge, not an honorable discharge. They said it was because of my illness.

Sarge wanted to unceremoniously kick me out of the service for disobeying orders. I filed a grievance; I had fought valiantly in many battles and deserved to be treated better.

"Jesus, Sarge. Would you give Whitey the same choice? Is it because of the color of my skin?" I thought he was going to punch me in the gut.

"Look," he said, "general discharge for illness or dishonorable discharge for going against my command. Take it or leave it."

Chapter 24

GILBERTO "BERTO" ABUEG

January 1945

Curious folks bombarded me with questions, the answers to which were none of their business. "Why were you medically discharged? What injuries do you have, Gilberto?"

"They are internal, Respicio." I addressed Glory's father by his first name; he disregarded my insult. It was the first sign that I was not myself. Before, and while I was in the army, I was very respectful using the titles of Nana and Tata. Now that I had been discharged, I opposed every kind of rule and authority.

Glory confided to Liling only that my discharge was related to a psychiatric disorder.

Respicio shook his head. "I am sorry for you, Berto. Tens of thousands of Filipinos wounded, fighting the war."

Maria sympathized. "Lucky you, Berto, that you didn't lose an arm or a leg; even more lucky that you didn't lose your life."

"I lost my best friend."

Liling tensed. "You know something, Berto?"

I stammered. "No. No. I meant he is lost and can't be found."

• • •

Was Raul captured by the Japon and hung upon a mango tree? Killed by machine gun? Rocket? Did he commit suicide? Did lightning strike his vehicle? There were rumors he had gone AWOL, and even tales that jungle beasts had devoured him.

The most unbelievable piece of gossip circulating—I had found my best friend's head. Who the hell started that string of assumptions? Thankfully, the story was dismissed by Liling and the villagers—just too gruesome to be believed.

Almost everyone was concerned and uncertain about Raul's disappearance.

The Army, the Hidalgos, and Ligaya would never *officially* come to know. Raul was initially listed as MIA, Missing in Action, not KIA, Killed in Action. What meager benefits his parents could have received were delayed. Raul would have wanted to designate Ligaya as a beneficiary so she could collect some support, but the couple was forced to postpone their wedding because of the war.

At first, I did not want to inform Ligaya about Raul's death. Just telling the story triggered panic in me so great that I felt as if my body had turned to custard and escaped its crust.

I confided in Glory. She admonished me for lying to her family. It took days for her to decide whether to share the news with her sister. She recalled the anguish she herself felt not knowing the whereabouts of Jaime's father. The questions—what, when, where, how, why—whacked her brain like bati-cobra sticks. She was certain the absence of answers was torturing Liling.

Glory could not bear to be the messenger announcing Raul's death—no, not to her own sister. My darling begged me to let Liling know Raul was dead, not to lie about it anymore. But she asked me not to disclose the details of my experience. They were incredibly macabre.

Glory gathered the family at Mr. and Mrs. Hidalgo's home. The Christmas parols were torn and still up. There were no New Year's celebrations. We did not wish each other a happy new year. Who can be happy at a time like this? The Philippines had just entered 1945, the fourth year of World War II in the Pacific. And, well, Raul is…Raul was…

I shuddered, haunted by Raul's voice—*Happy Christmas! Prosperous New Year!* His last words to me.

Everyone dressed in black. Quiet tears either dribbled or streamed down our brown cheeks; thankfully no one wailed. Mrs. Hidalgo had aged ten years since I last saw her at the port where Raul and I had departed for basic training. Liling's eyes were already swollen.

I looked around the hut. Jaime sat on Mr. Ugale's lap. Mrs. Ugale had situated herself next to him. Mr. and Mrs. Hidalgo stood, having given the best seats in the house to their guests. It was the Filipino way. Liling sat directly in front of me with Glory's arm around her shoulders.

Before I began my story, I took a deep breath. I shared that I had been hunkered in a cave with some other soldiers. That I had seen Raul because he delivered supplies to my platoon. He had left at the start of a monsoon. We'd heard an explosion. His truck had practically melted. No sign of him anywhere. We did a thorough search. It was presumed Raul had perished in the flames. A few minutes passed with people in quiet shock.

I looked directly into Liling's sad, sad eyes. "Raul told me he loved you and couldn't wait to marry his beloved."

Another few minutes passed.

Ligaya suddenly stood. "I don't believe you!" she said calmly and walked out of the house.

Ligaya was connected to Raul spiritually, not legally. They had been careful about cultural correctness pertaining to public displays of affection, but the villagers weren't blind. They had sensed and approved of Raul and Liling's deep love for each other. They had respected both of them and supported the couple's union. It had been certain Raul and Liling would marry after the end of the war, which everyone prayed would come sooner than later. The entire village grieved Raul's loss.

Mr. and Mrs. Ugale were disappointed that Raul's death had

caused the contract for the arranged marriage to be automatically null and void. Having been neighbors for decades, the two sets of parents vowed to be like family to each other regardless.

An earnest search for a new husband was initiated lest Mr. and Mrs. Ugale stayed stuck their entire lives caring for their "spinster" of a daughter.

Ligaya's parents were concerned that suitors might regard Ligaya as defective because of her headaches; they occurred only occasionally, but they were debilitating when exacerbated. Of course, potential prospects would more likely reject her for no longer being pure and chaste.

Chapter 25
LIGAYA "LILING" UGALE

January 1945

"You asked Berto to marry you? Oh, Glory!" I didn't know what to think. A woman never proposes. It is not the Filipino way. Papang would not accept it.

• • •

"Respicio, I respectfully ask for your daughter's hand in marriage." Papang nodded, even though Gilberto called him by his first name. Berto then turned to my sister, "I love you, Gloriana Consuelo Cruz Ugale. Will you marry me?" I'm sure Glory was blissfully surprised, especially when he placed an engagement ring on her finger.

Papang was quick to give his blessing. At twenty-nine, Glory was considered old for marriage in the Philippines. If the couple wanted children together, they would have to hurry. Papang often lamented that he was aged and infirm; before he lay on his deathbed, he wanted his eldest daughter well cared for and his grandson to have a father figure.

I watched Jaime and Berto together, often playing bati-cobra, soccer, or pretend pirates, activities Jaime's grandfather was unable to participate in. Jaime went with Berto willingly, smiled broadly, and often laughed when together. "My son" Berto called him—a comfort to Glory.

Berto and Gloriana were soon married in a simple court ceremony. A dozen bullet holes marred the walls of the justice hall. The splintered corner of the seat in front of me was evidence that the Japon had been here.

I must confess I experienced a momentary twinge of envy. I placed my hand over my heart and suppressed the urge to weep.

Glory looked beautiful in her tea-length gown. I had sewn it for her, fashioned from white brocaded curtains the Americano doctor's wife had almost discarded. The white had become dingy over time. Tea, used as fabric dye, evened out the discoloration. I winced when Papang remarked it was appropriate for Glory not to wear pure white on her wedding day.

As I pinned jasmine into my sister's hair, she reassured me that whatever infirmity afflicted Gilberto could be cured with the salve of her love. Glory deserved all the happiness in the world. I had met Berto only a few times, but my fiancé had loved his best friend, and I trusted Raul's judgment. Except for calling my father by his first name—I think because he regarded himself as a modern fellow—Gilberto was always charming and very polite toward the elders. He was a gifted conversationalist. And he worked hard. He had inherited his parents' hut and vegetable farm. He had all the winning qualities you would want for your daughter's husband.

Only enough people were present to fill one row of seats before the judge's bench, a sore disappointment to my mother, who worried that Glory's reputation had been too sullied. Perhaps the invited villagers did not want to be associated with the likes of my sister. Court instead of church—a smart choice, for you could never predict when Father Benito would be on his best behavior. Glory wanted no lectures, no snide remarks or rolling of the eyes, and no Bible readings pertaining to whores and fornicators. My sister asked the justice of the peace to remove the word "obey" from their wedding vows, and he readily agreed.

Gilberto had hoped to return to the university, but it had been decimated during the war. While the buildings were being rebuilt and the education system restored, the newlyweds settled in Gilberto's hometown, three villages from the river.

Glory's mat stayed folded in the corner. Our late-night, whispered sharing was suspended. In a way, I was glad Gloriana no longer resided with our parents, so the pitiful way I mourned Raul would go unnoticed. I admit to weeping often, and I hoped my mother and father would not also sense the depth of my sorrow.

Was my fiancé still alive? I refused to think he is dead. I prayed fervently to the God of Lost Loves. I set a deadline for my mourning, and after the end of the bereavement period, I pretended to return to normalcy. I looked fine on the outside, but within, a thousand bayonets continued to slice my soul.

Raul had said he chose to fight in the Philippine army for his "luscious." I returned to accepting the nickname he had given me. As farmers, we had accepted the fate of a hard life, but we had hoped it would be joyful, or at least tolerable because we loved each other.

In sorrow and anguish, my morbid and melancholic imagination ticked in my brain like the seconds on a clock. I tortured myself with the suspicion that my beloved might have found someone else. Or has been captured and held prisoner by the Japon. Or worst of all, was dead—sometime, somewhere. Mamang often found me with my eyes closed, emitting a heavy sigh. "Sighing is a silent scream," my mother would sometimes say.

Glory was right. Not knowing where, when, how, or why was torment.

"What am I to do without you, my love?" I whispered to no one. Time crawled. Almost everyone but me had come to believe with a certainty that Raul was dead.

• • •

"Oh, Lee-Ling!" my sister called out in her sing-song voice as she approached our home on her carabao. "Where are Mamang and Papang?" I shrugged. My sister's complexion glowed, her smile was broad, and she had a bubbly energy, effervescent, like champagne.

"Oh, Liling. I can't wait for Mamang and Papang to come home. I'm going to tell you first. I have the most wonderful news!—No, I have to wait for Mamang and Papang." My sister was giddy like a child who couldn't wait for someone to unwrap the gift she had brought to a party.

"What is it, Glory? Don't make me wait."

"You must for now. It's a secret."

Chapter 26

LIGAYA "LILING" UGALE

June 1945

Strong coffee with evaporated milk and a teaspoonful of brown sugar was my choice of beverage after poring over the tobacco farm's accounting books, during which Corazon and I shared many stories.

Cora admitted to me she was adopted. The documents remained sealed; she did not know her family history, only that Filipinos had raised her on the outskirts of the city's Chinatown.

I regaled her with my mother's memories about my dead brothers, born in the ten years prior to my own birth. Their passing had affected Papang so profoundly that he had devolved from a gentleman into a monster, according to Mamang. The monster, I was acquainted with, and Bartolome, Boy, and I exhibited the scars to prove it.

After The Event on that pivotal day in September 1944, Bartolome and Cora more frequently found refuge in each other's arms. One of the two would begin to cry, she said, and it would fall to the other to provide comfort and solace. The depth of their shared grief and the tenderness of their caring often turned into passion.

One day in November 1944, like a screenwriter for erotic films,

Cora had described intimate moments to me. At first, I was mortified, refusing to hear about my brother's lovemaking skills. She never blushed, and so I just listened.

I knew that, being almost blind, Bartolome's sense of smell was sharpened. "You are perfumed with the spices of a delicious cigar." Their wondrous, symbiotic relationship was a privilege to watch. My brother and sister-in-law had often laughed and embraced. Nothing could make them happier except to have another baby.

Cora scanned our surroundings first to ensure no one else eavesdropped. "Liling, first he would kiss my eyes and taste the saltiness of my tears upon his lips. A peck on my nose lightens my mood. It is a signal to me that foreplay has begun."

I reached for a sweet pastry. "Cora, you should write a romantic novella, make lots of money."

She put her hands up to stop my nonsense. "Bartolome would kill me, and I would be exiled from the country, or worse, executed for creating pornography." She paused and began to tell me of an incident.

"Sometimes my lover narrated, 'Once upon a time, there was a prince—' "

"A prince?"

"A very handsome prince." Cora nodded.

It was difficult for me to imagine my brother as handsome with his thick spectacles.

"The prince lingers upon a little hill with two tiny caves." The storyteller touched her nose. "He pauses to enjoy the warm breeze coming from within."

I shifted uneasily.

"Alas, the prince must move on. What does he find? Oh, a giant oyster." Cora parted her lips. "He enters it. It's quite dark. Oh, what's this? The most beautiful, bright pearls. He grazes the inside of my mouth with his tongue."

My breathing quickened.

"The prince wants so much to stay and enjoy this succulent oyster; however, he has a far distance to travel. What's happening? The prince makes a misstep and slides down, down along a steep hill." Corazon's fingers slithered down her throat and lingered upon her neck. "It tickles." She giggled, and then continued her narration. "I feign protests, but he sucks gently upon my soft skin, right above the inset in my clavicles. He tries to kiss every inch of my upper chest and finally reaches my breasts."

Cora was being playful. It felt naughty, but I remained riveted.

"What an adventure! The prince comes upon two mountains. Which one shall he climb first? The left one? The right one?" Through her blouse, she cupped her own breasts with the palms of her hands, trying to make a choice.

" 'What's this? Little creases in the mountains?' He kisses my nipples. They feel hard to his touch." Cora winced as if in pain.

She continued her tale, using the voice of a reporter.

"He suckles first upon her left breast and then shifts to the right."

Cora's voice changed; strangely, it sounded both angry and pained.

"Please do not do that, darling. I do not like it."

I shifted my posture, straightening the legs I had tucked under me, and sat with feet flat on the floor and hands on my lap.

"You don't want me to kiss your nipples?" The narrator's voice.

Cora growled deeply. "No! I do not like it. Yes, I used to, but not anymore." Had Cora become a character in her own story? I had read about multiple personality disorder in one of Dr. Billet's medical journals.

My sister-in-law closed her eyes and made guttural sounds—the sounds I had heard her utter during The Event. I could not bear to watch her suffering.

Cora paused as if changing her mind. She moved her hands to her muscular abdomen and parted her knees. I was alarmed. Was she talking herself into readiness? She continued speaking in haste. "Their joining—a multi-sensory ambrosia of moaning and mewing, moisture and musk, softness and hardness—I do not like it—The End." She panted and wept.

"The Event," I whispered.

Cora dropped to the floor.

I froze in shock.

. . .

No more strange, erotic stories followed. Instead, Cora began to complain about her husband, my brother.

"He wanted me on top. I resisted and crawled to the end of our bed. I told him missionary style only." She squinted.

"'Ride me, my darling?' He did ask me nicely. I said, 'No.' 'No?' He asked me again. Why don't men listen the first time? I said, 'No.' I thought lovemaking would exterminate the effects of The Event. During one session, however, Bartolome got carried away. I think he wanted a repeat of our early days of wild, raw sex. He growled, 'Ride me. Cora, move those hips. Sweetheart, ride me.' "

"My brother? My brother said th-that?"

"He pinched and pulled my nipples. Wanted to suckle them. I felt intense revulsion. I slapped his face—hard—covered myself and fled to the opposite corner of our house. I was frightened and furious. We slept in separate rooms for weeks."

"You are still not speaking? I'm so sorry to hear it."

"At last, my husband said, 'Come back to me, my sweetheart. I am lonely.'

"I told him, 'Me too. I am lonely.'

"Bartolome never again uttered crude and vulgar sex words. I refuse to allow him to paw my breasts like a Japon animal," Cora said angrily.

. . .

When the Americano doctor had confirmed Cora's pregnancy in January, I knew Bartolome and she would be overjoyed; their dead infant daughter was to be resurrected.

Now, I was to be present at the delivery. Bartolome fully expected Cora to sail through her third delivery as she had during Pacencia and Rosa's births, but this time, she moaned and screamed so loudly that my brother retreated to the quietest, most comfortable space he knew—the tobacco curing shed. For a while he was unable to bear any reminders of The Event—particularly any ungodly sounds of human torment. Cora's suffering pained him on many levels.

As a member of the Philippine guerrilla forces, he had spent weeks in the jungles searching for and killing enemy Japs. Even after he had mistakenly killed the two Japanese-American soldiers, he felt no remorse. All Japs looked alike; how the hell could he have known? He vowed revenge upon the Japon after his daughters were raped—one had died and the other entered a world of mutism.

Pacencia left the bedroom, I assumed to fetch her father. "Papang, come!" she beckoned loudly. She was trying to make up for his poor vision with sound and tactile cues. I watched Pacencia take her father by the hand as they rushed back to the house.

Bartolome tentatively entered the house. "Is something wrong, Cora? Is the labor going smoothly?"

"I don't think anything is wrong, Papang. Auntie Liling is helping her."

"Are you sure your mommy is all right?"

"I have a little sister." Pacencia could hardly wait to inform him.

"Already?"

"Papang, Auntie Liling said the baby came out fast."

"That was *very* fast."

"Oh, Papang, the baby is cute, cute, cute."

Bartolome found Cora cooing at the swaddled newborn. I sat nearby in quiet reflection.

"Sweetheart."

Cora answered, smiling, "Darling, we have another daughter. She is beautiful. In a way she reminds me of my adoptive father. Her skin is fair. Her eyes, they are..."

Pacencia completed the sentence for her mother. "The baby's eyes are so pretty. Oh, Papang, she is perfect." The girl was obviously quite thrilled.

Bartolome glanced at me. I just nodded and then turned away. Better he discover it for himself.

Chapter 27

LIGAYA "LILING" UGALE

June 1945

My brother wrinkled his brow. "Let me see our baby daughter."

The atmosphere seemed different, strained. I don't think my brother could decide whether he should be eager or reluctant to step closer. I hoped he would welcome his child the way a tender father should. He had received baby Pacencia and baby Rosa with so much love and joy.

Cora held out her arms and Bartolome reached for the bundle. He slid back the hood of the small blanket I had recently finished crocheting as a gift for the newborn.

Bartolome nearly dropped the infant.

"*JAPON!*"

...

My brother's breathing became uneven. He studied the baby's hair—lots of hair and black like Cora's and his. The nose—cute and flat like Cora's and his. Lips—pursed and pink. Skin—light-colored and faintly yellow-tinged. Brown pupils. *Slanted eyes.*

The new baby did look Japanese. Only Cora and Pacencia believed otherwise. The villagers tried to conceal their shock whenever they encountered the child. Despite her innocence, and beauty, and good nature, they thought she embodied evil. Her nickname—The Baby Japon.

Corazon named the newborn Luisa Rose—Luisa meaning "warrior"—and Rose after their late infant daughter, Rosa, who had suffocated during The Event. Pacencia never let us forget that Rosa also signified her favorite flower. Luisa was a noble name, and Cora intended her daughter to embody the strength and courage of a soldier who guards and protects. Never again did she want her daughters to suffer at the hands of the Japanese, or any other enemy, or any other man for that matter. She wanted Luisa Rose to be confident, fierce, empowered, and assertive as a child, especially when she grew up to be a woman.

People found it astonishing that Bartolome had not actually witnessed his wife being raped. To his knowledge, Cora had remained in the outer circle during the entire six hours of hell. Cora developed a clinical amnesia and dissociated herself from her memories. She never disclosed the sexual assaults to him. He had only recently begun to suspect something horrible had happened at The Event because of the way she sometimes reacted when they were trying to make love.

Bartolome's thick-lensed eyeglasses had been destroyed by the Japon. To him, the dark landscape of orgies and vulgarities must have been just a blurred maelstrom of midnight blues and olive greens.

The baby was alert and energetic, and she smiled often. Pacencia called her Dolly Puff-Puff because she was chubby and cute, like the expensive Japanese porcelain figures she saw in an old toy catalog. Everyone in the family was delighted with Luisa Rose. Everyone, that is, except Cora's husband. Bartolome tried hard to love his third daughter.

He secretly paid a visit to the Americano doctor, who was unable to assure him, one way or the other, who the baby's true biological father was.

When Bartolome held her, she babbled cheerfully and reached for his new eyeglasses—an act that would melt any father's heart. He currently felt like a loser, but hating his so-called daughter made Bartolome feel worse. The baby's eyes were what haunted him. They were marquise-shaped and tilted upward, representing the Japanese race he loathed the way the darkness abhors the light.

He could no longer be intimate with his wife. The thought that Cora was unfaithful devastated him, even though he had been told by witness after witness that she was forced—raped multiple times. That she did not surrender. That she fought her rapist valiantly, much like a lioness protecting herself and her cubs.

The child was plainly not his, Bartolome thought; to look at her flat-lidded, oriental eyes brought bile to his mouth. The seeds of prejudice had long ago been planted.

My brother and his wife again slept in separate rooms. Cora and the baby on one side, Pacencia in another, and Bartolome situated nearest the main door. He planned to rush out and defend his family and his land against the Japanese if need be. He refused to allow any Japon to steal from his farm again—not his tobacco, and not Cora or Pacencia. He could not have cared less if they kidnapped Luisa Rose.

Bartolome did not take into account that Cora might have been one of a million Filipinas who had Chinese ancestry. Her middle name, Meili, was Chinese. She was adopted and may have descended from a long line of Chinese merchants and traders who settled in the Philippines during the colonial era four hundred years earlier. Gotiangco, her maiden name, was common among Chinese mestizos. In those days, families combined names. "Co-" is the honorific title showing respect. Tiang was her great-great-grandfather's first name and Go was the surname of an ancestor.

Bartolome would never know who Luisa Rose's biological father was—*the unfortunate truth was the baby could very well have been his.*

Chapter 28

FATHER BUGARIN

September 1945

I might have picked the wrong life. I thought about Gloriana constantly.

As a mere fisherman, I was encouraged to know that scholarly life was considered second to the spiritual life in priestly formation. I joined the seminary at the beginning of the war, when natives were heavily recruited for the priesthood to spread the faith in the language of the locals. Our learning tracks were accelerated, and I was ordained sooner than expected.

I discovered that the senior clergy, most with European ties, believed Filipino priests were incapable of leadership, and therefore, could only be assigned to subordinate roles. The highest position I could hope for was associate pastor. I was deeply disappointed.

It was time to emerge from the safety of the seminary, the cocoon that had protected the weak butterfly all these years. Nervousness and excitement felt the same. I should have been excited, but anxiety made me feel unsure as a newly ordained priest. I was appointed to assist Father Benito at his church. I should not have felt frightened of him since he had long been like a father to me, the only son of a pious widow.

When I informed my acquaintances of my work assignment, they responded dully, "Oh, him," seemingly disinterested or disapproving of my news. As they turned away, I overheard their comments about how the pastor could cut the black hearts of sinners with the sharpness of his tongue.

On my way to my post, I crossed paths with an elderly, hunched man. He introduced himself to me as Respicio Ugale. He had just met his daughter on the path to the river to give her the red shawl she had forgotten on this cooler-than-usual morning.

"Father Bugarin, you say? A strong Filipino surname. I am happy to make the acquaintance of the new associate pastor for our parish." We shook hands.

"I am looking forward to ministering here, Tata Ugale."

"My grandson, Jaime, is too young to be an altar boy but, well, his mother has something against the Church. Because she stopped attending Mass, our pastor refused to baptize him, stating that the boy must not be raised in a sinful environment. We were informed that the pastor has the power to decide whether an illegitimate child may be baptized. We feel sad about that."

"I see."

"Our home is a humble place. There is goodness there now. Father, it would please me very much if you would come to meet my family and bless my grandson."

Truly, I could. I was a minister of God now.

"He is fatherless and was traumatized by The Event."

I knew little of The Event—only that the Japon had raped a village of women en masse.

"He was present when his mother...well, you know. He suffers from asthma. Please, prayers for his health."

"Tata, I'm happy to bless your grandson and you. And your wife?"

"Yes, my wife, Maria. She would be delighted."

"And Jaime's mother?"

"Well, his mama is my daughter, Gloriana."

I reeled backwards. How many Glorianas could there be?

"Are you all right, Father?" The old man touched my shoulder.

I waved my hand. "Yes, yes. Quite all right. Will she be home?" My breathing became fast and shallow.

"Glory is a volunteer in the army auxiliary along with my other daughter. Gloriana's the one I gave the shawl to. Forgetful, that one."

I clutched my rosary beads. I was suffocating and fought the urge to rip off my Roman collar.

I followed the old man to his small hut where I was greeted warmly by his wife. I noticed the four adult sleeping mats, folded and neatly stacked; a number of mahogany armchairs, and some women's clothing hanging on a rod. One set of clothes was in muted colors, conservative in style. The brighter colored dresses were… Could they belong to Gloriana?

"Hello," said a boy brightly. He looked to be around three or even four.

"Introduce yourself to the padre," the grandfather directed.

"My name is Jaime Luna Ugale." His wide grin revealed straight teeth. A bit thin. Shocks of straight black hair framed his face. A few small rips and stains set in his shirt, but his clothing was clean.

I was stunned. I could not help staring. A perfect likeness of me as a child presented himself. Could this be…could this be…? I studied the boy's features.

Hyperventilation and vertigo nearly overtook my body. The anxiety-ridden over-handling of my rosary caused it to break so that the beads spilled across the bamboo floor. I watched stiffly as a number of them dropped through the floor slats and landed on the dirt ground below.

Mrs. Ugale was cordial. "Father Bugarin, you must be tired from your travels. Please, have some mango juice. I'm sorry it is all we can offer you."

I accepted the cup and took a sip. To have refused would have been impolite.

Jaime ran after the wooden pellets, collecting them and placing the beads into an empty coconut shell. Energetic and polite.

"Ready?" I glanced at the three individuals present. I placed my empty cup back on the kitchen table. Mr. Ugale leaned on his cane. His wife dried her hands on her wrinkled apron.

I raised my hands, palms toward the boy.

> "Heavenly Father. Father of all Fathers.
> Source of life's breath.
> You have given us Thy son, Jesus.
> He blessed all children who came to Him.
> Look with favor upon Jaime and protect him.
> Grant him good health.
> May he grow in wisdom and strength.
> Surrounded with love from near and far."

I shall have to love you from afar.

I turned toward the boy's grandparents.

> "Bless Jaime's family who ask for Thy mercy
> and grace.
> May every sinful discord and the devil's wickedness
> be banished from this place."

Mrs. Ugale glanced at her husband.

> "Look with kindness on Jaime's mother, Glo—"

I coughed.

> "—Glo-ri-ana."

I lingered upon her name.

"Give her comfort in moments of weakness and sorrow.
And joy in the care of her son."

I hesitated and continued at a much slower pace.

"May she be forgiving of the deficiencies of others.
And be forever surrounded by love and peace."

I hesitated and hid my shaking hands. I faced Mr. Ugale.

"And what of the boy's dad?"

Mr. Ugale shook his head and tensed his jaw. "Only Glory knows the identity of Jaime's father. She refuses to disclose it. Bastard! I do not wish to know the snake who dishonored my daughter."

I understood Mr. Ugale's reference to the serpent in the Garden of Eden, a cunning trickster who tempted Adam and Eve with the forbidden fruit.

"She searched in every near and far place without success," Mr. Ugale continued. "And, Father Bugarin, she has mourned his loss for all these years."

Mrs. Ugale said dryly. "We do not know where this man is. We only know that our daughter has suffered for her indiscretions." She looked at Jaime with sad eyes. "We are mindful that Jaime is fatherless."

I gulped. I gestured a cross in the air as if brandishing a sword to cut the thick atmosphere. "We ask this blessing, in the name of the Father—" I paused a little too long. "*—the Son—*and the Holy Ghost."

All participants responded, "Amen."

"Thank you, Father Bugarin." Mr. Ugale shook my hand. I could barely look at the man.

I turned to the boy. "I hear you're a great helper, Jaime." He beamed. "And what do you wish to be when you grow up?"

"Me priest—"

"You would make a fine priest."

"—and mayor, and soldier, and volunteer, and doctor." I laughed. "And river fisher like my mama."

I felt my eyelids collapse.

"It sounds like your mama is a very special lady."

"I love my mama. She fighting the Japon to protect me. Lots of very, very, very mean people."

Oh, Jaime. I'm one of those mean people. Mean to you and your mama. My heart is full of sorrow that I can't protect you like she does.

Jaime ran to retrieve a shiny object under an armchair. "This yours, Father. You drop it." He held out a silver cross with a slumped Jesus wearing a prominent crown of thorns.

I covered Jaime's open palm with my hand and folded the child's fingers over the crucifix. "It is yours now, Jaime." Memories of that fateful day five years ago—of fishing, and hiding, and loving—flooded my mind. I felt the spark of our connection, like low-voltage electricity. My skin touching Gloriana's skin, and my skin touching Jaime's skin now.

"Thank you, Father." And in a spontaneous moment of pure joy, Jaime stepped toward me. He wrapped his arms around me. I hugged him back, tightly. I peered over the boy's head and looked contritely at Mr. and Mrs. Ugale. They were smiling.

I placed my hands upon Jaime's shoulders and looked deeply into his brilliant, brown eyes.

"Bless you, *my son*."

...

A lump was lodged in my throat as I bid the Ugales farewell, and quickly exited before they could see me cry.

I moved hastily toward the church where Father Benito waited to orient me to parish work. But then I paused, changed my mind, turned around, and walked away, tearing the white clerical collar in a gesture that resembled slicing my own throat. Tears coursed down my face. I ran toward the river to our favorite fishing spot. I recognized the monkeypod tree where Gloriana and Ligaya had hidden from the Japanese soldiers. It had grown much over the last few years.

I lay on the patch of grass where Gloriana and I had joined body to body, heart to heart, soul to soul. I continued to weep uncontrollably—confused, remorseful, and incredibly sad.

I reflected upon the poignant choices I had made that long-ago night under the full moon. I had abandoned the woman I cherished. Abandoned the son I did not know I had. And now I was abandoning the Church I loved.

I have a son. A beautiful son. Oh, God, how can joy and agony coexist within the same hourglass of time?

Wonder of wonders! I had held my son and experienced the child's exuberance for life. How unlike my own habitual melancholy!

As in many times previously, I contemplated the taking of my own life. Suicide was a means of coping. What plague of transgressions set upon my soul! Fornication, masturbation, self-righteousness, disobedience, deceit and dishonesty, all manner of depravity. In the shadows of my sins, I believed the world should be cleansed of unholy matter.

I am damned and will burn in hell.

I slumped over a large rock on the pebbled shore strewn with driftwood, bent my head, closed my eyes, and recited the Act of Contrition.

> "Oh, my God, I am heartily sorry for having offended Thee.
> And I detest all my sins because of Thy just punishments.
> But most of all because they offend Thee, my God,
> Who art all good and deserving of all my love.
> I firmly resolve with the help of Thy grace to sin no more.
> And to avoid the near occasion of sin."

After removing my outer garments, I waded into the river, and immersed myself fully, as if cleansing my sins in holy baptism. I attempted to drown myself but was neither courageous nor committed. I tried to drown myself again, and again. I sputtered, gulped air, and groped my way back to shore.

Add failed suicide to my long list of immoralities.

My thoughts were interrupted by the sounds of a river—the braying of water buffalo, fish jumping to escape predators, the clucking of feral hens, and the hoopla of a distant night fisherman who must have snagged a fine catch. I glanced toward the path to the barrio and noticed a woman disappear around the bend. She was wearing a red shawl.

...

At the bishop's office, I informed my superior of my desire to trade a diocesan's life of service for a monastic life of silent prayer.

During the period of mandatory discernment, the bishop discussed the solemnity of a priest's vows of chastity, poverty, and obedience. He extolled upon the profound need for the institution of family. The bishop, of course, referred to the community of priests and other religious, but I thought of Gloriana and our son, Jaime.

The Church had helped me rediscover the grandeur of religious vocation, serving in the name of Jesus.

"Father Santiago Bugarin, you are called to love." I shuddered at the bishop's words.

At the end of a period of intense introspection and guidance, the bishop asked me, "What say you?"

"It is my destiny to pray in solace—for world peace." The realization that my beloved and our son were traumatized by The Event pained me. World War II was still raging on without a predictable ending. More battles ensued throughout the Philippines.

I added, "To pray for depth of healing—for the world." In my mind, I prayed for a cure for my own spiritual, emotional, and mental illnesses. I accepted the responsibility of praying for my own kin, for I was the one who had triggered their trauma.

I would never see my son again. Would never watch him mature. Never behold the major milestones of his life. Never would, never could, and never should.

My only acceptable influence was through prayer.

Satisfied with the depth of my reflection, the quality of my supplications, and my commitment to service, the Church granted my humble request for transfer to a contemplative order. They assigned me to a monastery in Europe. Already ordained, I was still to be addressed as Father, but I was adamant about changing my name. I announced my new moniker—Vincent Judas. Vincent, after the patron saint of spiritual needs, and Judas, the apostle who had betrayed Jesus.

...

Every evening in my cell, after prayers and before retiring, I looked down upon my nakedness and studied the scars on my arms, abdomen, and thighs. I pretended they were badges rewarded for my so-called bravery.

Insomnia plagued me like tomcats screeching under my window. In my wakefulness, I relived every kiss and every caress with Glory on that special moonlit night in December 1941.

...

After our lovemaking, Gloriana had left me naked on the riverbank. I had turned back to my pile of clothing. I saw my neighbor's carabao tied to a tree on the shore. *Strange, why would it be here?* I also saw stalks of bananas and a stash of eggs. Stolen goods.

The two Japanese bathers, whom I recognized by the river that afternoon, grabbed me from behind. Still unclothed, I tried to fight against their knives. I was more fit than the hairy Japanese, but being two men against one, they eventually overpowered me.

One of the soldiers, the bald one, held me down on the ground, knee on my upper back. I took a mouthful of coarse sand when he smashed my face into the shore as I continued to fight. The one Glory called Gorilla pulled on my hair like reins on a horse, making it too easy for him to ride me, rape me. Was God punishing me for fornicating? To be a man and raped by a man was, to me, the epitome of degradation—a night of sin upon sin. Just the day before this heinous incident, I had considered myself a pious person, a responsible citizen, a moral man.

I did not cry out. I loved Glory intensely. I watched her with fear as she proceeded toward the village; she was still close enough to hear. A commotion would have compelled her to turn around and investigate. No, safer, I decided, that I surrender.

A night bird squawked. This distracted the Japanese. I then heard rustling from behind the trees and the murmurings of other Japanese men. This caused the rapist to stop, rush to redress, and join the others.

The Japanese army would not have been too angry about any soldier raping the Filipino enemy. I discovered that male homosexuality was not illegal at the time and censorship was lax in Japan; nonetheless, the hairy perpetrator took a risk by engaging in sodomy, considered to be a perverted sex act.

I rescued the carabao and returned all stolen property. Seeing the extent of my injuries, everyone remarked that I must have been strong and brave against the Japon. I did not correct them.

In less than twenty-four hours, the lover within me had become a rape victim, and then the imposter village hero.

...

To sustain our livelihoods, we monks tended our vineyards for the purpose of making altar wine. We grew our own fruits and vegetables, and raised poultry and livestock, all without talking. But our main purpose as a religious order was to pray.

The monks and priests prayed in shifts, and I was frequently scheduled for the evensong. Although the chapel was sublime in its simplicity—without ornate carvings and antique tapestries—I preferred to pray outdoors in the manicured flower gardens where the scent of jasmine, Gloriana's favorite flower, perfumed the air.

In the few periods when soft conversation was allowed, a couple of the monks complimented me on my piety because, they said, I often lifted my eyes toward the heavens. What a laugh! Did they not know that, actually, I kept watch for the mango-colored disc in the sky? I took comfort in knowing that the moon that shined over the monastery in Europe was the same that illumined a certain village in Asia. I imagined my loved ones and I were so connected that the three of us simultaneously gazed at the luna.

My external and internal scars would forever remind me that I, Father Vincent Judas, formerly Santiago Bugarin, fled like a fugitive into a cloistered life to ensure that no one, most of all my Gloriana and my son Jaime, could ever locate me. I was not devout. I was gutless.

Chapter 29

LIGAYA "LILING" UGALE

July – December 1945

"We were like two starved beings who came upon a banquet and stuffed themselves until sick." Glory had confided that for the few weeks after their January wedding, she and Gilberto were ardent with passion. Three months later, she revealed her "secret" and happily announced that they were expecting a baby. Everyone, especially Jaime, was thrilled.

Some time went by. Glory complained to me that their intimacy had decreased in quantity and quality. "Now we are tired of each other." Gilberto had been short with Jaime, and this upset my sister.

* * *

"Berto, you are different," I addressed my brother-in-law.

"Come back to me, my love," begged my sister.

"Jesus, I came back, didn't I?" Berto seemed uncharacteristically irritated.

"You did come back from the battlefields," I replied.

"It is as if you are a completely different person returned from the war," added Glory.

Berto emitted a groan.

"Yes, and I do not like it." Glory placed her hands on her hips.

Gilberto stomped out of the house and slammed the screen door behind him.

"I'm sorry for starting this, Glory," I said. "I felt I needed to speak up."

"I do not want my son around that bastard. Jaime needs a caregiver, not a crazy man. Liling, God has abandoned me yet again. I feel betrayed by a man yet again. I despise my husband. I am planning to flee."

"Dear sister, divorce is not only illegal, it is immoral in the Philippines. This is a Catholic country. Besides, you're having a baby."

• • •

My concerns about my sister grew. I initiated a visit.

"How goes it, Glory?"

"I'm fine, Liling."

"Really?"

"Yes, I assure you, I'm fine."

"Then why is your face not showing it?"

Gloriana reached up to cover her cheeks. "You got me. I'm worried, Liling. There is something wrong."

"Tell me, sister. What is it that's wrong?"

"I don't know, exactly. I just know something is wrong."

"Glory, you are fortunate to have a husband who cares much for you and Jaime. Me, I wait for my Raul." I sighed. "God of the Lost, bring Raul back to me."

"Liling, Raul is dead." Was that a kind thing to say to me? I ignored this. I refused to believe it.

"Shall I ask the God of the Lost to bless Berto?"

A tear slid down Gloriana's cheek. "No, Liling."

"Bring back Santiago?"

"No."

"Well then. Amen." I tried to be optimistic.

I noticed my sister cupping her belly with her arms, like a hen wrapping her eggs within its wings.

"You will be delivering soon." I smiled. Glory did not.

. . .

Our mango tree shielded my sister and me from view of our parents and the afternoon sun. I shooed away the fruit flies and waited for Gloriana to speak.

"I don't believe Gilberto is one bit sorry for hitting me last night."

I gasped. My sister was advanced in her pregnancy. "No, Glory. No."

"I am too exhausted to haul water, too fatigued to chop wood. I nap frequently. Gilberto came home to a dark house. He was thirsty. The water pot was empty. The stove was cold. No dinner ready. He threw his walking stick at me, leaving a flaming mark across my abdomen.

"I buckled over in pain. I thought the contractions were starting. Too early. My due date is not until the moon is like a mango again. I even prayed your kind of prayer, Ligaya. 'God of Birthing, it is not time yet. Please, I beg Thee. It's too early.' "

Pensively, I said, "Amen."

"It took almost all of my energy to hoist myself off our sleeping mat. My husband was hungry, and it is my responsibility to feed him. Why he just doesn't cook for himself is beyond my understanding. A grown man who cannot cook. I moved as briskly as I could lest he beat me again.

" 'Just make sure breakfast is ready in the morning,' he said. And he guzzled his beer. Who does he remind you of, Ligaya?"

"Papang. The old version of Papang."

"The next morning, I searched for chicken eggs. I nearly panicked when I found nothing in the coops, but then your God of Hens was kind that day. I spied a lone egg balanced on a soft pile of dirt, leaves, and feathers. While scrambling the egg, I sobbed. I spied Gilberto stumbling down the road with a hangover, an indication that he would be especially mean that day. I did not have time to milk the goat. After I served Berto the egg topped with a chopped tomato, he helped himself to the large bananas and the rice, left over from our previous evening's meal. He did not offer any to me, or to Jaime, who watched everything unfold from his corner."

"Oh, Glory." There was nothing much I could say. We hugged, trying to divide our sorrows.

. . .

Jaime rode the carabao to our hut. He urged me to come as quickly as possible. "Mama need you, Auntie Liling. She screaming. I stay here with Lola and Lolong."

"Yes, yes, Jaime. That is a good idea. Go see if Lolong will play the clapping game with you."

I overheard Jaime say to my father, "Papa Berto call me bastard. He say, 'Shut up, bastard!' What is *bastard?*"

Papang was angry. "Why that dirty, dirty..." He stopped in time and looked at Jaime, who had learned well not to complete the perverse Filipino phrase.

With a pretend smile, Mamang started the game. "Let's clap!"

. . .

No mango-colored moon shone to nullify the darkness that shrouded my sister's hut.

When I arrived, Gilberto was at the table chewing loudly, then smacking his lips. Glory stood silent, stirring rice porridge.

I observed a trickle slowly roll down Glory's thigh into a small puddle of congealed blood. I directed her to lie down. She drew her knees to her chest in a protective pose. With a sudden wave of nausea, Gloriana lifted her shoulders off the mat, making the sound of dry heaves.

Gilberto yelled, "Jesus, can't you see I am *eating?*"

She must have felt a sudden piercing in her uterus because she thrashed about in agony. "Help me, Liling. My body is tearing, exploding, ripping, searing." My sister screamed the way I imagine spooks sound on a black night.

Gilberto paced like an enraged carabao. "You're making a ridiculous noise. You embarrass me."

Gloriana reclined with her huge belly pitched left. The undulations under her skin reminded me of puppies writhing soon after birth.

Screams followed pauses, as if the fetus were abrading Glory's womb, followed again by another pause and another scream. Gloriana's lips became parched and cracked. She was too weak to sip from the cup of water I offered, and Gilberto was too preoccupied to think of her needs.

I'm sure Berto regarded this delivery as an intrusion. The wall calendar revealed a square outlined with a red circle; the eve of harvest season, probably the worst time for a farmer's wife to give birth.

Gilberto growled, "Let's get your labor over with so I can finish my labors."

Glory's contempt was evident even in her weak voice. "Then slink to the whorehouse, Berto?"

"Your mother's cunt! You are big as a pig and refused me. What is a man to do?"

I needed to see the moon rise. I exited to leave the couple alone for a few minutes. There was no moon.

I returned and Berto was still there, grumbling. I ignored him.

"Oh, sister." I held Gloriana in my arms and kissed her forehead. "You can do this. I am with you."

• • •

"What an ugly sound coming from an ugly woman." Gloriana's high-pitched screeching bothered Gilberto. I glared at him.

"How I could have had sex with you, impregnated you, is beyond comprehension. Jesus, I gave up university for this?" He smirked.

Raul's best friend, the friend who would have been best man at our wedding, dares to speak to my sister in this rotten way?

Most villagers were already familiar with the side of Gilberto that was charismatic, compassionate, and intelligent. The sterling reputation that preceded his medical discharge disguised his changed personality. He hid the emotional scars from his time in the army under a public façade of charm. The people could not know the immensity of his pain.

The loss of his best friend, Raul, was expressed as rage, which he tried to quell with liquor. His newfound thirst for alcohol turned him into an intimidating and abusive drunk.

• • •

My wish was for Gloriana to forget her suffering for an instant when at last she heard the baby's cry. "Head out!" I announced happily and waited for the body to slide out.

With a mighty scream, Gloriana pushed. "Wait. Is that another cry?" she asked.

I saw the tops of two bloody baby heads. I was not surprised by her having twins; multiple births ran in our family. I expected to see two arms, two legs on *each* baby. Two heads meant two babies. I shut my eyes and opened them again. Two arms, two legs, two sets of male genitals. Two heads. *One body*. After pushing the birth sac away from their shoulders, I picked up the babies. Or should I say I picked up the one torso with two heads.

My voice cracked, "Oh, God of Birthing!" The twins were Siamese. Deformed. Conjoined from shoulder to hip.

Gilberto advanced slowly. His eyes were full of horror and hatred. He shook and shouted, unleashing terrible obscenities.

"Jesus! This baby...these babies...this monster—is not mine. Devil's progeny. Disgusting!" Gilberto swept his arm across the bedside table, flinging an alarm clock to the floor. He fled, leaving me alone with my distraught sister.

Gloriana drew her knees up and wide to examine her twins between them. "Oh, Liling!"

Very tiny newborns. Contortionists. Another week of gestation and they would not have been able to pass through the birth canal. Glory would surely have met her death.

Struck speechless, I cleaned the babies of blood and the waxy vernix of birth, then wrapped the twins in the rough, nubby fabric of a rice bag. They were born prematurely; the crocheted blanket I was working on lay unfinished. Bundled up with only their heads exposed, they appeared quite normal.

The babies cried weakly. One was bluer than the other. Gloriana placed her finger near the pursed lips of one baby as the other infant searched for her left breast. Baby One sucked with no gusto. Baby Two, the smaller, began to cry. She carefully placed her right nipple near Baby Two's mouth, but it turned its head. Her breast was firm, and hard to the touch. Drops of a thin, light-gray substance formed through the dark brown pores of her nipple.

She focused on her sons' eyes. They were bright and full of life, even with body frail and somewhat limp.

"Hello," Glory muttered, greeting her babies as new mothers almost always do.

The infants ever slightly turned toward her sweet, soft voice. Could it be that Big Baby was already bonding? Small Baby smiled. My heart opened. Surely, Gloriana's heart opened too.

I turned up the flames in the oil lamps and peered at my nephews. I interlaced my fingers and prayed. "God of Twins, forgive Glory, said to have danced with the devil." My words came out wrong; I meant Berto, my devil of a brother-in-law. "May the babies die sooner than later."

My petition was unintentionally loud enough for Gloriana to hear. She chastised me, "They are my babies, Liling. How dare you?"

I continued my prayer. "God of Twins, I beseech Thee. Take these children unto Thee. Amen."

Said with a gentle voice,"I know, Glory, Sister, you are in shock.

You must think rationally." I peered into my sister's sad face. "What kind of life will these babies have? Think, Glory. Think. You must be rational. As they grow older, will you be able to feed them? Clothe them? Take them to school? Will they be able to walk, to lift, to labor on the farm? Will you continue to diaper them into adulthood? Who will care for them when you are gone? Berto? Jaime? Think of Jaime, sister."

I continued after a pause. "They are premature. They share organs. They are going to die, Glory. I'm so, so sorry. They are going to die."

A drunken Gilberto returned, yelling, "Maybe Father Benito was right; you are in disfavor, and these freaks are the proof. You have given birth to freaks. I'm going to take the freaks to the river and drown the freaks."

"No!" Gloriana lay dumbstruck and defeated.

Berto made it abundantly clear he wanted a boy to call his own, like all Filipino fathers, to pass his name through the generations. He left again, muttering something about a whorehouse.

"You are right, Liling. We have no food to spare for two extra mouths. They will be of no use on Gilberto's farm. What kind of life will they have—locked together from shoulder to hip?"

To assess the newborns further, I placed my ear on the babies' chest and listened with an intense focus. I shook my head. "Only one heartbeat."

"Miss Queen of Brutal Honesty."

"I learned that from you, sister."

Gloriana saw beyond the deformities; she held her twins more securely in her arms. "My heart is your heart, my sons."

I removed the babies from their mother's hold and realized they could not lie flat. They were connected at an odd angle. Against all forces of the fatigue and fear that had set in, Glory moved to fashion a makeshift bed in a tobacco crate. She lined it with pillows and the partially finished blanket.

The twins became weaker. Gloriana sang to them, held them closely, kissing their eyelids, their crowns, their fists and feet.

"Do you want to name your babies?"

"No." Gloriana sobbed. "I am unable to give my sons anything, not even the gift of a name."

"So be it." I acknowledged Gloriana's wishes.

Pacencia arrived unexpectedly with fruit for the family. She saw the conjoined twins as Glory loosened the makeshift blanket. The girl backed away, dropping her basket. I snatched the youngster's arm.

"You are not to speak of this to anyone. Do you hear? No one." I spoke too harshly.

Pacencia nodded. Her voice was shaky. "Yes, Auntie Liling. No one."

"Promise me."

"I promise, Auntie Liling. No one."

"*No* birth happened. You did *not* see attached babies."

Pacencia nodded.

"If you break this confidence, the God of Tattletales will place a curse on you, and you will be struck dumb again."

Pacencia cried and ran away. She had never seen a deformed baby and her Auntie Liling had never before threatened her with such vehemence. I asked the God of Wretched Aunties to forgive me.

Gloriana stroked her sons' faces with the backs of her fingers, pressed their noses lightly, and caressed their broad singular chest. She laid them tenderly in their makeshift crib.

In the morning, they were dead. Sweet cherub faces like the wood-carved motifs at the church. Gloriana cried—the twins lay in final repose, *each with an arm embracing the other.* Rivulets of tears coursed down my face.

"Go with the angels, my sons." She kissed their cold lips again and again and handed the lined container to a repulsed Gilberto. I was sad that he did not show grief for his infant sons.

"A proper burial, Berto." I should not have had to say this. I was in such shock over his insensitivity. Gilberto seemed to be a stranger, not at all like the friend I had met through Raul. Could he, would he, throw the babies away like trash? My brother-in-law left with the crate and returned empty-handed sometime during the night, doused with liquor and cheap rose perfume.

No one knew where he took the twins. Rumors abounded that Gloriana gave birth to normal twin boys and the priests at the seminary took them in as assurance to increase their numbers. By giving their sons to God, Gloriana and Gilberto would be assured of their place in heaven.

Once in a long while, a neighbor or two would speak of another rumor, the one where Gloriana had delivered a monster, part of a curse for consorting with the devil.

Many months later, Jaime and his one-eyed cousin, Vicente, chased after a monkey into the jungle. They were drawn to a half-buried, badly disintegrating rice bag containing bones, two skulls, and a crocheted scrap. Jaime informed his stepfather, who came up with a scheme to make some pesos. He contacted an archeologist from his university. The science department sent a mere intern to examine the skeletons. Marks had been made by wild animals that feasted upon the joints, the most succulent parts of the skeletal remains.

A journal article was eventually published about an astounding find—a tiny and queer creature, a monster with two heads.

• • •

My grief finally began to decrease, but the approach of the Christmas season stoked my feelings of loneliness and longing. Everyone in the family seemed to have renewed faith that the war would soon be over. Their uplifted emotions helped to prevent me from sinking again into further despair. We promised to stay strong for each other with the goal of surviving past the New Year.

The annual parol making was held at the Ugale hut. Conversation was cheerful enough. We even received a letter from Boy in Hawaii, who generously included money orders for each family member. It was to be a happy Christmas.

The villagers looked forward to gathering at the plaza for the New Year's Eve rituals. The bonfire was lit, around which folk dancing and singing contests occurred. Men and teen boys strung long lines of firecrackers on bamboo poles—the noise was believed to frighten away the evil spirits. Pork chops and goat meat sizzled on the grill. Woks of vegetables were prepared for the traditional community meal. It was usually a feast, but in wartime, the amount of food was limited. The villagers shared what they could and made sure no one would go away hungry.

I tapped my sister on the shoulder. "Glory, Berto is acting strangely."

At midnight, fireworks exploded, producing a lot of noise and smoke. Men who had guns were allowed to shoot as long as they did so safely. Jaime coughed several times so he was sent home with Cora and Pacencia; we could not risk a flareup of his asthma.

It was easy to find Berto, for the crowd had parted to reveal a pathetic man in a stupefied state. He looked at me and folded into the ground. He screamed, his eyes shut tight, his hands over his ears.

The villagers responded, not with empathy, but with laughter and disdain.

"What is he doing?"

"Sick in the head?"

"Like a baby."

"A dirty, dirty, dumb-dumb soldier."

I knew that for a while now Glory's husband had been prone to apathy, irritability, flashbacks, memory loss, and an inability to concentrate. At first, my sister described his symptoms as mild, but they intensified gradually.

Gilberto's panic attacks were triggered by any loud bang; the smell of barbecued meat; fires, big and small; and black birds.

The village children taunted him "*Loco Loco*"—not just crazy—double crazy. When within his vicinity, juveniles whistled in piercing glissando, imitating the sound of a rocket seeking its target. And then they made loud booming noises like human explosives. The teenagers discovered that coconuts triggered an extreme psychopathological reaction. They rolled coconuts to Gilberto's feet every chance they got. Berto was as fragile as a toy soldier made of crystal. I wondered when he was going to crack.

Chapter 30

LIGAYA "LILING" UGALE

January 1946

"Glory, I'm here!" I called out. I had ridden the carabao, carrying a large container of mangoes for the Abuegs.

"Liling, wait there. I'll be right out. Wait, okay?"

"Can Berto help with this load of fruit?"

"He cannot," Glory said nonchalantly as she tied up the carabao. That's when I saw the purple-blue marks on her arms.

My sister began to breathe more rapidly, and her face became flushed. Was that an impression of a hand slap on her face?

"Glory! What has he done to you?"

"Nothing, Liling. It's nothing. I fell picking papayas."

"Those are bruises. You would tell me, wouldn't you, if he is hurting you?"

"Of course, Liling, I would tell you."

"And Jaime? Is Jaime all right?"

"He is not hitting Jaime, and he is not hitting me."

Oh, God of Love and Peace and Honesty.

"Looking at you, I sense that something is wrong, sister."

Malaise, like a cancer, had metastasized and eaten into her sense of humor. Gloriana was uncharacteristically melancholic and unenergetic.

"Nothing is wrong, Liling," she said unconvincingly.

"Where is Berto?"

"Gone."

"Gone?"

"He left."

"Maybe that is a good thing," I said.

"I'm lonely, Liling."

"I know about loneliness. Tell you what, I'll help you with dinner, and then when it's Jaime's bedtime—"

"Liling, can you take Jaime to visit Mamang and Papang?"

"Are you sure? On a school night?"

After our early dinner, Glory and I lay side by side on our mats at the Abueg hut just as we had since we were youngsters.

"I love you," said Glory.

"I love you."

Glory started sniffling.

Departure time arrived too soon. My sister kissed the top of Jaime's head. "Be good, my son. Listen to your lolong. Brush your teeth." She dabbed Jaime's sticky lips with the hem of her apron. "Eat your vegetables. I will see you tomorrow."

"Enough, Mama. Mama, 'nough." The boy wriggled away from anyone who was overly attentive and provided too many maternal ministrations.

"Sorry, Jaime. It's just that I love you much more than you know. Go with Auntie Liling now. Give Lolong and Lola hugs for me. I love you, my son."

"I love you, Mama."

And then mother and child said simultaneously, "High like the moon, and the sun, and the stars." I was delighted to witness this special moment.

Jaime and I rode past the church graveyard on the carabao.

. . .

Gilberto had developed a mental illness triggered by the traumas of war. The soldier had been in constant fear for his life, not just while in active combat but in the eeriness of quiet when it seemed deceptively safe. When sound dies, warriors die; snipers surreptitiously, silently slit the throats of the unsuspecting.

Gilberto was never the same after his discharge from the army. I wondered what sent him into a psychotic tailspin, like an incapacitated war plane out of control, heading for an imminent crash and burn.

There were episodes in which Gilberto punched his own head. Occasionally, he wrapped his arms around the back of his skull as if shielding himself from harm. One might find him with his head resting on his elevated knees, tenderly caressing his own hair.

Family and friends no longer visited the Abueg abode because Gilberto's daytime flashbacks were frightening and perilous. Visitors risked being the target of his vitriole, Satan-like stares, and his threats of murder.

Violent images in his nightmares caused him to view Gloriana as the enemy. The present had evaporated, and he was back in the jungles, on the rice terraces, in the caves, or in the river. More than once, he bashed his wife as she slept. The fear of harm, especially to Jaime, caused Gloriana to lose precious sleep. Her insomnia only served to compound her problems with recurring depression.

"Mama? Something wrong with Papa Berto? He no smile. He no laugh."

"He is sick, Son. Give him time; he will improve," Gloriana said without much conviction.

Gilberto was eventually disowned by his family of origin and separated himself from Gloriana and Jaime. He became the homeless town drunk. Sleeping in horse stables, eating from the pig troughs, stealing fruit from the villagers' trees. In the worst of times, he survived on grasshoppers and grubs.

The elders whispered to each other and shook their heads. "Ay. Loco loco. Dirty, dirty, dumb-dumb."

. . .

"Glory!" I called from outside my sister's hut. "Glory?" No answer. "Gloriana, it's me. Open the door. I have a big basket of vegetables for you from Mamang." I waited one minute and called again, louder. "Glory!" Annoyed, I heaved the basket up the stairs and knocked on the splintered door. "Glory. Are you okay?—I'm coming in."

When I entered, I saw my sister lying prone on her sleeping mat. It cheered me to see Gloriana was taking a much-needed rest. "There you are. Mamang is worried." I bustled about, putting the vegetables in their respective bins. "She gathered these squash and eggplants for you."

"I left Jaime at Auntie Soledad's to play with Vicente. It's good that you live very close to Auntie. I told her to send Jaime home in about an hour; she can keep an eye on him from her stoop. Glory, where do you want these avocados? Glory?"

I turned around.

"Gloriana Consuelo Cruz Ugale Abueg!"

Glory had not responded—it was so unlike my sister to be silent for long. I moved slowly toward the resting figure and gingerly poked my sister's sheet-covered upper back. I pulled back the linens.

I gasped. My sister's hand was cold and stiff. There were lacerations on her palms and fingers, and defensive cuts on the sides of her forearms. My pulse skipped beats.

I gently turned my sister so she was face-up. Glory's eyes were open, and gray, and blank. My breathing became even more ragged. A large blood stain on her blouse covered her abdomen. A fly escaped from her left nostril.

"Oh, God of...God of...OH GOD—OH GOD—OH GOD!"

. . .

The room swallowed me with icy blackness. I rushed outside, heaving, hoping the sun's energy would fortify me to act in a mature and halcyon way for Jaime.

I immediately suspected Berto. Troubling memories besieged my brain—images of Glory's bruises and scratches. His nighttime attacks upon my sister; in his delusion she was the Japanese enemy. Memories of verbal vomit spewing forth from his twisted tongue.

I rushed to the constabulary to report my sister's murder. I was not surprised that Gilberto Abueg was already well known to the policia. They had accumulated records on him for simple assault, petty theft, public intoxication, disorderly conduct, trespassing, vandalism, and indecent exposure.

I needed to intercept Jaime. I ran back to the house, now a crime scene.

. . .

"Mama, I'm home!" Jaime called out brightly as he skipped up the garden path.

"Jaime!" I yelled from inside the house.

"Hi, Auntie Liling. Where's Mama?"

"Jaime!" I called out nervously. "Wait outside. I'm coming outside."

"Look what Vicente and I drawed." He pulled out a hand-drawn map of Hawaii from his pocket and pointed to the island of Oahu. "Uncle Boy lives here, right, Auntie Liling?" He pointed to Pearl Harbor.

"Right."

"I want go Hawaii with Mama."

I sat on the front steps, effectively blocking my nephew from entering the house.

Jaime was chatty. I didn't know what to say. I pressed my fingers against my face and felt tension in my muscles. I noticed that my hands then moved jerkily, signing, writing in air. I think my strange behavior alarmed Jaime.

"Auntie Liling, where Mama?" he asked in a suspicious tone.

"Shh, Jaime. She is sleeping."

"Sleeping?"

That is a lie. I choked. "She is gone, Jaime."

"Gone? Gone where?"

"She is—oh, Jaime." I began to sob.

Jaime's eyes widened and his shoulders dropped.

"Mama…gone?"

"Yes, dear."

"Mama coming home?"

"No Jaime—Jaime. Your mama is…."

"Auntie?"

I decided to be direct but use a gentle voice. I placed my hand over my nephew's heart. "Be still, my love. I am here." I choked. "Jaime. Your mama is—dead."

"Dead like Rosa?"

The wind caught the paper Jaime was holding in his hand, and his map of Hawaii wafted away. He did not try to chase it.

Jaime walked into my open arms. Auntie and nephew clung to each other tightly and we cried and cried a very long time.

Chapter 31

GILBERTO "BERTO" ABUEG

January 1946

The policia tracked me down as the most likely suspect. I do not remember anything. Oh, Glory, Glory? Glory, where are you my darling, beautiful Glory? Slut!

I am living unauthorized in an abandoned tobacco shack on Bartolome's farm. My head is speaking rightly, but the authorities hear only gibberish. "This is what I am saying!" I shout, and shout, and shout. "Hear me! You are not listening!" I give up. It is evident they don't understand the sounds emanating from my mouth.

Injuries—a distinct bite with canine punctures on my hand, and on the back of my right leg where the dog had ripped through my trousers and chomped on my calf. Served by Benedicto, the dog, whose name means *blessing*. I laugh like a madman. Jesus. Benny. The dog!

The only clothing I owned was worn on my body—filthy khakis and a stiff T-shirt—the original colors now obscured by brown muck and thick with sweat. A search of the premises revealed nothing of use to them—a filthy mat on the dirt floor where I slept. Spoiled scraps of food wrapped in a faded red bandanna saved for a later meal. A five-gallon container of feces, set in a far corner, the stench overpowering. "Human feces." The policia asked, "You shit in the bucket, Berto?"

"What human would collect feces? Absurd!"

When I was interrogated, it was clear I was impaired. My eyes rolled back into my head, and I laughed like a maniacal creature from the deep jungle. I flapped my arms like a bird and danced like a bird and cawed like a bird, waiting, waiting to take bites out of my carrion.

I brought out a cured tobacco leaf, compliments of my brother-in-law, Bartolome. He hates the Japs. More than I do? I don't think so.

"What the fuck is he saying?" asked the tall policia.

"Sounds like roll. Roll tobacco? Roll cigar? Roll something."

I muttered again. My fingers were not nimble.

The policia talked among themselves. "I heard roll cocoa. Roll co-co-nut?"

The other policia shrugged.

"Shit."

"Roll a coconut."

"Yeah, well. This guy's loco."

Nothing more than curses spewed forth from my mouth. I rolled the leaf into a cheroot, reached into my pants pocket, and brought out a medium-sized army knife. I was cutting the ends of my cigar when the policia noticed a streak of blood on its blade and handle.

"Drop your weapon," ordered the taller policia.

I tried to slash the officer. I had to; he was the Jap enemy. Can't you see? They say things. Loco. Loco. They pronounce it Rrrow-Ko. Rrrow-ko. Jesus, what kind of stupido language is that? I go to university. We pronounce L correctly! "Rrro-Co... Roll. Coconut. Jesus, roll coconut!" I yelled. I stabbed the air.

"Shit!" shouted the tall policia.

Without warning, I transformed from an attacker to a blubbering baby curled into a ball, easy then to restrain and easy to cart away. I give up, Jap enemy. I give up, black dog. Jesus, he kept barking nonstop. I slammed my ears.

I don't know where they took me. To prison? To a mental institution? I don't think anyone knew. I don't think anyone cared.

"Sir," I asked the policia. "Where is my wife? Where is Glory?"

Chapter 32
LIGAYA "LILING" UGALE

January 1946

The funeral procession moved exceedingly slowly as it necessarily started and stopped for Papang, who stumbled several times along the rock-strewn path to the cemetery. Jaime held his hand. "Come, Lolong. This way, Lolong." Father Benito, impatient as usual, showed little compassion.

He recited the funeral rite from rote memory. He said "My condolences" in a terse tone and then offered a limp hand to my parents.

"Like squeezing bread dough," Mamang later said.

I couldn't believe my ears. "Sinners die a violent death, deservedly so." Did I actually hear him say that?

"Mama gone?" Jaime turned to his grandfather.

"Yes, Jaime. Your mama is no more."

Did Jaime not understand that his mother had passed away and was not coming back? He showed little emotion. The boy seemed to study his relatives. Almost everyone he loved was weeping. Vicente's black eye patch was soaked. Old Auntie Soledad was wailing to the farthest boundaries of heaven. No one flinched; drama was expected from her.

Nobody dared roll their eyes when Mamang sang the Filipino hymns loudly and sometimes off key. She blew her nose delicately but often. Yet another of her children gone. Children should not precede their parents in death.

My father used his cane to steady himself. He laid his other hand, shaking, on Jaime's shoulder and occasionally patted it.

I declared myself the saddest of all, but I was not tearful. I stood stoically, as I once used to when punished by my father. Except now I believed I was being punished by God, the Father. My sister, who was my best friend and confidante, had been murdered. How could you? God of... How could you? I had turned my anger from Gilberto to God.

The time came for the memorial photo. Because photography was very expensive, picture-taking was reserved for funerals so the living could remember their deceased relatives. A morbid practice—to see only funereal photos in a family photo album could be unnerving.

The coffin lid leaned on its side upon the box. A wooden cross remained propped against the lid.

Everyone, dressed entirely in black, lined up behind the simple wooden coffin to look at Gloriana, whose hair had been lovingly brushed by Mamang. I placed my black mantilla over my sister's shoulders and draped the ends to cover her nicked arms, remembering the times when we had played "nun" as little girls. Cora and Pacencia arranged a few flowers, sprigs of jasmine and frangipani, into Gloriana's hands—another unsuccessful attempt to cover her nicks and bruises.

It could be said that Gloriana was more beautiful in death than in life. Her face less askew. The mole seemed to have shrunken.

"Mama sleeping, Lolong?"

"No, Jaime. Your mama is not sleeping. Quiet now, while the man takes our photo. We do not smile, Jaime."

"I cannot smile, Lolong, even if I try."

Bartolome and another man moved to cover the coffin. It would soon be time for burial.

Jaime yelled, "Wait, Uncle!" The men paused. I watched intently as the dear boy reached into his pants pocket. He removed a figure of a stooped Jesus with a stylized crown of exaggerated thorns. He laid the silver crucifix gently on his mother's chest, near her heart. "God of My Mama..."

Jaime broke away from the coffin, ran to me, and collapsed in my arms. We clung tightly to each other, and finally, like the brewing dark storm clouds on the day Raul was reported missing, released torrents of tears.

Chapter 33

LIGAYA "LILING" UGALE

February 1946

I timed my arrival ninety seconds after Bartolome's entrance into the church sanctuary. I waited while he fastened his precious eyeglasses to his face using hemp cord. My brother dared not fire his weapons when his vision was out of focus. He had learned a powerful lesson from the incident in which he had machine-gunned a pair of Japanese-American soldiers. His fighting could never again be reckless and impulsive. Since then, Bartolome had developed into a proficient warrior who planned his offensive tactics in meticulous detail.

Bartolome and a high-ranking Americano military man, both part of an intelligence network, I think, held one of many clandestine meetings in the confessional of Father Benito's church. They continued their strategizing in whispers so churchgoers would think they were penitents making contrition. My brother posted me nearby as a guard. I was to pray the rosary very loudly if I saw anyone looking suspiciously like an enemy spy.

Who knows what they planned in secret? Soon after these meetings, I heard news reports of the sabotaging of Japon communication lines, bombing of a Japon weapons storage site, and major battles won by the Filipino guerrilla fighters. I wondered whether Bartolome had anything to do with these victories. Even if I asked him earnestly, I knew my brother was forbidden from speaking the truth.

Bartolome's guerrillas, loyal to the United States because of its promise to grant the Philippines their independence, were fiercely determined to avenge the Japon slaughter of civilians and the forcing of thousands of women into sexual slavery—comfort women, the Japanese called them.

Bartolome could take things very personally. My brother's underlying anger had mushroomed when Glory was murdered, an indirect victim of the war. His hatred was projected less toward Gilberto and more toward the Japon. The rape of his wife, Cora, gnawed at their relationship like a voracious cannibal. The Japanese had marred his daughter, Pacencia, the gem of his life, dulling her sparkle. He abhorred his alleged baby, Luisa Rose, who looked like the enemy.

"We are losing the war, Bart. We're outgunned, outmanned." I only heard the Americano soldier's words because I sat nearby, attentive.

"I will never, ever surrender. Never!" Bartolome punched the interior wall. "Let's go. I want to check the supplies. Then I transfer cigarillos to your vehicle."

The generous donations of tobacco products from Bartolome's small company held him in good stead with the allies who, in turn, supplied his underground militia. Cigarettes in exchange for modern artillery: guns, explosives, and radios. The two men exited the confessional, walking quickly past a surprised nun. I followed a short distance behind.

"Don't forget we need provisions," Bartolome reminded the soldier in still hushed tones.

"You'll find stuff in your shed, Bart." I surmised the Americano must be referring to the old tobacco curing shack from which our brother-in-law had been ejected.

"Hey, Bart! Got some dip?" The Americano turned the wad of tobacco in his mouth; a rivulet of spittle dripped down his chin. The soldier looked about, took careful aim, and fired a brown projectile into the largest spittoon he must have ever seen—the baptismal font.

. . .

I received news that Gilberto was incarcerated indefinitely without consideration for any of the psychiatric treatments he needed. Not much care or compassion existed for the insane in those days. The legal system was preoccupied with other war criminal matters. I tried to visit; after all, Berto had been Raul's best friend, my sister's husband, and Jaime's stepfather. Locked behind a thick metal door with huge steel rivets, he blathered something about a coconut. I never went back to the prison. Gilberto was literally locked away and forgotten.

. . .

Four years after The Event, the guerrilla fighters savagely resisted the Japon, forcing them to retreat into the mountains. Bartolome marshaled his Filipino comrades to move covertly through fields, jungles, and rocky terrain, waging war through underground aggression.

The villagers divided themselves into three groups and congregated once again around the only three radios in the barrio. News about Japan's surrender in August 1945 caused a mix of relief and joy with a sprinkling of doubt. Didn't Bartolome say there were hot spots still occupied by the most indomitable Japanese?

The announcer reported, "One million Filipinos, including tens of thousands of military men, have been killed during the war against the Japanese. Hundreds of bodies were left by the roadsides. Death has been caused not just by gunshot or explosion, but also by disease and starvation. Manila has been extensively damaged with many hectares decimated. Broken concrete, splintered lumber, glass shards, and stucco dust have settled where once stood historic, ornate, and stately buildings erected by the Spaniards. It is the end of World War II. Ladies and gentlemen, World War II has *ended* in the Philippines."

The peasants continued for a long time to live their daily lives with the same intensity of fear. World War II was over? Many could not be fully convinced. The Japon were still in hiding—Bartolome and other mountain-bound guerrillas were certain of it. Unsure and still filled with suspicions, the guerillas did not celebrate.

The radio announcer described a prideful US military parade in Manila. The city folks celebrated, joyfully crying out, "Americano! Americano! Americano!"

The villagers in the Chinese restaurant joined them and chanted, "Americano! Americano! Americano!"

Papang joined in the jubilation. "I have always said the Americanos are good people!" I shook my head.

I drew Jaime close to me. God of All People, may this boy grow up in a peaceful world."

Little Jaime turned to me in earnest. "No more war! Auntie, now we move Hawaii?"

PART III

CONSOLATION

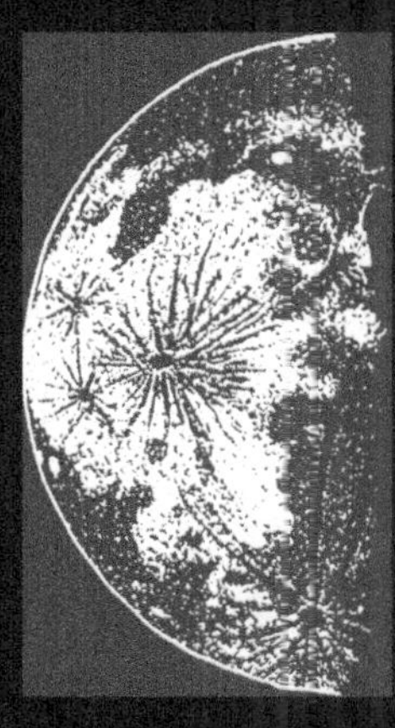

Chapter 34

AGAPITO "PITONG" MACADANGDANG

February 1946

On September 2, 1945, World War II had ended throughout the world with Japan formally signing the United States-prepared instrument of surrender. I was glad to finally be rid of my rank, Private First Class, since I had been ordered to perform scuttle work and had been called to battle in the worst conditions. Big rats had plagued us by raiding our rations, morsels in discarded tin cans. They even feasted on the rotting dead whose burials were postponed because we were busy in active combat.

A stray bullet grazed my right thigh. Some thought it was due to friendly fire. Hah! No way. I bragged that a Jap had attacked me. I showed off my scar. I stuck to my story—I fought so hard and moved so quickly that the enemy's bullet just scraped my skin.

Whenever I huddled in a trench, blasted Japs in the jungle, or slept in the barracks, my wild imagination comforted me with illusions of Salome. They sustained me on the worst of my army days.

I returned to my parents' town after my honorable discharge and looked forward to resuming the position of Sergeant-at-Arms. I had sharp instincts and could smell trouble like a trained hound dog. My reappointment gave me the compensation I needed to afford a family with my woman.

"Mother, Father, I'm eager to meet Salome. I dream of the day we will marry. I want to now secure my future with her."

My parents glanced at each other, anxious.

"You are the father; you tell him."

"You are the mother, and *you* chose Salome; you tell him." My father fled in a huff, slamming the door behind him.

"Spineless." Mother jabbed her hands on her hips.

"Tell me what, Mother?"

Mother enunciated her words in an exaggerated way that indicated I had to proceed cautiously. "I will tell you what has happened in the years since you joined the army, but only after our afternoon repast."

She took her time preparing coffee and coconut pastries. She moved like a *Philippine slow loris*, a sluggish creature.

Finally, my mother, settled in her rocker, smiled at me, clutched her mug, claimed the beverage was too hot, blew into the liquid to cool the coffee, set the mug aside, reached for a rice cake, and nibbled ever so slowly.

I cracked my knuckles, then cracked them again. I scratched the scar on my right thigh. I knew better than to rush my mother.

. . .

Usually a woman of many, many words, my mother fed me the short version of the disturbing news. "Salome is promiscuous. She may be a prostitute in the city."

My hand muscles slackened. I dropped my coffee cup. I howled, not just because hot liquid spilled on my lap; my fantasy about pure and chaste Salome had burst.

That was all my mother said. Back and forth, back and forth, she rocked and took another small bite of her pastry.

I refused to marry a woman with a tarnished reputation. A whore. That's how my mother described Salome.

I picked up the broken pieces of ceramic. "A contract is a contract. A covenant is a covenant. Salome should have kept her end of the marriage agreement."

My mother kept rocking and nibbling. Maddening.

No legal recourse for me. Nothing in writing. The business of arranging marriages between children belonged to the parents. This contract was struck long ago, and my parents had lost track of Salome's parents, rumored to have since died. Would she have still been available if I had come home after my first tour of duty?

What a fiasco! Salome had made me look like a circus clown. I'm thirty, too old for drama.

. . .

On one particular safety and security patrol of the town, I noticed a recruitment poster tacked onto a pole in the plaza. It was written in English; I sounded out the words phonetically.

> ATTENTION
> Sugar Plantation Hiring
> Able-Bodied Men Wanted
> Willing to Labor
> Includes Passage to Hawaii
> Up to Sixty-five Cents Per Day

As I tore the flyer down, the vessels in my neck pulsed fast and strong. Sakadas! World War II had interrupted the organized migration of unskilled Filipino laborers to the USA.

I showed the bulletin to my army buddies. "You see? I told you they need workers in Hawaii."

They all spoke at once.

"Pitong, let's go."

"I heard the wild animals there will gobble you up."

"What? What kinds of animals? You mean a whale?" My friends laughed.

"Pitong, that poster is a hoax. It sounds nice, but I bet they will make you a plantation slave," one said hesitantly.

"What do we know about sugar cane?" asked another Pinoy.

"I know farming," I said and waved the poster.

"You think growing sugar and growing rice are the same?"

"I don't care. This flyer says *sixty-five* cents per day. We will be rich. I'm ready for golden pineapples, golden beaches, and golden hula dancers."

• • •

When I applied to work for the plantation in 1946, I recognized that the broken marriage contract was a blessing. Salome, my shattered dream. The USA, my dream come true. I boarded the ship bound for Hawaii.

I accepted my appointment to an irrigator position. I pitied the Pinoys who immigrated to California. Instead of laboring for one employer, they moved with groups of Mexican migrant workers from farm to farm, and field to field. Imagine learning how to harvest many different crops: oranges, strawberries, grapes, cauliflower, asparagus, lettuce, and sugar beets.

At first, I regretted turning down higher wages at salmon fisheries and canneries in Alaska where the average temperature is thirty-seven degrees Fahrenheit. But I was satisfied working in balmy weather with one crop: sugar cane.

The bachelors' dormitory, decorated with pages from smut magazines, stank of smoke and local beer. I lived there with eleven other men from different Asian countries, speaking in broken English. My coworkers and I yacked all the time about sex. We compared the tiny Filipina "hens" to the voluptuous, topless, blonde and red-headed girlies on our walls.

Friday nights were a time for relaxation, crude jokes, and drinking.

"My girlfriend is small. Flat. I hate the way she make giggling. Her hand always make covering her mouth, make hiding the gold tooth in the front."

Laughter.

"Lucky some of you have *real* brides. Some of you have picture brides. Me, I have only dreams—mmm—of pink nipples in my mouth wondering if 'down there' is as red as her ponytail." More laughter.

Another Pinoy said, "Guess how I want to die." We shook our heads and shrugged our shoulders. He pointed to a busty brunette on a pornographic poster. "I pray to suffocate with my face between this rabbit's tits."

I said, "You mean bunnies, not rabbits. Ay, ay!" We elbowed each other and drank more beer.

After several weeks of debate, my friends decided white women were far sexier than their girlfriends back home. Pinays are conservative sexual partners, not open to experimentation. Missionary style only. No moaning, no screaming, no crude terms, just absolute quiet. If the Filipino man is too eager, the woman is guaranteed to say, "No. Jesus is watching."

In America, white women preferred white men. It was rare for a Caucasian woman to date a Filipino man. First of all, she was taller. She did not speak pidgin, and if from the mainland, she was impatient with our thick accents. White women did not think we earned enough money. Complained that we workers had rough hands. I couldn't marry a white woman—not anyone smarter or more cultured than me. Worst of all, their gossip—Filipino men had small penises.

I also would not marry a Japanese female. I saw the damage of World War II; I simply hated the Japs.

A few of my friends abandoned their Filipino wives and families back in the Philippines and took up with local Hawaiian or Chinese barmaids.

I wrote my parents, asking if they would kindly search the region for spousal candidates, for I desired a wife. Four weeks later, I received a letter from my mother stating that, in fact, she had found someone very special, and this time, my father fully approved. I ripped open the envelope containing Mother's correspondence, eager to know more about the arranged marriage. The chatty nature of her letter annoyed me.

> Pitong, my dear,
>
> Are you eating well, my son? The baby carabao died. Your uncle in California married a Mexican lady. Will I ever see him again? I cry. Your other uncle is freezing in Alaska. Don't worry, he said. He wears thermal underwear, fur coat, gloves, scarf, beanie, thick socks, and heavy boots. What is snow? What means thermal? What means beanie? The Hawaii plantations recruited more laborers. Remember your cousin in the barrio? He is going to Ho-no-ka—Ho-ka-ka—Ka-ko-ha— Wa-ki-hu. Anyway, a place that starts with the letter H or K or W. Is that near you? Make sure you welcome him.

Mother. Almost every place in Hawaii starts with an H or K or W. Ah...at last. About the girl...

> Who would not want to marry you, my hardworking, generous son? Thank you for the ten pesos you sent us.

Blah, blah, blah. Ma, come on already.

> The MAIDEN is Ligaya Valeria Cruz Ugale. Liling for short. Be a good boy. Don't forget to pray. God bless you.
>
> Mother

I am sure my mother capitalized the word "Maiden" so I would be certain my potential wife was pure and chaste. Like the majority of Filipino parents, my mother ended her letter, "God bless you." Not "I love you"—a phrase too sickly sweet for the older generation. My parents understood duty, obedience, respect, and caring. Love could not mean both bonding with children and romantic love, so they hardly ever said the word at all.

I immediately replied.

> Mother and Father,
>
> I met a Mrs. Ugale, but she said Gloriana is her daughter's name, not Ligaya. I am arriving soon to meet my betrothed.
>
> Pitong

• • •

Our Caucasian plantation supervisor purchased a brand-new automobile and drove around the camp to show it off. I whistled when I saw it and came up with a scheme I believed would make Ligaya fall in love with me. It took courage, but I asked my supervisor for the use of his car.

"Oh, no. No one can drive this car except me."

I made a request. "I like take poto [photo]."

"Poto?"

Like other Filipino immigrants, I rolled my Rs and tended to mix up my F and P sounds.

"You want to use my car as a prop in pictures? Oh, good idea. I got fins and chrome, the latest model."

Just as I reached to slide my hand across its teal blue body, my supervisor squawked, "Don't touch it. I don't want fingerprints on the wax job." So, I went for the door handle. "Stop. Don't go inside the car. The fabric—I don't want any darkie to dirty the upholstery."

I felt disappointed. I wanted to show Ligaya how handsome I

looked behind the steering wheel.

I borrowed a summer suit. The shoulder pads and peak lapels made me look huskier. The straw fedora was my supervisor's idea. My foot was positioned on the tire near the driver's side, right elbow on my raised knee. I looked and felt rich.

"Smile." My supervisor snapped my photo with his Brownie box camera.

Who knew how long it would take for the postal service to carry my letter to the remote village? I planned to hand-deliver my picture to Ligaya.

On the back, I wrote *Love, Aggie*. Much more American than *Pitong*.

• • •

Many of the workers lived frugally and put away every spare penny—some banked at the credit union and others hid their savings. One idiot lined his pouch of tobacco leaves with cash. One night, in an alcohol-induced stupor, he rolled himself a cigar, not realizing until the next morning that he had smoked away all of his life savings. I was one of the smart ones who understood the concept of compound interest. My savings grew enough to afford a visit back to the Philippines.

On the evening before departure, my friends paid for a round of beer at my "Aloha Party."

"Lucky you."

One drunken pal begged, "Bring back a wife for me."

A roommate asked me to join him in conspiring to be deceitful to his wife. "Tell my spouse and family I am coming to get them pretty soon," he said as he played with his mistress' fingers.

"I'm not going to lie for you." He shrugged his shoulders.

"Don't, eh, puck [fuck] too much."

"We'll miss you at the bachelor's dorm."

"No. We won't."

Everybody laughed. "Is your long eggplant still working? Use it or loose [lose] it."

Chapter 35

AGAPITO "PITONG" MACADANGDANG

February 1947

I flew back to the Philippines one year after relocating to Hawaii, eager to meet Ligaya and arrange my marriage to her. On the flight, I reflected upon my time in Hawaii. Plantation work was hard, but I earned much more money than any nonprofessional in the Philippines. I learned all the stages of farming sugar—planting, growing, ripening, and harvesting. Harvesting required setting massive fires to burn the outer leaves. I almost burned to death in a wild cane blaze—except for that near tragedy, I felt grateful for making the decision to immigrate.

Something seemed to be amiss when I arrived.

My mother paced. "Did you not get our telegram?"

"No. Something wrong, *again?* Did I waste my time and money crossing the Pacific to be here?"

She handed me a yellow form with a carbon copy of her message.

> "Son. Stop. Don't come. Stop. Liling used goods.
> Stop. Ma. Stop."

It was unlike Mother to spend the money for a telegram, unlike her to communicate so concisely.

Father spoke up, "We told you Ligaya is pure and chaste. We are upset because we discovered she is a victim of wartime rape."

"You only found out recently?"

"Yes, Pitong. We read about The Event long ago, but the village is so far away from our town we did not see a connection. I'm sorry. And—"

"There's more?"

"Ligaya's sister, Gloriana—you had mentioned you met their mother, Mrs. Maria Ugale. Well, Gloriana had a child out of wedlock with a man who abandoned her. She then married a soldier who turned crazy and murdered her." My father circled the air around his ear with his index finger, then drew it across his throat. "Her son, Jaime, is well-behaved, but no one except Gloriana knew who the father was."

I slumped into the nearest chair. What melodrama!

Mother said softly, "I'm sorry, Son. Be patient and we will find another more suitable woman for you."

"So, that is all, Son. Now you must decide whether you want to pursue this marriage."

The first question out of my mouth was, "Is she beautiful?" A stupid question. Truthfully, the loss of the sweetly exotic Salome, as I had always imagined her, still upset me. Even though we were strangers and had never met, I believed she had betrayed me.

"Yes, she is pretty."

"How pretty?" Another immature question.

Father shrugged. "She has black hair and brown eyes."

I groaned. My father did not care much about looks, only that the woman I would marry be Filipina and Catholic.

Mother said, "Ligaya had many suitors. I heard that even the Americano doctor's son pursued her. Does that not tell you she is a catch?"

"Mother, Father, I will try. I am an old bachelor. You both say she is good-looking and intelligent. Malicious gossip—I won't let that faze me. The Event affected every female in that village. If a woman was not raped in body, she was raped in mind. The Event—I'm sure Ligaya is a strong survivor because of it."

I took a deep breath. "I, Agapito Macadangdang, will marry Ligaya Valeria Cruz Ugale."

Chapter 36

AGAPITO "PITONG" MACADANGDANG

February 1947

I walked the three miles to the Ugale home, being careful not to step in the carabao patties. It had been one year since I had left for Hawaii. I was excited to return to my barrio.

I was dressed in khaki pants, which Mother had ironed for me, and a light-yellow Hawaiian print shirt showing palm trees and surfboards.

When I arrived, I stood for a moment, wiped the sweat from my forehead, cleared my throat, and called up to the open, unscreened window for Ligaya's mother. The Ugales' hut was one of the older ones, with narrow gaps between the walls of bamboo slats fastened side to side. The roof looked newly thatched with nipa grass. A black dog leashed by rope to a large mango tree by rope sniffed at the baskets of vegetables I was carrying. The dog growled and I playfully yipped back.

"Benedicto! Benny. Benny!" a woman scolded. She shooed the dog away. Mrs. Ugale did not appear to have aged at all since the last time I saw her in 1942.

I waved. "Nana Ugale, ma'am, my father grew these vegetables and I harvested them." I used a respectful tone. Mr. Ugale nodded, indicating I had scored points.

Mrs. Ugale accepted the basket that included squash, eggplant, bitter melon, lima beans, and long green beans. "Thank you, Agapito. What beautiful squash! It has been a while since we have had so many fresh vegetables."

"My siblings and I shelled the lima beans ourselves. I have a young adult brother and a teen sister."

Ligaya stopped crocheting for a moment but did not look up. Her father was seated but leaned heavily on his cane.

Mrs. Ugale peered at me closely. "Oh, Agapito. When I met your parents during the marriage arrangement, I did not realize you were the intended groom. How could I not remember? You and I had a nice chat a while back."

"Please, ma'am. Please call me Pitong. I remember you were looking for Santiago, and I was looking for Salome."

"Certainly, Pitong. This is my husband." Mr. Ugale faltered as he attempted to rise from his mahogany armchair.

What is Respicio Ugale's nickname? Almost everybody in the Philippines earns a nickname, which Westerners find peculiar—Boy, Boboy, Dodong, Dong-Dong, Munding. *Peping? Pepe?* I peered at the old man. Mr. Respicio Ugale did not look like a Tata Pepe.

Mr. Ugale struggled to stand, but I walked quickly to shake his hand in formal greeting. He looked frail, but he squeezed my hand a little too firmly and for a little too long. He looked deep into my eyes.

"My name is Respicio Ugale. Respicio means *respect.*" I am glad I wisely decided against the informality of nicknames. What hidden meaning was Respicio trying to convey? *Conduct yourself in an honorable manner, or else?*

A little boy pointed to himself and impatiently asked, "How about me, Lola?"

"You must wait, Jaime. I did not forget you."

I smiled at the boy.

"This cute little character," said Mrs. Ugale, "is our grandson."

He turned to me. "Hello, Tata." In practiced English, the boy said, "My name is Jaime Luna Ugale. I'm pleased to meet you, sir."

"How polite you are! Tell me, do you like vegetables? I brought a big basketful."

"I did not like vegetables, but now I eat them for not to be blind like Uncle Bartolome or crooked like Lolong."

"Oh!" I was caught off guard. Ligaya smiled.

"Jaime! Come help me." Mrs. Ugale was busy readying a tray of warm colas. I knew they must have spent a lot on the sodas to make a good impression. "Now, Jaime." The boy skipped to the kitchen table and tiptoed to place Filipino pastry on a platter. Benny entered the hut sniffing about for treats.

A funereal photo was tacked to the wall. I could see that Ligaya looked very sad, but her eyes were not puffy. "I was very sorry to hear about Gloriana, ma'am. I never saw Santiago again after you made your inquiry. My deepest condolences." I felt sympathy for everyone there; this family might be my family.

"Ay, Apo Dios." Mrs. Ugale made the sign of the cross.

Ligaya gave her mother a puzzled look.

"I must confess," said Mrs. Ugale, "I never told anyone about my search for Santiago. Our eldest daughter was—"

"My mama is in heaven!" announced Jaime.

I sensed discomfort and quickly said, "Again, my deepest condolences. May God bless you in your grief."

"And you, Pitong, did you ever locate Salome?"

"No, ma'am."

The mood was somber in the hut. Thankfully, Mrs. Ugale quickly changed the subject by introducing her daughter. "Of course, I would like you to meet your intended, Ligaya." The woman blushed.

She was indeed pretty, not gorgeous by American Hollywood standards, but her face did not hurt my eyes. She cocked her head. I knew she was listening.

"Nana and Tata Ugale, as you know, I have come from Hawaii

where I currently reside in bachelor quarters. I plan to move into a plantation house, which will need a woman's touch."

I was careful with my words. I tried to convey much information in only two sentences—I was employed and lived in the United States, saving money for a home. I was lonely, tired of being single, and looking for a wife.

"Liling is skilled at many things, son." A shrewd sales pitch. Mrs. Ugale said *son*, indicating I had garnered her acceptance and affection. Additionally, her use of Ligaya's nickname gave me permission to be less formal.

I tested the use of Ligaya's informal name. "Liling, your crocheted curtains are lovely." No one cringed. I studied the window coverings while offering the "sideways" compliment. I hoped Ligaya caught the hint that I thought she was lovely. Courtship in the Philippines was a convoluted, slow-motion game.

Mrs. Ugale spread a bit of butter on the sweet roll and then stirred my coffee with the butter knife.

"Beautiful," I said as the yellow globules of floating fat melted into the coffee. I was again referring to Liling, whom I hoped realized the compliments were indirectly meant for her. She resumed her crocheting at an excitable, faster pace. "I mean, crocheted curtains like those would make the house look very fine and fancy."

"You work?" Ligaya's father finally spoke.

"Yes, sir." Enough about window coverings. "I work as a sugar cane irrigator. I hear that your son, Felipe, also works for a plantation."

"Uncle Boy was almost killed near Pearl Harbor," Jaime chimed in.

"I was in the military here. Private First Class."

"First Class! I want to be a first class private, and a priest, and a doctor, and a fisher like my mama. What is it like in Hawaii?"

"Hawaii is warm like the Philippines. I wish more of our people could move there. Food on the table every day. You can own a real house made of wood, not straw, and I am owning a vehicle now."

"We studied Hawaii. My mama and me, we wanted to go." The boy's shoulders slumped. "But the war. Then she died."

Ligaya opened her arms and Jaime quickly stepped into them. Woman and child embraced. It was the remedy Glory's son needed to soothe his momentary grief. He then brightened and ran toward the door.

"I'm going to play bati-cobra with Vicente."

Ligaya called after him, "Be careful, Jaime." She finally spoke.

I did not expect my reaction to her nurturing response; I was touched by her tenderness. Her voice was melodious; smooth and sweet like the melted butter in my coffee. I fell in love with her then.

Chapter 37

LIGAYA "LILING" UGALE

February 1947

I lifted my hand to my cheek, which felt warm to the touch. I was under Pitong's scrutiny. I glanced toward our visitor, hoping not to catch his eye. *Oh, God! He's staring at me.* I looked away quickly but was unable to resist turning back. *He's still looking at me!* I felt more than just flushed; I felt feverish.

Gloriana used to tease me about having too high expectations of men. She warned that it would doom me to forever remain an old maid. I had a history of quickly dismissing potential suitors, including Dr. Billet's son, who had been persistent in trying to court me. I rejected them if they had even a tiny bit of dirt under their fingernails. Agapito had to pass my inspection. I so wanted to take the time to study him.

I had told myself that if Agapito's fingernails were clean and well-groomed, it would be God's sign that the match was meant to be. I peered in Pitong's direction, but not at his face this time. His fingers were not stubby. Slender yet manly. No hair on the knuckles. His fingernails were short and unsoiled. In fact, they sparkled. Confirmation from God.

My gaze moved from Agapito's hands to his face. Our eyes met and I gasped. Was it attraction that made my heart flutter? Or was it my feelings of guilt at letting go of Raul?

I love you, Raul, but you have gone from me. Send me a sign that you approve.

Papang said, "I heard that you were almost killed."

"Yes, sir."

"Oh! Tata, please, tell us the story." Jaime leaned forward.

Agapito adjusted his posture. "It was harvest time, an unusually dry period. We were burning cane to get rid of the dried leaves on the sugar stalks." Agapito peered at Jaime. "You see, the stalks are full of raw, liquid sugar, so they don't burn."

"I love chewing on sugar cane," said Jaime. "So sweet."

"The wind picked up and shifted. I was trapped in the middle of the field."

"Oh my! How did you get out?" Mamang turned her good ear toward Agapito.

"I jumped into the irrigation ditch."

Agapito continued. He was a master storyteller.

"And then?" asked Jaime. There was a pause. "And then?"

"I heard a voice—it said, *Be still.*"

My crochet needle clattered to the floor. I jerked my head up. What?

Pitong said, "I heard the voice clearly. I looked around and could see no one. And then the voice sounded again, *Be still.*"

"Ay, Apo Dios."

"I closed my eyes, crossed my arms over my chest, and stiffened my body like a log." Agapito demonstrated. "Slow-moving water took me under the flames. I heard explosions. I felt the water heating up. I thought I was going to boil to death."

"Oh, my. And then?" Mamang stopped eating.

Jaime shushed Benny so that he could hear. "What happened?"

"I was afraid of drowning because the flow of water turned rapid. I choked. I hit several small boulders and felt my skin split. My body was hurled against the granite with terrible force. I thought my bones were going to break the way a tree trunk can sometimes splinter in a logging river."

Agapito looked around at his audience, who was captivated by his dangerous adventure. No one interrupted.

"I wasn't sure how far I was going, or whether the fire had jumped to another field. I only knew I could barely breathe."

"Like asthma?"

"Yes, Jaime, very much like asthma. I was wheezing and I had pain in my chest. I coughed a lot."

"I have asthma." He demonstrated breathing through pursed lips.

"Burning sugar cane leaves fell from the atmosphere. It looked like black snow. I heard what sounded like bombs and missiles, frightened men yelling—some terrified and some with authority. It reminded me so much of World War II."

"Ay, Apo Dios," Mamang said again. She clutched her ever-present rosary. Jaime scooted closer to the storyteller.

"And then I got stuck in the ditch blocked by an irrigation gate. I thought for certain my life was over. The battleground noises subsided, and suddenly I felt a rescuer grab me under the arms and pull me to safety. I must have been disoriented and fighting him off because this time the voice said reassuringly. '*Be still. I am here.*' "

I choked and dropped my crochet work. My eyes were moist.

Agapito continued. "I coughed and dirty water was released from my nose and throat. God saved my life."

A flashback to the last time Raul and I were together. His last words to me. I placed my hand upon my heart, the last place he had touched me. *Raul has sent me a sign of approval.*

I took a deep breath and stood with confidence. "Mamang, Papang, please inform Mr. Agapito Macadangdang that I would be happy to crochet his curtains."

...

I could not help comparing Agapito with Raul. Pitong was shorter, darker, less playful. He smiled less, but it was brilliant when he did so. A hard worker, certainly, but not well read. No plans to attend university. A little socially awkward and nervous at times, as if a military order to stand at attention was suddenly going to disrupt the moment.

Whereas my match with Raul was made in heaven, the couple consisting of Agapito and me was a match made on earth.

...

A Filipino daughter's family needed an adequate period, sometimes months, even years, to assess the beau's suitability. The elders, especially, gave due consideration to his respectfulness, work ethic, and family values. Could the man support a wife and afford a home? Would he care for his parents and his in-laws in their old age? Would he be a good father? Was he a diligent worker? Was he ambitious? Did he waste his money on beer? Were his teeth stained from tobacco? Did he have a wandering eye? Was he able to save his earnings?

Time was insufficient to fully evaluate Agapito. My family and I only knew he went beyond expectation by shelling the lima beans, he owned a vehicle, he would settle in his house with a wife, and he used kind words to describe my crocheted curtains.

My extended family weighed in. Auntie Soledad interpreted his words and gestures, not as industry or generosity but as a way to bamboozle the family into acceptance without proper vetting. There were no obvious indications that Agapito possessed any negative traits. However, an astute observer might have assumed he had a quick temper, for as he departed, Pitong kicked dirt at the aggressive dog, Benny, who was gentle around the Ugales. Mamang said she heard growling. Was it the dog or the man?

Chapter 38

AGAPITO "PITONG" MACADANGDANG

March 1947

I considered myself fortunate that my parents had selected a good-looking, Filipino, Catholic woman, but she was already almost thirty. For a short while, I had trepidations about having perhaps accepted old, unwanted goods. I did not have wet dreams about Ligaya.

Our cyclonic courtship lasted only three weeks because I was mandated to return to Hawaii by the end of the month to resume sugar plantation work. My parents believed Ligaya was eager to pursue the relationship because she was approaching the age when conceiving and childbearing might be difficult.

An engagement required numerous meetings between the families. Even though I was thirty-one, custom dictated that the parents accompany the son to make a formal appeal to marry the daughter. I did this in the presence of all Ligaya's maternal and paternal uncles while the aunties twittered in the kitchen corner preparing coffee and treats. Mr. and Mrs. Ugale joyously gave me their blessing.

Unlike the American tradition in which the bride's side pays for most of the wedding expenses, in the Philippines the groom's parents shoulder the responsibility. At a subsequent meeting, both our families discussed finances, guest lists, the date, venue, and wedding details.

Mr. Ugale had splurged and bought cola for his guests, which my parents and I, following Filipino convention, politely refused.

"Oh, how very kind of you," Mother said.

Mrs. Ugale then insisted. It was part of the protocol.

"You must be thirsty after your long trip. You came such a distance. Please." Mrs. Ugale gracefully waved her hand over the distinctive bottles of ebony liquid as if she were a beauty pageant queen at the fiesta.

"You went through so much trouble for us. We appreciate your hospitality." Though quite thirsty, still we did not help ourselves to the beverages.

"Thank you. Oh, but no, thank you," Father chimed in.

"Go ahead. We insist." Mr. Ugale was such an accommodating host.

"We want you to be comfortable in our home," said Mrs. Ugale. "After all, we will be family soon."

"Well then, if you insist," my mother said. Still, we Macadangdangs did not reach for the drink.

Mrs. Ugale opened the bottle and poured the fizzing room temperature beverage into coffee cups. "Here you go."

Good manners. It was a prolonged act of give and take, push and pull. To accept an offering too soon was egocentric, showing lack of constraint. Filipinos believed that rushing to partake meant one was too hungry, too thirsty, and therefore at poverty level. On the other hand, to not partake at all would have been an insult, for the host had spent good money trying to make a positive impression. It was the culturally correct way to do things.

The dowry included payment for a passport and visa, ground transportation to the airport, and airfare to Hawaii. I also gave the Ugale family, for the length of Ligaya's life, the use of one hectare, almost two and one-half acres, of the rice fields I still owned in the

Philippines. They could use all harvested grain as food for themselves or sell the rice to make some money. A water buffalo calf, a pig, and a dozen chicks enhanced the dowry package. I also promised Ligaya's parents that I would have our home ready by the time she relocated.

Mr. and Mrs. Ugale gasped when they heard me describe my gifts; they were more than pleased and thanked me profusely. Ligaya was not getting younger. They remarked how fortunate their daughter was to be marrying a man who was generous, had a steady job, owned a house and a vehicle. The Ugales' reputation would soar simply by association. Their daughter was moving to the United States of America.

...

Filipinos living in the poverty-stricken, rural parts of the country were still financially and emotionally recovering from the war. All parties understood it was prudent to keep things simple. Mr. and Mrs. Ugale were very agreeable to almost everything my parents suggested, lest I withdraw my proposal and they end up with an old maid of a daughter. My mother and father were relieved when Mr. and Mrs. Ugale agreed to their recommendations because they secretly had an extremely limited budget.

"One more thing to discuss," Mr. Ugale said with authority. "Jaime is an orphan now that his mother is gone. We do not know who his father is. Maria and I are getting old and we will not be able to raise him for long."

"Yes?" I said anxiously.

"Liling wants to adopt him, and we are asking you to be a father to Jaime."

I glanced at my parents.

"We shall leave the decision to you, Son," my father said.

Everyone stared at me. "I must think about this new development and will give you my answer shortly."

After a time, Mrs. Ugale, trying not to show her anxiety, said pleasantly, "You may go for a walk now. How about the town square?"

I smiled. At last, some time alone with my betrothed; I had many questions for Liling. I'm sure Ligaya, who had been sitting demurely with her back very straight, legs crossed at the ankles, with folded hands on her lap, also had many questions for me.

I called out, "Jaime? Would you like to come with your Auntie Liling and me to the plaza?"

Jaime whooped and ran to hold my hand.

Liling and I stood simultaneously, and a split second later Ligaya's aunties ran to put on their walking slippers. I felt disappointed but chuckled—two adults—still chaperoned.

...

Ligaya and I strolled leisurely. The four old, chattering females followed behind us. Jaime held hands, first with me, then with Liling; he never came between us. Auntie Soledad and the others kept their distance but watched us with hawk eyes. Feeling like teenagers, we schemed to break away from our entourage of chaperones. With Jaime in tow, we sprinted toward a crowded food court, leaving the aunties behind; some like cross hens and others like panting old donkeys.

The three of us laughed. Then we looked behind and laughed some more. I handed Ligaya an envelope, which she quickly slipped into her purse just as the most physically fit of the aunties rounded the corner.

Her auntie Soledad gave us a good scolding. "Two people so juvenile and disrespectful perhaps should not be getting married."

Jaime did a somersault. I started, "I am Romeo."

Liling caught on and in exceedingly dramatic voice called out, "Oh, Romeo, Romeo, wherefore art thou, Romeo?"

Auntie Soledad harrumphed.

We had so much fun, then apologized profusely. To atone for my teasing, I asked Jaime, "What do you think I should do to guarantee the old aunties' forgiveness?"

"I know. I know." He skipped quickly to a colorful booth where the hawker was selling a cold dessert. I treated everyone to *halo-halo*.

The jackfruit, bananas, mangos, layered over cracked ice and then drenched with sweet condensed milk, were refreshing after the chase. It was enough to appease the relatives, especially Auntie Soledad, whom I hoped would report that Ligaya was fortunate to be marrying such a thoughtful and generous man.

Jaime ate the extra cherry that the vendor gave only to him and licked his lips. He hooked arms with his Auntie Liling and looked earnestly at me.

"Mister. Tata? Will you marry me and be my daddy?"

Chapter 39

LIGAYA "LILING" UGALE

March 1947

I loved my sister so much that I wanted to fulfill her wishes. Gloriana had dreamed of immigrating to the United States to escape poverty and pursue a better life for her son. Pitong and I discussed the pros and cons of adopting Jaime. If we left my nephew in the Philippines, he would likely have to quit school and work on the farm. A bright and energetic youngster deserved a fine education and all the opportunities the USA had to offer.

"Pitong, I will understand if you do not wish to complete this process of marrying me. I will talk to my parents about releasing you from the marriage contract so you can find the woman you desire, one without a ready-made family."

"Liling, there is nothing I want more than to parent with you. Will you accept me as Jaime's father?"

"Thank you. I love you more and more every day. Come; let's go tell our little boy the good news."

...

I felt overjoyed when Pitong said he was eager to marry and found it easy to accept the idea of adopting Jaime. Especially because of this, I fell in love with him.

With deliberate care, I opened the envelope Pitong had secretively handed me. I pulled out a black and white photograph. In it, my fiancé was wearing a white summer suit, aloha shirt, and fedora.

I pressed my thumb on the photo where the car ornament was printed, as if claiming the vehicle as my own. I traced the fender on the shiny, sleek automobile. Pitong's elevated foot was posed on the tire and his elbow was perched on his bent knee. He looked as sharp as the car.

Settling in the Buick next to my handsome husband, wearing a sun hat and dark glasses like the starlets of Hollywood, was what I envisioned. I pressed my fingers to my lips to stifle a girlish reaction. The God of Goodness was being good to me.

Pitong agreed to parent Jaime, but he informed me he would like us to have children of our own. I scrutinized his likeness, then tried to imagine what our offspring might look like. Our children would have black hair and brown eyes; that was a given. I hoped they wouldn't inherit Pitong's bushy eyebrows and shorter stature. I especially prayed they wouldn't be as dark-skinned; I wanted to blame his olive-colored arms and face upon the Hawaiian sun and not on his genes. Pitong should be clean-chested, with no hairy buttocks. For if we have a son, I did not want him to remind me of the ugly Japanese Gorilla or Fuku, the Oriental Bull.

I wanted our daughters, if so blessed, to have his cute nose and full lips.

I would have wanted Pitong to be taller and more rugged-looking. But he drove a new automobile, admired my crocheting, had clean fingernails, and agreed to adopt Jaime; that was enough for me.

I flipped the photograph over and was amused. In very fancy but legible letters, my soon-to-be husband, Agapito Macadangdang, had written with a flourish—*Love, Aggie.*

Chapter 40

LIGAYA "LILING" UGALE

March 1947

My sister's death left a crater in my heart. Thoughts of Gloriana wafted in and out of my awareness every day. On the eve of my wedding, the sadness caused by her absence became acutely intense. Oh, Glory, how different life is than we had planned! I miss you. Sister, I love you. I promise to take care of Jaime.

Memories of Gilberto stabbed me, like he had stabbed Glory. My jaw tightened. You would have been our best man. Something happened in the war to make you go crazy. What? And why, why did you murder my sister? I loved you. Now I hate you.

The moon, my companion, had offered solace and hope every lonely night since Raul left for the army. It witnessed my daily ritual—laying my hand over my left breast and whispering, "Be still, my love. I am here."

My connection to Raul faded in bits. I became desperate to lock his image into my brain for I owned no photo of my beloved. I tried but could no longer feel bonded to him. Rumination about the *What ifs*—what if you and I were marrying instead? What if we had children?—plagued me. My determination to abandon such thoughts sometimes waned. Abstaining from focusing on Raul made me feel like a traitor, but I had to do it.

Like a child on Christmas Eve, Jaime was restless, unable to sleep. To be a "ring guard" became the sole subject of his chatter, so excited was he.

Coughing. Coughing some more. Papang awoke almost immediately. He had learned a powerful lesson the day Jaime almost died of respiratory distress, while he was sleeping off a beer binge. He hobbled to Jaime's mat and stood watching a long time.

Fog shrouded my sleep; I was exhausted but still alert like other "new" mothers. "God of Asthma, please keep Jaime healthy. Do not take his breath away. I am to be wed tomorrow. Amen."

...

My wedding dress fell just below the knees, a short, white button-down, more reminiscent of a nurse's uniform than a bridal frock. I refused to spend a centavo on anything I would wear only once. A sheer, white mantilla and simple shoes with thick, clumsy heels completed my look.

No money for a formal bouquet. Father Benito, now looking much older, hastily pulled three plastic lilies from the church's stock of Easter decorations for my use—the first act of kindness the priest extended toward me. I politely declined. Jaime had picked a nosegay of jasmine, his mother's favorite flower. What a lovely gesture! The scent was a sign that Glory was with me today.

Papang wept when he saw me. "Today I am happy that you will start a new life with a good man. Liling, I give you a father's love." Papang and I hugged. He kissed my forehead. I do not remember him being this affectionate with me. I was touched. It was his roundabout way of saying I love you. I would treasure this moment; he rarely shared his sentiments.

"You will walk me down the aisle, yes, Papang?"

"Oh, how I want to, but I'm afraid I will be too slow, or I will stumble and embarrass you."

"Papang, I want very much for us to walk *each other*. We will move carefully."

My father nodded and smiled.

Chapter 41

AGAPITO "PITONG" MACADANGDANG

March 1947

I had packed the only three T-shirts and three aloha shirts I owned.

My younger brother asked, "What will it be? The Filipino shirt or the tuxedo?"

"I'm going to wear Americano style. I prefer the look of success."

I studied my original pick, the *barong Tagalog*, a traditional embroidered shirt. But then my long-time friend had let me borrow the white tuxedo he used while working in the dance band, playing sax.

My brother took a sip of his beer and gave a critique of the formal suit. "That jacket is a bit too wide for your shoulders."

"But the lengths of the sleeves and trousers are just right," I said.

"Stripes of black satin on the pant seams and the jacket collar. You know that black is bad luck for weddings, right?"

I shrugged. "Yes, but it is mostly white with only a little black. If I am granted mostly good luck, I will be able to tolerate a bit of bad luck."

"You know, I would be happy to be your best man. I am your best man, right, Brother Pitong?"

"Yes, I consider you my best man. Best at getting into trouble," I chided.

My brother stuck out his lower lip.

"I'm sorry. If times were better, of course, you would be my official best man at the wedding." Liling and I did not plan to have a wedding party of attendants and groomsmen. Our bridesmaids would not be maidens, after all.

"Nah. No other musicians in the band wear my size; I wouldn't have a tuxedo to wear."

We laughed.

"Well, good luck, Pitong. You're going to need it."

"Ha, ha." I threw the Filipino shirt at my brother.

...

It was as if a magician had cast a spell on my money and made it disappear; I had used up all of my savings for my travel and dowry. No wedding ring could be afforded, not yet. My early arrival at the church gave me time to relax my nerves as I wandered into the sanctuary. I found a handmade poster on the bulletin board next to the baptismal font.

One Ring for Weddings. Fair Barter.
~~One Two Three Four~~ Five Six Seven Eight Nine Ten

"Pitong?" I spun around, surprised to find a young but haggard-looking woman at the entrance to the nave, holding a skinny newborn. She had two other scrawny children in tow.

"Yes?"

"You need a ring, Pitong?"

On my guard. "How do you know my name?" My voice sounded harsh.

"I happened to read your banns of marriage in the church bulletin. That's how I discovered your wedding is scheduled for today."

"I see." I tried to wear my Sergeant-of-Arms face.

The stranger laughed. "No, we do not know each other, but we know *of* each other."

"What?"

"We were supposed to get married, Agapito. I'm Salome."

"Salome?" Disbelief in my voice. My parents had described her as a loose woman, a prostitute.

"Yes, we were supposed to get married."

"My parents lost track of you."

"The connection between us broke when my parents died."

Should I say, *Oh, I've had dreams about you, Salome?* She'd had a special effect on me. And others? A seductress who so easily cast a spell over men. I was taken aback. The woman standing before me did not appear anything like the object of my dreams. Fatigue, defeat had taken away from her beauty. With three children so close together, I imagined her body doughy, with stretch marks. Her loose abdomen spilled over the waistline of her skirt. And a cleft lip. *Stop staring at it*, I scolded myself.

"Waiting for you made me impatient. No one knew where you were or the date of your return so that we could meet and marry."

"Fighting in the war." To be warm toward this woman was not easy. Could she have been traumatized by The Event and other horrors of World War II? Exposed to broken man-boys, sour and immature? Did they focus on her cleft lip and want her only for sexual favors?

I tried to be sympathetic to her need to escape to the city where she consorted with many men, perhaps in search of love, safety, and security. I was supposed to be the husband who provided those things to her.

"Will you allow me to lend you my wedding ring for some food, Pitong? A chicken, or a few eggs, or some vegetables for my pinakbet. My children are hungry. My husband is in jail. In the Philippines, I cannot divorce him."

It took me a few moments to fathom the gravity of her circumstances.

"You would be my number five," the woman said.

"What?"

"You would be my number five. Number five wedding, that is. Nobody can afford rings, Pitong. Not after the war. So, they borrow mine—only for the ceremony, of course. There is no shame in that. I help you; you help me. I need to feed my children."

Ring for rent. The woman looked too destitute to own a ring of genuine gold.

"And your husband, he does not mind?"

The woman shook her head. "I have not told him."

I waited expectantly. She took a cue from my silence and said she had met her husband in a strip club. He was Middle Eastern, a Muslim from the southernmost island of the Philippines. Tall with chiseled features. I asked her what she did for a living.

"Dancer."

She said that, at first, he watched over her with love and protection, but it had turned into jealousy, ownership, and manipulation. The woman's husband became her security guard, bouncer, pimp, and lover.

"In jail, you said?"

"For stealing goods from the strip club. They pay hardly anything, and we were starving."

Feeling generous and having pity for the family standing in front of me, I said, "I will give you food from our wedding luncheon. Today, you do not starve. You will feast."

"I am grateful." The woman placed the gold band with the tiny diamond chip into my palm. "Your bride, she is a lucky woman, Pitong."

"Lucky marrying a man with no ring to give?"

"She is lucky to be marrying at all due to the shortage of eligible men." During and after World War II, the ratio of men to women was lopsided, so many men had been killed.

To ward off misfortune, Filipinos believe the groom should not be allowed to see the bride prior to the matrimonial service, so I was not given the chance to explain why Ligaya would have to give back the piece of jewelry.

I carefully slipped the gold ring on the cord that had at one time carried Jaime's silver crucifix. "Secure this with your life, okay, Jaime?"

The young "ring guard," playing pirate, saluted and promised, "Aye, aye, sir. With my life."

Chapter 42

AGAPITO "PITONG" MACADANGDANG

March 1947

We were simple people—the wedding service had to be simple. Liling and I decided to stick with tradition and included several Filipino rituals in our wedding. First, Ligaya, Jaime, and I each drew light with tapered candles from the "unity flame" to symbolize the inclusion of Gloriana's son in our family.

After the lighting ceremony, Mr. and Mrs. Hidalgo, as our sponsors or godparents, draped Mrs. Ugale's white mantilla over our shoulders, thus wrapping us in a "cloak of love." The cord ceremony followed the veiling. Each loop of a cord, tied to make a figure eight, was placed over our heads. The cord symbolized being "bound together" for eternity with devotion and faith.

Father Benito said, "Repeat after me."

My bride said sweetly, "I, Ligaya Valeria Cruz Ugale—take you to be my husband—to have and to hold from this day forward—for better, for worse, for richer, for poorer, in sickness and in health—."

The priest continued, "—to love, cherish, and obey, until death us do part."

Ligaya made a clear pronouncement. "—to love and cherish until death us do part according to God's holy law."

The churchgoers gasped, her omittance of the word "obey" obvious. The "error" made both sets of parents squirm.

A younger Father Benito might have lectured Liling that wives should submit to their husbands in everything out of reverence for Christ. What would I do if he gave my thirty-year-old bride a scolding? Weddings should be blissful. He took in a deep breath and continued the service, probably too old to care that I, the poor groom, would have to deal with a stubborn wife.

Father asked me to recite the vows—a man's wedding vows do not contain the word "obey."

No other problems with the ceremony occurred except for the presence of a haggardly stranger in the last pew trying to shush her constantly crying newborn.

"I now pronounce you man and wife. What, therefore, God has joined together, let no man put asunder. You may kiss the bride," Father Benito said dully.

Ligaya froze with sudden bashfulness. Without hesitation, I leaned in to brush my lips against hers. It was the first time we had ever kissed. Jaime smiled. Such a wide smile. Liling bent to kiss him on the forehead and I shook his hand.

Both sets of parents clapped, obviously relieved that their old bachelor son and old maid daughter were finally joined.

Father Benito gave a quick apology for not coming to the luncheon, but for an extra offering he would bless our wedding meal, long-distance from the church. I overheard Mr. Ugale call him a "dirty, dirty, dumb-dumb" under his breath. The godfathers and godmothers collected what meager centavos they could offer the priest. He huffed with disappointment, then prayed three short sentences of a blessing.

The female stranger charged toward Ligaya and demanded her wedding ring back. Liling looked astonished. She said that the woman looked vaguely familiar. A beautiful face and a cleft lip. "The Event?" Liling asked Salome, who nodded, tearful.

Liling begged me with her eyes to do something. I simply nodded my head. My new wife reluctantly removed the gold band and handed it to the woman who, as if jolted by electricity, rudely pulled her hand away. The ring fell to the Spanish tile floor and rolled under the baptismal font. I hissed and Ligaya's eyes grew wide with horror. According to Filipino superstition, a dropped wedding ring means marital misery. I glared at the woman, unconvinced she was my former betrothed. I decided that since the ring did not belong to us, the bad luck was not ours either.

Jaime, good at retrieving anything found underneath anything, helped to recover the stranger's gold ring, ready to be loaned to the next poor couple in exchange for food.

I felt a strange relief that Salome had broken our marriage contract. Would I have wanted to parent three howling children? I glanced at Ligaya. My wife was attractive, not hard to look at. Smart, but not too smart. I didn't quite know what love was, but I was happy.

In the postcolonial period, the Filipinos adopted the Spanish custom of rice throwing, a gesture of "showering" prosperity upon the newlyweds. But it did not occur at our wedding—to do so in a place with starvation was arrogant and wasteful.

Only thirty people had attended our late morning wedding reception—both sets of parents, godparents of the bride and groom, and the aunts and uncles.

Bartolome was present, but he chose not to bring his wife, who stayed back to care for the baby with the Japon eyes. I never once saw Bartolome carry her or care for her. I observed that having others fuss about the child greatly aggravated him.

The Ugales probably had conflicting emotions. The family was thrilled that Ligaya had married; however, they realized that after her move to the USA, they might never see her again.

"You be good to my sister, or else," Bartolome jokingly warned me, his face sad.

"Bartolome, my brother-in-law, it does not need to be said."

I tried to analyze our guests' thoughts. Joy, envy, hope, relief? I worked my way through the crowd and overheard a lot of chatter. Small minds make small talk.

"Pitong is *finally* married."

"A bachelor until age thirty-one, there must be something wrong with him," whispered several guests independently.

"Maybe something is wrong with the family. Ever think about that?" I squinted my eyes with concern.

"He's handsome enough."

"Maybe he has 'played' with the Hawaiian girls. You know, the hula-hula," said a guest, swaying his hips and waving his hands like a native dancer.

"A bachelor son in his thirties might convey he is not covetable or that his family is deficient or damned." How quickly the gossipers forgot that I was a hard worker, courageous in venturing to a new land. I do not smoke. I rarely drank. "A good boy" unfortunately, still a virgin. I looked forward to my wedding night.

"They say he's wealthy. Owns a Buick."

"Rich? But see her hand? Where's the ring?"

"Perhaps she's allergic; cheap metal."

"Liling is mature."

"Yes. Very likable."

"You think they match?"

"Everybody matches when lying horizontally." The guests burst out laughing. The crudeness made me cringe.

"They say the first marriage arrangement was rescinded. People called her a slut. Sal—. Salo—. A biblical name." The guest struggled. "The woman who had St. John the Baptist's head brought to her on a platter. What's her name?"

"Salome."

"Ah. Yes. Salome."

"You don't say."

The stranger's hungry baby cried nearby. The woman who called herself Salome met me at the commercial kitchen door. I gave her the paper boxes with helpings of our banquet entrées.

"Thank you for your kindness, Pitong. Best wishes." The woman with the cleft lip pivoted with her children in tow. I relaxed and returned to the reception to be with my beautiful bride.

Chapter 43

MRS. LIGAYA "LILING" MACADANGDANG

March 1947

Pacencia, our mature flower girl, or rather, our junior attendant, would not stop swishing left, right, left, right. I had taken one of Gloriana's crinolines and adjusted it to fit my niece. The tulle fabric peeked from under the lace-trimmed hem. The dress I had sewn was rough and stiff against her skin, but she seemed thrilled to wear a brand-new outfit, not an ill-fitting hand-me-down. I stitched crocheted lace onto the neckline and armholes. I must say, a very pretty creation. No one would have recognized the fabric—extra from that used to upholster Dr. Billet's new waiting room chairs.

My brother, Felipe, wrote a letter of congratulations and slipped in a money order for a generous amount. In American dollars, it was almost half of Boy's monthly salary and worth at least three to six times more in Philippine pesos.

In better times, much of the entire neighborhood, including children, would have been invited, but we joined the hosts of the reception in deciding that to be frugal was wiser than to be showy and inclusive.

To help, one of Pitong's uncles, a pig farmer, arranged for our local Chinese restaurant to cater the wedding reception. To cut his out-of-pocket costs, he delivered a squealing pig, on the slender side, for the chef to butcher. The eatery specialized in Cantonese cuisine, but his uncle asked for a mixed menu that included Filipino foods. The chef angered Uncle by saying that sautéed onions, tomatoes, and garlic, adding a bit of fish sauce and lots of pork fat, was the basis of almost all Filipino foods. Change the protein, change the vegetable to make different dishes. But the basic ingredients were always the same. He said, "No wonder Filipino food is not considered gourmet, unlike Chinese, French, or Italian." What an insult! Uncle threatened to pull his business from the restaurant.

...

The crowd cajoled Pitong and me to the center stage of the restaurant for the first dance. We both historically loathed being the center of attention. I felt quite shy as we swayed together to a love song airing on radio.

"You look nice," Pitong whispered to me.

"You, too."

"Must thank Uncle for the whole roasted pig."

"Yes, we must."

"Haven't danced in years."

"Nor I."

Pitong said, "Your skin is soft."

"Your fingernails sparkle."

I had not envisioned an awkward conversation when I dreamed of marrying Raul. The romance novels describe couples who stare lovingly or longingly into each other's eyes. Pitong and I had little eye contact.

Pitong said, "I cannot promise that I have the answer to many problems, but I can promise that you will not face them alone." A beautiful thing to say. I made him repeat it so I could memorize the words.

"Pardon me?"

"I cannot promise that I have the answer to many problems, but I can promise that you will not face them alone."

"Thank you, husband. You are very kind." The word *husband* sounded strange on my tongue. I would have to get used to it.

Pitong's uncle announced the start of the "money dance," a Filipino custom to raise funds to help couples start their new lives together. Usually, wedding guests pin currency onto the bride's veil, but I did not have a traditional headdress to wear. Instead, peso bills were placed between our lips as we danced. We then tugged the notes from each other's mouths, like kissing. The guests squealed with delight. It was too soon after wartime for our guests to have much to give. No matter, it was fun for all.

As the first song continued, we were surrounded by other couples who waltzed rhythmically around the room.

Pitong then danced with his mother. She appeared lighthearted and chatty. Papang barely moved because of the pain in his back, so little Jaime asked his grandmother for a dance. Mamang laughed because it included some modern shake-shake moves that the older generation scolded the younger generation for. I'm sure Mamang did not mind. She loved things that made her feel youthful. Besides, Jaime would also be moving to Hawaii. Lola and her grandson needed to create many more memories before our departure.

Papang raised his glass and called for a toast. "May our children be joined for life, and may our families always remember this fine day. We waited long for Liling's union to Rau—er, Agapito with happy anticipation." I don't think anyone detected Papang's near faux pas. "Here is to my daughter and her new husband. To my wife, my dutiful"—Mamang stomped her foot (*Oh, good, she is smiling*)—"er, beautiful wife. And I drink to you, our dear friends, neighbors, and in-laws. May we all share in happiness, good health, and prosperity. Mabuhay! Mabuhay! Mabuhay!"

The Chinese proprietor shut off the radio, signaling the need to speed up the reception and shepherd our guests out the front egress.

He must get the restaurant ready for the Saturday happy hour and first shift of diners, he said. Pitong's uncle grumbled, refusing to be bossed around by a Chinese. He had paid big money for a decent celebration and donated the pig. He decided to prolong the reception by turning the radio back on, and in so doing, irritated the restaurant owner.

Noticing the increasing tension between Pitong's uncle and the Chinese, the senior Mr. Macadangdang contributed an extra round of beer for the men, and colas and orange sodas for the women. The extra purchases of liquor and refreshments seemed to placate the Chinese owner.

I approached my father-in-law.

"Thank you, Tata Macadangdang."

He smiled. "Call me Papa."

"Papa."

"Take care of our Pitong."

"I will, Papa. I promise."

Our warm exchange was interrupted by Pitong's brother, still a bachelor.

"I want to go to America, too. I dream of all the modern things in the USA. Television. Telephone. The latest model car."

"Well, you must first find a rich American woman," Pitong advised. His brother frowned. Then Pitong added, "Or I shall have to become a US citizen and order you."

"It will be faster for you to be a citizen." The siblings laughed.

The Chinese restaurant owner reluctantly agreed to several more dances like the swing and cha-cha, which made people thirsty. The unexpected profits from extra liquor sales satisfied him. It was well-known that liquor orders and bar tabs increase in times of war and poverty; maybe the alcohol helped these poor Filipinos forget their unfortunate stations. Merriment, jokes about wedding night sex, congratulations, and good wishes were all around—I would say our celebration was a grand success.

Chapter 44

MRS. LIGAYA "LILING" MACADANGDANG

March 1947

After the short reception, we arrived at the Macadangdang home by carabao and carriage. No money for a honeymoon getaway, not even for a cheap motel. The hut was old, and the flooring worn in several places, but sturdily built, and comfortable and cozy. Oil lamps lit the home. Mr. and Mrs. Macadangdang were already asleep, or so it seemed. I had a feeling that Pitong's mother feigned slumber on the floor mat, hoping to be an aural spy.

When we entered the only bedroom in the house, I saw his parents had garnered a twin-sized mattress for us, likely a cast-off from one of the Americanos. No box spring or frame, but the bed was made up with clean sheets pulled taut. I found a vase filled with fresh, fragrant jasmine on the wooden footstool.

Pitong and I stood facing opposite walls and slowly undressed. We both folded our clothes neatly. Pitong placed the tuxedo into a paper bag to be returned to the saxophone player in the morning. I laid my white dress upon a small dresser, near the basin of water with more floating petals of jasmine.

Pitong hopped onto the mattress wearing only his blue boxers. He reached for his bottle of cologne and splashed a few drops of musky scent upon his face.

I felt terribly shy about the white cotton briefs I pulled off, wishing I had had the money to purchase prettier, more delicate lingerie. I quickly dismissed the idea; even if I'd had the money, I would never have splurged on teeny see-through underwear. After a sponge wipe using the basin of water, I pulled on a light cotton nightgown, a hand-me-down from the Americano doctor's wife.

"Do you like sherbet green?" Mrs. Billet had asked me.

Even before I had answered, the missus had thrust a parcel containing the nightgown, a sweater, and two blouses into my hands. The used articles of clothing looked brand new.

"Thank you, ma'am." I hurried home with the gift.

"What is *sherbet*, Mamang?"

"I do not know."

I held the nightie against my chest. Sherbet must be something of a pretty pastel. The neckline, cut in a deep V, was still modest. The lacework around the armholes and along the bodice was intricate and delicate. The dozen pretty, pearl buttons sewn down the front were too fashionable for bedtime.

I released my hair from the claws of my side combs. A tumble of black, shiny tresses framed my face. The deep V cut of the nightgown revealed just a bit of cleavage.

When I turned toward the mattress upon which Pitong had already reclined, he gasped. My first thought—*I am too ugly*—but he said clearly, "You are beautiful."

I lay shyly next to my husband. Through the sheer fabric of my night dress, I'm sure he could make out my triangle. On the twin mattress, we only fit by lying on our sides or with one partner on top of the other. We faced each other. We did not say anything. Pitong kissed my neck and I giggled. It tickled.

Pitong excused himself and opened the bedroom door. He said he spied his mother with her head cocked toward the bedroom to listen. She was giving her husband a dirty look. Perhaps her annoyance was due to Mr. Macadangdang's gargled snoring with mouth wide open. I was willing to bet she wished he would shut up so she could hear better.

"Mother, go to sleep." He shut the bedroom door quietly.

Pitong kissed the other side of my neck and I giggled. Could my mother-in-law tell that foreplay had begun? I was sure this was foreplay. Cora had defined it in one of our many woman-to-woman talks.

Soon, however, Pitong smashed his lips upon mine, hard. It startled me. He shoved his stiff tongue into my mouth. I gagged.

Suddenly, my mind turned bitter with memories of the Japon who had invaded my village and raped its women. Captain Fuku, the Oriental Bull, had snorted and humped me as he slid his thick tongue across my teeth.

Had my husband ever been informed that I was an involuntary member of a sorority of World War II rape victims? I certainly didn't want him to find out. I had vowed never to discuss it with him. In fact, the fewer people who knew, the better. No, no one would ever understand that I hid trauma in the secret places of my body.

Something hard pushed against my thigh and the hem of my gown rode up. Pitong tried to unfasten the delicate pearl studs. After a few minutes of struggling unsuccessfully with the top six buttons, he pulled hard at the front and three of the iridescent buttons popped off.

Other women might have been aroused at Pitong's eagerness. I had read so in love stories, but I had a flashback to the violence of The Event. I became frightened, shut my eyes, and shut my mouth. I turned off my brain. Before I turned off my heart completely, Pitong jerked in a series of spasms and kissed my neck again. Just like that, the consummation was complete. A grunt and a moan. Had my mother-in-law heard? Was she duly satisfied?

I was bewildered by my girlfriends' enthusiasm about sex as if it produced pleasurable and transcendent sensations. Now that I had experienced it for the first time, I decided it was an unwelcome but necessary wifely duty. I knew I would have to surrender to Pitong if I wanted children, and I wanted children intensely. If he had been a romantic man, perhaps I would have been open to a more spiritual enjoining. But he was rough and fast, and he convulsed in his release. I shall continue to resort to shutting my eyes, shutting my mouth, and closing my brain.

Clumsy is the descriptor one might use for our wedding night. The whole act went quickly, but I felt sore. We turned away from each other and slept on the narrow mattress with our backs against each other's.

My tears spilled in silence. I dreamt of Raul.

Chapter 45

MR. AND MRS. AGAPITO MACADANGDANG

March 1947

PITONG

"It pains me to see my bride's bare left hand." At the outdoor market looking at wedding rings, I tried to bargain the prices down, but I still could not afford even the cheapest diamond jewelry.

"Perhaps I can help."

I swung around to see a suntanned old man looking lonely, melancholic. He held out an old tobacco pouch.

"You can help, Tata?" I took the pouch and examined its contents.

"It's my wife's jewelry."

"Your wife?"

"She died yesterday."

"Tata, I'm so sorry to hear that."

"I will sell her jewelry to you. I need the money for her funeral and crypt."

"I can't do that."

"Please, young man. Or her body will be dumped in the paupers' grave."

I desperately wanted to give Ligaya the circle, a symbol of my eternal love for her. I examined the jewelry; one ring, only without diamonds. It must do, for now.

"How much? For the ring? Just the ring."

The widower's voice quivered. "Enough for a decent burial for my wife."

I closed my eyes for a moment, trying to decide. I bought the ring I could scarcely afford. It had five large, unusual, dark gems roughly cut. Pyrite? More substantial than the tiny glass on Salome's ring.

"A ring is a ring is a ring," said the old man.

"Today, this ring must be *the* ring."

The old man dug into his pocket and produced another tobacco drawstring pouch. "I had these extracted from my dead wife. They are worth much money, but I will give them to you for a bargain price."

I emptied the contents onto my palm. Two gold-capped molars and a front tooth outlined in a frame of gold. I nearly dropped them.

"No thank you, Tata. Someone else will have better need for them."

...

LILING

At the airport, surrounded by bustle, Pitong presented me with the ring, unique if not beautiful. I urged myself to feel satisfied with Pitong's gift. I had never owned a piece of jewelry before and should have felt overjoyed, but the gems disappointed me; they were not diamonds. What is the American saying? Beggars cannot be choosers. Even back then in the Philippines, diamonds should tell a story not only about the depth of one's love for his wife, but they should be symbolic of the wife—precious, sparkling, high quality, rare. Clear, white diamonds could convey all of that.

I studied my ring of shiny, gray-black stones. I called them "my black diamonds." They were not ugly. But the dark gems, they were not pretty. Why would Pitong, a man of wealth, purchase something other than diamonds? What story does that tell of me? I am dark. Of lesser quality. Cheap. The second choice. The consolation prize.

I came out of my reverie and refocused. "Thank you, Pitong."

"Call me Aggie." He smiled. I smiled.

"Thank you." I chose not to call him Aggie. What a silly sounding name! "I realize you worked hard for the money to pay for this ring and then searched all through the village market for the perfect piece. Pitong, I shall cherish this gift from you. I am grateful."

Agapito had been in the Philippines for three weeks, and much had happened to us in that short time. A considerable number of tasks needed to be completed when he reached Hawaii. High in priority was preparing a home for me and Jaime. He had to get busy studying for the citizenship exam or he would be stuck forever in the bachelors' dorm and I would be stuck in the barrio. Pitong was smart. I'm sure he would pass.

"I *will* call for you and Jaime as soon as I can. I am sad that we must part ways. I will call for you. And soon we will be together again, I promise." Pitong kissed me on the cheek and ran across the tarmac to climb up the steps to the airplane bound for Hawaii.

I waved when he glanced back. "Bye, husband."

Chapter 46

MR. AND MRS. AGAPITO MACADANGDANG

LILING

August 1947

Stuck in the village, I flipped the pages of my calendar, free merchandise from the Chinese restaurant.

Pitong corresponded with me first. He was not a romantic writer, but he did attempt to write in English.

> Dear Liling,
>
> I am count the days until we meet again. I am study hard for the citizenship test. I am try memorize the First Amendment. I am try memorize the Bill of Rights. Freedom of speech, religion, assembly (whatever that means), press (whatever that means. I think means newspapers) and right to petition (whatever that means). Pray to the God of Immigration, Liling, so that learnings will not leak from my brain. Soon (I hope) I will be able to petition for you and Jaime, and we be together in our own home.

> Tell Jaime that I am look forward to going fish with him, not in a river, but in a ocean.
> Love,
> Aggie

We each received only three letters from the other. The postal shipping line added extra ports of call to its already overextended distribution schedule. Delivery to our rural area was slow, taking as much as a month for mail to arrive.

I marveled at the idea that Jaime and I would follow Agapito to the United States of America. My dreams duplicated the American movies, dubbed in Filipino, that my friends saved money to watch. Rarely able to afford entertainment, I relied on them to describe the scenes and dialogue in detail so I could experience the movie vicariously. When I am in Hawaii, I will watch as many movies as I want.

I envisioned American men tough like John Wayne. The good guys always beat the bad. I believed all American children were as cute as Shirley Temple and could sing and dance. My favorite star was Esther Williams, the famous actress whose movies featured her talents as a swimmer and diver; she always looked gorgeous, even emerging from a pool. Life should be like synchronized swimming—beautifully choreographed ballet with swimmers who demonstrated great endurance, flexibility, artistry, and precise timing. In adversity, I wanted to be like Esther, able to control my breath and arise with strength and grace.

God of Adversity. Please, no more misfortune and hardship in America. It's supposed to be the land of opportunity. Amen. Please?

...

PITONG

March 1948

Back in Hawaii, each square of the Glamour Girl Pinups calendar was marked with big, broad Xs. I will have to get rid of this. It has been twelve months since our whirlwind courtship and simple wedding—making me impatient with the immigration process.

I had to earn my American citizenship before I could bring my bride to Hawaii. English is a difficult language, but I studied hard. I knew who George Washington was and what the thirteen stripes and forty-eight stars symbolized in the American flag. I learned about Abraham Lincoln and the Civil War. I could hum the national anthem. I understood the American views of the Japanese and Hitler's Germans in World War II. During a class show and tell, I proudly showed off my bullet scar.

I memorized the Pledge of Allegiance, which I recited slowly so that the instructor and then the judge would be able to understand me with my Filipino accent. "I fledge [pledge] allegiance to the plahg [flag] of de United States of Ame-rrrica."

Finally, I passed. Now I could order my wife and adopted son.

Though legally married, I had remained in the single men's dorm for more than a year because of the geographical separation from Ligaya. With immigration papers confirmed, I was overjoyed to be assigned to housing for married couples and families. The plantation subsidized my rent, making it possible for me to save more quickly to buy a house. Next to marriage, home ownership was my top goal.

I moved to a tiny two-bedroom structure—blue-green stained wood, white trim, a patio, and corrugated tin roofing. It stood beside a hibiscus-lined red dirt road where the mud pulled on my slippers when it rained. Under the large avocado tree, a separate garage protected my corroded Chevy pickup from the bombing of overripe fruit. I wished I could afford a new car like my plantation supervisor's.

...

LILING
September 1948

It seemed the entire village was at the Ugales' "happy-sad" house to wish Jaime and me goodbye. I did not know if I would ever see my family and neighbors again. Fortune shined on me; not many of the villagers had the privilege of moving to the United States of America.

"Your adventure begins, Liling, my dearest daughter," said my weepy mamang. "I pray that Pitong treats you well. Ligaya, please find your brother. It is a mother's hope that her children are close."

"I will, Mamang. I did plan to connect with Boy, and I am excited."

"Ay, Apo Dios." She slipped her rosary into my pocket.

"God bless you, Mamang."

Papang patted me on the shoulder. "I pray that you find happiness with Pitong, and prosperity in Hawaii. It is what we have wanted for you."

"Oh, Papang." I carefully hugged my hunched father. "You are a good man, Papang." Tears slid down his cheeks. His intimidating face and fierce eyes of a time long ago were gone.

"Am I forgiven for all the...?"

"Oh, Papang. Shh. Let us forgive each other."

I surveyed the group in a bittersweet moment. Auntie Soledad handed me a brown paper bag containing white crochet thread, with unsolicited advice. "Liling, my dear, for a successful marriage, you must be obedient and submit to your husband."

My body stiffened. "Yes, Auntie Soledad," I said, just to appease my elder. No. Glory had taught me to use my own mind and my own mouth. I would not be blindly dutiful to a man at his command.

Vicente, who could usually be found running, jumping, or climbing about, was able to control his boisterousness as if a witch had placed a spell on him. He looked somber standing next to Jaime, who had just given his bati-cobra sticks to his cousin. "You can have these. I'll miss you. Try not to get blown up, okay?"

"Jaime, when you get rich, can you send me a real American bat and baseball?"

"Sure, Vicente!" It was hard for the playmates to say goodbye to each other.

Cora carried Luisa Rose and stood a distance apart from Bartolome, who was not tearful. His eyes expressed pain—he was unable to reconcile his love for his wife and his hate for his baby. His behavior was confusing to all around him. I squeezed my brother hard.

I moved to kiss the beautiful little child with the "wrong" eyes and gave Cora a gentle hug. "Take care of yourself."

Pacencia stood close to Jaime with Benny in her arms. The dog licked Jaime's face as if it realized this was farewell to his boy owner; he was going home with his new girl owner.

"Pacencia, you have learned to crochet well. You can now sell lace to the Chinese merchant. Make sure he doesn't cheat you; he must pay decent cost for goods plus labor. Oh, there is so much more to teach you." I kissed my niece on the forehead and stroked dear Benny's soft fur. Jaime hugged his grandmother. "I love you, Lola, to the moon, to the sun, and to the stars." They held each other a long time.

But he attached himself to his lolong the longest. Jaime must have instinctively known this would be the last time they would be with each other. Grandfather and grandson stared deeply into each other's eyes. Without words, they said goodbye.

...

PITONG

September 1948

In just thirteen hours, I would be reunited with my wife and Jaime. The flower leis were strung using the plumerias I had picked at dawn. In the Philippines, these blossoms are called frangipani. My finger bled when I stuck it twice with the sewing needle.

Restlessness mixed with excitement. To make a good impression, I worked extra hard to clean the house, making sure I picked my clothes up from the floor and sent them to the Chinese laundry woman the bachelors tended to hire. My dishes were washed using Pure Brand soap, and I scrubbed the hardened rice from one of two pots I owned.

Cockroaches and cane spiders were squished—I didn't want my wife and little boy to be squeamish about Hawaii's super-sized bugs. The cobwebs from around the light fixtures and sills were swept away. It had been a while since I had dusted. It would be good to have a wife who could take over the housework. Then I washed the windows and screens, knowing full well Ligaya would be measuring them for crocheted curtains.

The cows and chickens were fed. A mewing kitten was found in the coop—no wonder the hens had clucked angrily this morning. I enticed the medium-haired feline over to the porch where I used a clean tin can for water and another tin can for last night's leftover fish. It gulped greedily. "Slow down. There is plenty more. Oh, little boy kitten, you lost your mama? Don't worry; there is a little boy coming to adopt you. He lost his mama too."

...

LILING

September 1948

With entry papers completed at long last, I traveled with Jaime.

"We're on the airplane, Mommy!"

"Mmm. You know what my favorite word in the whole wide world is?"

"What is your favorite word?"

"Mommy!"

"Mine, too. Mmm. Mommy! And Mama. Mama Glory and Mommy Liling!"

I hugged him tightly. "Oh, Jaime, how you have grown! And you look so much like your mama! God of Angels. Bless my sister, Glory, who is with you in heaven. Show her that her son is living their dream. Amen."

I worried incessantly on the long flight that included a scheduled fueling stop in Guam. What if Jaime had an asthma attack during the flight, necessitating the airplane to boomerang back to the Philippines? What if the plane crashed? What if we got lost at the international airport? What if—? What if?

I smoothed Jaime's hair, and he, in turn, smoothed the fur on his dark brown teddy bear, a farewell present from Dr. Billet.

"My boy," the Americano doctor had told him, "you're going to have a mighty fine time in Hawaii, mighty fine. Here's a present from me and the missus. His name is 'Brownie.' " I cringed but said "Thank you" to my former employer.

The toy was more appropriate for a younger boy, but Jaime's eyes lit up.

"Mommy Liling, my bear is Pinoy!"

...

"I am in the United States of America." With absolute jubilation, I made the sign of the cross as Jaime and I stepped off the enormous propeller plane.

I saw Pitong waiting for us with two frangipani leis in hand. He looked happy, situated beside an old rusted truck. I paused. *Where is the Buick?*

Jaime clung to his "Brownie."

Pitong joined us at baggage claim. A figure stepped out from behind a column.

"Boy!" My brother Felipe surprised me. We hadn't seen each other in about fourteen years. We wept and held each other tightly.

"Oh, God of Dreams Come True. How we have suffered! May thy mercy and love draw me from the dark on the inside." Jaime and I walked hand in hand toward the light of our first day in the USA. "I am grateful. Amen."

Now in the bright Hawaiian sun, Jaime stepped on his shadow. He said joyously, "Amen!"

DARK ON THE INSIDE BOOKCLUB STUDY GUIDE

1. What did you know about World War II in the Pacific Theater before you read this book?

2. What feelings did the book, Dark on the Inside, evoke in you?

3. What did you learn about the Philippines and its people through Dark on the Inside?

4. Which characters could you relate most to? Why?

5. Which characters did you like least? Why?

6. Why do you think the author titled the book *Dark on the Inside*? What title would you have given it?

7. Do you think the wartime interactions between the Caucasians, Filipinos, and Japanese are realistic as depicted in this book?

8. Describe any prejudices and discriminations you have personally experienced.

9. Are there any lessons from this book that can be applied to interactions in today's world?

10. How does one develop multicultural sensitivity and competence?

Thank You for Reading My Book!

Dear Reader Friends,
Please leave a review of *Dark on the Inside* by finding the title or my author name, Virginia Cantorna, on Amazon. Click on "Write a customer review."

Thank you!

Free short story

To join my cultural historical email list and receive a World War II story about Liling's brother, Felipe "Boy" Ugale, send me your email address. :)

I would love to stay in touch with you.
Website: www.cantornabooks.com
Email: CantornaBooks@gmail.com
Facebook Group: www.facebook.com/groups/cantornabooks/

Thank you very much!
Aloha,
Virginia Cantorna

Find out what happens to Liling and Pitong in Hawaii
Virginia Cantorna's next novel

Dark on the Outside

Ligaya "Liling" Ugale Macadangdang was excited about immigrating to Hawaii from the Philippines with big dreams of an easy, happy, and prosperous life. She is disappointed, however, when she settles in a rural sugar plantation camp and discovers her new husband is not whom she believed him to be. The newlywed misses her homeland and the family she left behind. The "American way" is a challenge to adapt to. Worst of all, her neighbors are Japanese, so they remind her of The Event and other atrocities of World War II in the Pacific. Her beloved son, Jaime, is sickly. What will happen to him and to the American-born children she wants desperately to bear and raise? She is not used to being treated poorly because of the color of her skin; in the Philippines, almost everyone is brown. She does not seem to be thriving like everyone else, which causes her to be overcome with sadness, insecurity, and anxieties. Allow Ligaya to inspire you with her faith and courage as she emerges from the darkness into a new world called America.

. . .

ACKNOWLEDGMENTS

What a difference you have made in my life! I am utterly grateful.

For Expert Writing and Publishing Guidance

Scott Allan
Jasmyne Boswell
Susan Friedmann – Publisher
Meredith Lindsay – Cover Design
Toby Neal
Sara Patton
Patrick Snow
Self-Publishing School
Tyler Tichelaar – Editor
Ramy Vance
Viki Winterton

For Teaching Cultural Competence

Argosy University – Honolulu:
  Dr. Yvonne Awana
  Dr. Joy Tanji
The Center for Multicultural Training in Psychology – Boston University:
  Dr. Mari Carmen Bennasar
  Dr. Connie Chan
  Dr. Kermit Crawford
  Dr. Linda Daniels
  Shani Dowd
  Dr. Roxana Llerena-Quinn
  Dr. Olivia Moorehead-Slaughter
  Dr. David Trimble
  Dr. Jackie Vorpahl

For Inspiration, Encouragement and Support

Kaulana Aina
Rowena Dagdag-Andaya
Dr. Elizabeth Ayson
Mischel Berg and Mike Rodby
Danielle Bergan
Alfred Cantorna
Emily Cantorna
Esperanza Cabbab Cantorna
Christen Chargualaf
Evie Chargualaf
Justin and Jodie Chargualaf
Daisha Dagdag
Fred and Judy Dagdag
Robert DeVinck
Annie Gorman Diggs
Pamela Saharah Dyson
Reiko Fukino
Roberta Gately
Kenn Grimes
Jessie Cantorna Harrington
Anela Hew
Lindsey Hew
Sandy Hew
Maui Academy of Performing Arts:
David Johnston, Carolyn Wright
Rosemary Himuro
Lin McEwan
Carol McNulty-Huffman
Peter Mellen
Cindy Paulos
PsychPhiles:
Adrianna Flavin, Amber Kawamura, Marlene Maneha, Satoko Miki-O'Donovan, Maria Thomas

Robin Sagon
Amorah St. John
Kristi Scott
Cornelia Soberano
Kalei Sombelon
Laurin Toegemann
Unity Church of Maui
Manuel Vazquez, Jr.
Jennifer Welcome
Elizabeth Winternitz
Writing Circle facilitated by Jasmyne Boswell

For Bringing Joy
Mateo Ikaika Kalani Cantorna-Aina
Persephone Hew
Ashton, Caleb, Averiana, and Coledon Chargualaf

In Loving Memory Of
Marissa Antonio
Esperanza Cabbab Cantorna
Casey Chargualaf
Patrick Ramos
Cornelia Soberano

Made in the USA
Las Vegas, NV
19 May 2021

23261403R00204